HER VAMPIRE TEMPTATION

ALEXIS ALVAREZ

MIDNIGHT ROMANCE

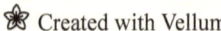

PROLOGUE

B^{ri} *"On your knees, beautiful. Now. Spread those thighs for me."*

I obey with hesitation, my naked body aching with desire for the man in front of me. His voice, so deep and powerful, is an erotic drawl. The glint in his dark eyes is at once wicked and sexy.

His bare chest, rippling with muscles that lead down to the sexy V, makes me want to undo his jeans this second.

"You know what I want, don't you?" He steps closer to me. Teasing me with his proximity. He laughs. "And I know what you want, too. You'll get it…eventually."

He leans over and grabs a handful of my hair, pulling as he speaks into my neck. "As long as you're a good girl. Do what I say."

I gasp in arousal and moan a little, my eyelids fluttering shut. He smells like rain and forest and mystery. I part my lips and lean forward, hoping for a kiss.

He obliges. Touches his lips to mine. Electrified, I melt into the contact, opening my mouth for his tongue.

But he pulls back too soon. "Just a taste. You'll earn more." He chuckles. "'We'll start with this, hmmm?"

My eyes fly open as I hear him unbuckle his belt. The swish of the leather through the loops of his jeans makes me wet between the thighs.

"You know what position I like," he murmurs.

I look up. I just want to see his expression, and then I'll do every dirty, depraved thing we both crave —

But a screaming alarm splits the air, and he dissolves into a mist of colors.

My bedroom swims into focus, my alarm clock blaring into my eardrums, reminding me:

1. I'm alone.
2. My sexy mystery man doesn't exist.
3. It's time for work.

I close my eyes and try to resummon him, even as I shut off the irritating alarm, but he's gone.

"Damn." I rub my eyes with one hand and sit up, then push my red curls out of my face.

At 7 am on Monday morning, it's dark as midnight because of my black-out shades, which makes it even more tempting to fall back into slumber. But I have a busy day ahead of me, so I'll have to leave mystery man for another night.

I unwind the sheet from my arm and wince as I accidentally poke one of my most recent scars. It's puffy, all sealed up, but still sensitive on the edges.

My stomach flips with anxiety, and I push back the feelings as hard as I can. Dr. Su said worrying doesn't help, and I know she's right.

Easier said than done, though.

I rub my skin softly in silent apology as I flip on the lights and blink against the onslaught of incandescent brilliance.

"It's you and me again, babe," I say to myself. "Us against the world." I take a deep breath and try to speak with conviction. "We can do this."

I'm used to being alone, and really, I prefer it. No lie.

But at times like this, it sure would be nice if my dream man were real… just for a single night.

CHAPTER 1

B^{ri}

I take a deep breath of the fresh desert air. It's evening; I've made it past the last poisonous ray of sun, and now I'm free. Driving down a long desert road in Oro Valley, I have the car window down to enjoy the cool October on the way to my web design client.

Too bad my car won't cooperate. *Check fluid level* flashes again—crap. Good thing I have a spare jug of coolant in the trunk.

I pull over down a short drive and park in an empty lot by a newly constructed building. I hate expansion into the desert, but this structure is well designed, with beautiful waves of steel and glass.

One orange cone and a trailing piece of construction tape are the only remnants of what work must have gone into it. No signs, though.

I fetch my coolant and prop the hood to pour. Suddenly, I know I'm not alone. My skin prickles and my body electrifies—there's someone behind me.

"You can't park here. Private property."

It's a man. He has a hint of a European accent. I can't see his face, but his tone is velvet and steel, full of confidence. Sexy.

"This is car trouble." I speak into the engine of my old Honda Civic, not looking up as I pour coolant. "As soon as I finish my champagne, we'll be out of here."

There was no one here when I pulled in. Did he materialize out of thin air?

The pale blue fluid gurgles and chugs into the opening. "But thank you for the helpful lecture on road rules, Professor." It might not be wise to talk this way to a stranger. But sometimes I feel like words are my way to feel truly free, limited as I am in other ways.

"I do like to teach the uninitiated." His voice is lower and closer. "If I find it worth my while." He's stepped nearer to me, and damned if I can't sense his presence. It's like a magnet, pulling me.

From the sound of his voice, I imagine he's handsome or powerful. You only speak with that kind of effortless confidence if you offer exactly what society thinks it wants.

I finish pouring and stand up, wiping my left hand on the thigh of my jeans and check to see if his voice matches his face. And…he's hot. He makes *handsome* look old and worn out. He's simply phenomenal.

And I swear to God, he's the man from my dream last night.

Tall and built, lean. Dangerous. Dark brown hair, nearly black, tousled and thick. Green eyes. Thick lashes and lips that look sensuous and cruel at the same time. Mid-thirties, maybe, about ten years older than I am?

My neck tingles. I've never felt such instant attraction to anyone before. And from the look in his eyes, he knows. And he knows I know.

And he likes it.

He smiles, then his expression changes from mocking to something more serious.

We stare at each other for a few seconds, and I can't fight the oddest feelings—that one of us is predator, one prey. But who is who? Because I want to hunt him hard, even as I want him to chase me and catch.

Then he smiles. My bloodstream has turned to fire, to ice, to liquid sunshine. I don't understand his effect on me —the bottle drops from my fingers as I flush, nervous and a little embarrassed at my reaction.

I bend down to pick up the bottle, breathing a little hard. "Fuck." I only mouth it, head down, and there's no way he can possibly know what I said.

But somehow, he does. "Mm. That does pair nicely with a good champagne."

"Ex*cuse* me?" Did he really just say that?

My entire body begins a slow burn as images flash in my mind, X-rated, beautiful images of this man. Naked.

"Champagne goes with anything, doesn't it? But at the risk of being repetitious, you are on private property. This isn't open to the public for leisure picnics."

There's something about the ferocity of his gaze, the tilt of his mouth, that makes me realize at once that this is a man you don't cross. He's smiling, and there's the powerful attraction, but there's something else in his eyes that isn't about humor at all.

But nobody is going to make me back down.

"At my own risk of repetition, and no offense intended, but as any human with any modicum of basic logical reasoning skills could probably comprehend," I wave my hand at the popped hood, "This is no snack in the park. Engine issues trump no trespassing signs."

"I think you do."

"What?"

He quirks a brow. "I think you do like to offend." His smile is back. "And see what happens. Throw caution to the winds and let the words fly. Am I right?"

I put my free hand on my hip, heart racing at how astute he is. "What does that even mean?" I shrug a shoulder at the car. "Your judgement about me is off. And by the way? A gentleman would ask if I needed help."

"Oh, I'm no gentleman." He crosses his arms and tilts his head at me. "Did you make a mistake in judging me, as well?" He looks me up and down, bold. "I think you need to be careful with that mouth. Someday you'll push too far and end up provoking just the wrong person."

"Are you implying that you're that wrong person?" I narrow my eyes and act scornful. Although my heart pounds, sparring with him is exhilarating.

This is one inappropriate conversation. If there was a master list of "things not to say to a strange man in an empty parking lot," my sentences would be at the top of the page.

But I haven't actually met someone this attractive in a long time. Too long. Is it wrong to seize the moment, especially if I don't know how many more will come my way? Anyway, I don't get the feeling that he's dangerous —to me.

"Rest assured, I'm absolutely wrong for you," he says. A beat goes by. "But I'd take the time to demonstrate just what happens when you offend me." His eyes drill into mine. "If you asked. Quite nicely."

A thrill of desire shoots through me, so hard and immediate that I catch my breath. I'm wet between the thighs, just like that.

Fuck. Is it written on my face that I like a good dominant man? Can he tell that I'm aching for a scene? "I can be nice when it suits me." I give him a smirk. The engine makes a single ping!—and I glance back at my car. "Too bad my car isn't being nice."

"Too bad you waited until it was too late to get it repaired." His tone is dry. "And here you are, stranded at night, in an empty parking lot with a stranger."

"Car troubles can strike at a moment's notice." I cross my arms. Act like I didn't know there was a slow leak and that I was putting off taking it to the shop. It's just hard, when you can't go out during the day —

"A lot of things happen in the blink of any eye," he agrees. "Both for good or not." He sounds exasperated and–to my surprise–slightly tense. He glances around him as if checking for something, then relaxes nearly imperceptibly. Like his whole body is a bit lighter.

"Ah, insightful." I roll my eyes. "Next, please tell me that sometimes you can go left or right. Things are hot or cold."

He steps in an inch. "Pleasure or pain."

My face gets hotter than before. "Sure, if you're into that."

By the little smile that hovers on his lips, I'm sure he's read me loud and clear. He knows what I like.

Then he tilts his head, as if he hears something I can't. "Your work is done, I assume?" But it's an order. He's demanding that I leave, even though it was masked as a question.

He steps over and runs a hand over the side of my car, the way one might stroke a racehorse. He frowns, closes his eyes, then smiles. "You'll be okay."

I roll my eyes. "Thanks for your exquisite assistance." I smirk at him.

"If you had any idea."

"I was being facetious. In case you didn't notice, you were absolutely no help at all." I give him a look.

"Did you really need my help, though?"

I put the bottle down and cross my arms.

My left arm tingles at the spot where the needle went in this morning, not once, but three times. It was a new phlebotomist, a trainee. But I'm so focused on this man that I don't even feel the usual anxiety about waiting for the results.

"I don't need anything from you." What I *want* from him is another story entirely.

He laughs but looks around him again. He seems very alert, on edge.

I wonder if he's waiting for someone important. Is it a woman? Jealousy flows through me, completely unwarranted, yet powerful. I roll my eyes at my own reaction.

I step back to the front of the car, remove the metal holder and drop the hood into place.

"Drive safely." He's right next to me, holding the bottle.

"Or else?" I shake my hand out and dart him a little look. I can't help but smile, a little cat grin, and then bite my bottom lip. Why do I want to provoke him so badly? Push him until he...

He narrows his gaze. "You only think you want to find out."

A thrill of arousal shoots directly to my clit at his tone, warm honey and sex, but his eyes–they're fierce. I step back and blink.

His voice softens, and he taps the bottle. "I'll throw this out for you. Get that leak checked tomorrow, so you don't need to pull over again."

"Yes, sir." My tone is insolent. For a split second, when his eyes darken, I envision images of the two of us, naked. Him ordering me to do dirty, wicked things. Me, obeying. With pleasure.

My face is hot. I swear he's reading my mind, the way he smiles.

He locks eyes with me. "All right, then."

I nod. "All right."

There's something unsaid between us, something hot and bright and powerful, growing by the second. If he asks for my number, I'll give it. Or if he gives me one more smoldering look, I'll just fucking toss my phone at his head along with my panties.

But he doesn't ask me for anything.

And I'm not going to beg for his attention.

He raises a hand, then turns and walks to the building.

He was larger than life, and I feel it even more so in his absence. It's the way the air around me seems to deflate slightly, the very molecules drooping as they silently file back in to fill the area he just occupied with his presence.

I glance over. The bottle's disappeared although I don't see any trash can. He's lounging against the brick wall like he just fucked someone good and hard.

It's in his smug little smirk. The way he looks me up and down and lets a smile light his lips up for a split second before he shakes his head, still smiling, and bends his head down to a lighter.

I imagine the click but don't miss the flare of fire against the black night before he cups it with his hand and turns his profile to me. For a second the heat in his hands is brighter than the sun. Then it's gone.

He's a smoker? Usually that's an immediate turn-off, but at this moment in time, I don't care one fuck. I bet his lips would taste delicious with whiskey and smoke on them.

He blows out smoke–a deliberate puff, and I imagine it curling toward me through the cool October night air, tendrils tenderly winding around my body, teasing, touching. My nipples tingle.

He smiles. Laughs a little.

Fuck, he can't possibly know what I'm imagining! I suck in a breath as my face gets hot. *It's just smoke.*

Okay, I can't just stay here staring. Plus, I have a meeting with a client.

So I get back into my car and pull out of the empty lot in the middle of nowhere in the wilderness outside Oro

Valley, leaving him behind at the—what is this place, anyway? I don't even know what this building is for.

Well, it's not worth obsessing about since I'll never see him again.

But later in the evening, even as I show the boutique manager her new website on my laptop and as I show her how to set up the customized order tracking system, I think of that man. How the thrilling, dangerous banter with him made me feel more alive than I have in—years.

And I dream about what I want him to do to me.

a^{lain}

"Alain Marchmont. My liege." Karl gives me a mock bow and smiles, showing his fangs. "What a pleasure to be summoned to see you." He glances around the empty parking lot towards the newly erected building. "What is this place?"

"None of your concern. We're here to talk about other things." My tone is sharp.

He shrugs, then narrows his eyes. "Are there humans near?" He sniffs.

"Do you see any?"

The scent of the feisty redhead lingers in the air, available to only those with the finest scent ability: FBI dogs. Shifters. Vampires, like us. But she's far away by now, in that clunker of a car.

"I smell one." He licks his lips. "Fertile and young. A girl. Fine, warm blood. "I thought you brought me a treat." He smiles, but it doesn't reach his eyes.

A chill runs along my spine, thinking about the innocent in the hands of Karl. At his disposal.

"Do you feel you deserve a reward, Karl Gustavus Platt?" I raise a brow and cross my arms. "After what you did?"

I stare him down until he averts his eyes, but it takes a long minute.

"I was only trying to protect myself. I don't see why you have to question me." He crosses his arms and glares.

For some reason, Karl seems more powerful than usual —it's odd.

Vampires change slowly, over time. Like glaciers. But Karl has become different in just the past few months; more conceited and, somehow, more robust. Like he's bursting with energy.

But I called him here to discuss his behavior, not his demeanor. I frown at him. "What you did. It's not code."

He scoffs. "Just because you made up a code doesn't mean I need to honor it."

"I made more than the code. I made you." I step in an inch.

His eyes go wide. He's still just a brash bully underneath the bluster. I laugh. Partially with relief.

He snarls and leans forward. His breath stinks of rotten things, old dead and recently dead mixed, with the sweet iron tang of blood. Odd—the underscent of blood is refined, delightful—not the kind Karl enjoys. He usually goes for fast and easy.

"How dare you laugh?" His eyes are small and beady now, pellets under his protruding brow.

He has a shelf of a forehead, almost like an awning for

the rest of his face. He's a modern creature now, but he would have been at home in a Holbein painting. "Do you think that because you turned me that you own me?"

"You swore an oath of loyalty to me in return for the gift of eternal life." I raise a brow.

"It's been a long time, Alain," he snaps. "Is there no statue of limitations?"

"Statute," I correct automatically.

Now he's embarrassed, and that turns him nearly feral. He hisses and steps in, baring his canines.

I put up a hand, mind racing. Surely, he won't be foolish enough to attack his creator?

But no: he steps back, breathing hard, eyes glittering. Shiny with rage, like little new buttons in the holes of his sockets.

"Don't do that again." I pierce him with my stare. I'm stronger than he is, by far, and more agile. I'm smarter too, and he knows that. I think he hates that part most of all.

He swallows and looks away. "Understood." His shoulders are taut and his body tense.

"Karl, last week you killed a young woman and her entire family in cold blood for no good reason."

"They learned who I was." His voice is flat.

"You could have wiped their minds instead." The frustration wells up, and the words snap at him, bullets in the air. "The daughter was just eighteen. The boy, ten." I run a hand through my hair. That was the age of my brother, eons ago, when he was killed.

"She made fun of me." His voice is bitter. "She said I was ugly." He giggles, high pitched, a sound that doesn't

17

match his physique. "Her blood was delicious. I drained her dry."

He makes a fist and raises it, and the muscles bulge in his biceps and triceps. He has the face of a dullard, but the body of a champion weightlifter. "The second when you suck that last drop of blood? The very last one the body has to give? It's the sweetest one. Hers was the best I've ever had."

He has a look of bliss on his coarse face. "It almost makes all of this worth the pleasure." His words roll off his tongue as he waves his hand up and down his body. At mine. His eyes roll back in his head before he seems to remember he's talking to me. He snaps back into position and shakes his body, as if sloughing off a winter's sleep.

"We don't do that." I snap.

But I remember how it feels to take the last drop, the one infused with the very essence of life. My salivary glands start to produce, and I shut my desire down hard. "We take what we need and leave the host to be."

He shrugs. "Your rules. Not mine."

"You know that's accepted across the globe by the majority of vampires because it keeps us safer. And you swore to me —"

He breaks in. "Who will ever notice a few more dead humans here and there? They're all going to die someday, anyway." He leans in, expression earnest. Like he's the master, and I'm the acolyte.

For a minute as our eyes lock, my mind sways. He's not wrong about their impending mortality, and when I think about his words, the ancient urges well up.

I take a deep breath. "Why were you even talking to

the girl in the first place?" I shake my head, forcing myself not to betray my reactions. To show him that I'm still the stronger of us.

"Maybe I wanted to find a pretty sweetblood for some sex and dinner," he drawls. "Is that okay with you?" He pauses. "But she wasn't interested. So I showed her my fangs and threatened her."

"We don't kill those who don't wish to fuck us," I snarl back. "We definitely don't tell them our true nature. That's reserved for the select we can trust."

"Humans are supposed to be scared of vampires. Do what we tell them." Now he's querulous. "But she didn't. She was a bitch." His mouth twists. "She deserved what she got. And so did her family."

"I had to call in favors, Karl. Set it up like arson and fix the body so the coroner wouldn't find the lack of blood and the broken necks. It was a world of trouble to cover for that."

And beyond that–it didn't feel good. It made me sick.

He shrugs. "Isn't this your job, oh great and gracious father? To look after your offspring?"

I bristle. "It's all of our job to protect each other. And them."

Lately, this past century, I've come to feel that vampires have a purpose beyond mere existence. I feel it in my gut: We were chosen for a reason, and that is to protect and guide the weaker species. Especially humans.

Oh, I know how that sounds, especially to vampires who've lost any touch with humanity save that of the taste for their blood. But I feel it pulsing in my veins: There is a greater purpose for us all.

So far, I haven't convinced many. Certainly not Karl.

He shifts his stance. "If you're so concerned with who I drink, why don't you find me the human that was here before?" He takes a deep inhalation. "What a delightful smell." He narrows his eyes. "Maybe I'll go see if I can find her, later."

Karl has a better sense of smell than most vampires, yet even he can't track her when she's already driven miles away. I think.

But I remember the look of ecstasy on his face when he spoke of killing, and the urge to protect the redhead rises up suddenly with a power I can't resist.

"You'll do no such thing," I snarl.

"Want her for yourself?" He smirks. Then his smile fades. He looks at me with an expression of surprise, then a smug knowledge. Like he's figured something out.

Fuck, I'm usually better at hiding my emotions. How can he tell?

"This has nothing to do with her." I lower my voice.

"Would it upset you if I took her?" He rubs his hands together. Giggles.

God, he's offensive tonight. It's like he has no fear. And he's oddly in tune with my emotions—more than usual.

"No more killings, Karl."

"Fine." His eyes slide away, and I don't trust that he means it. "I don't need her blood, anyway. I can get plenty." He's so confident.

He licks his lips and touches his face, where his cheeks glow, red and bright. He's the epitome of health, in a sick sort of way.

"You look refreshed." I make my voice sarcastic. But I can't resist the impulse to dig.

"You have no idea." He smirks.

"Then tell me." I stare him down, hoping he'll want to brag and drop some information.

He laughs. "Don't you wish I would?" But it's like he can't help himself. "Maybe I have a new supply," he says. "A really good one."

"Oh?"

He bounces one leg, like he can't hold back. "You're not the only one who can do things. Get rich." He gestures at my lab building. "You think you're so smart, but I've figured a few things out myself."

"Such as?" I raise my brow.

"Oh, but I've said too much." He smiles, but it isn't pleasant. "May I go now?" His tone turns obsequious. "I do so hope you've forgiven me, my dear creator. My Lord. Oh, maybe I should get down on one knee."

Karl waits in front of me, obviously loathing me but still beholden to me by the power of his oath. It keeps him there. It makes him stand back a few feet and tilt his head down, even if he doesn't know he's doing it.

It brought him here at my summons, even if he's unpleasant and ugly. It means something to him yet.

And although I know he's up to no good, I can't push at this moment. I need more time to figure out what he's doing.

"Go." I nod. Karl vibrates in front of me and blurs away without a word.

I'm left with the odor of his mouth, the heavy scent of death overtaking the delicate night odors of creosote and damp earth. But the foulness of his breath carries a spark note of beauty—he *has* been into some good blood. Really good blood.

That, as well as his attitude, leaves me with a lingering feeling of unease. What is he up to?

I wish I didn't need to care. But he's still my responsibility. When you sire a vampire, it's like giving birth, and forever after, you own the effects of what you created.

I step away from his effluvia into the freshness of a mesquite and create my own contamination by lighting a cigarette.

I take a deep draw, and my mind goes back to that human. I smile as I breathe out the smoke, remembering how her heart sped up when I smiled at her.

Oh, she wanted me, that one.

I contemplate finding her. Bringing her to Club Toxic as my very own sub for the night. Imagine her luscious, nubile body squirming on my lap as I spank her hard, turning her ass pink.

Think about the sounds she'd make when I drive my cock into her pussy and make her come. The feel of that red hair, thick, in my fist. Those tight, pert nipples in my fingers. A nick on her neck, the taste of her sweet, fresh blood. My God.

But then the night would end, as all nights do.

And I'd be left with the responsibility of the human, who would either need to be mind-wiped or brought into the circle of trust—a tedious effort that more often than not ends in a mess.

I already have a human I trust. I can't risk adding another one to the mix.

And there's something about this girl…I don't want to risk wiping her. She's sassy and smart, and it would be an utter tragedy to ruin something so lovely.

She's best left alone.

I scowl at myself and toss the cigarette down, and grind it out hard, ensuring that there are no sparks left. I don't want to start a fire. I've been around long enough now to see that global warming is very real, and so is human-related environmental damage.

Human. Ha.

I smile to myself, then pick up the butt from now and the one from earlier.

If I want to find a plaything for Club Toxic, I can pick up a beautiful little subbie in downtown Tucson. There are many vapid little lovelies there who are dying for a taste of the exotic…and I know how to deliver. And then disappear from their lives and their minds afterwards.

But later that morning, before I turn in for the day in the safety of my lair, I tug my cock. Imagine that it's the redhead's small fingers, her pretty tight mouth on me.

And when I come with a strangled cry, I see her vision in front of me so clearly that I almost think I've summoned her here with the power of my release.

CHAPTER 3

*B*ri "I got a message to call the office?" My heart thuds. It's Friday afternoon, and instead of feeling excited for the weekend, I'm filled with anxiety.

It's been five days since my blood draw, and the results are probably in. Usually I get a message to check the patient portal for an email from my doctor. Every time, the anxiety gets worse. Sometimes it seems like I just can't keep doing this, year after year. It certainly makes it hard to concentrate on anything else.

"Just one minute." The receptionist is pleasant but impersonal. "Oh, yes. Dr. Su wanted to talk to you."

"Personally?" Panic hits my nervous system like bird shot.

"Just one minute." The phone goes mute for a second before I can respond. Then she's back, and I can hear chatter in the background. "Oh, here it is. You'll need to repeat your blood work."

"Was something wrong?" I think I'm going to pass out.

"Just one minute." She sounds uncertain. "It looks like… Gila Diagnostics lost the results, it says."

"How do they lose results?" If she says *just one minute* again, I'm literally going to scream.

"I'm sorry, but I don't have that information. Dr. Su said to call you, so you could reschedule a new blood draw ASAP? And you might need to talk to insurance to approve?"

"Okay."

"Have a great day!" She hangs up without waiting for a reply.

I take a deep breath to calm my racing heart. It's okay. It's not bad news, not yet. But I can't seem to relax.

"Fuck it." I grab my phone and call my best friend, K.

It's a complete relief when I hear her cheerful voice. "Bri Baby! What's up?"

I hear her girlfriend, Mani, in the background: "Tell her hiiieeee!"

"Ugh. Just freaking out." I shut my eyes and try to imagine K's small face and blonde braids. Her blue eyes. She and Mani are probably twined together on the couch in her front room, watching some kind of history documentary.

"Why?" She sounds concerned. "What happened?"

"The lab lost my blood test results. How does that even fucking happen? Now I need to wait at least another week, maybe two, to find out."

"Oh, Bri. I'm sure the results will be great. You're going to be fine." She answers automatically, and I know she's only trying to reassure me.

"You can't know that." I sound bitchy, but it's only because I'm anxious.

"Didn't Dr. Su tell you that she was confident they got it all after the last surgery?"

"Yes, but still. I need the test results to relax." I bite my lip.

"It's going to be okay. Wait, don't you have Gila Diagnostics?"

"Yeah, why?"

"Maybe they lost your results during the break in."

"What break in?"

"It was on NPR." Her voice cuts out then comes back in. "Mani, can you move Arthur?" Arthur is her ancient arthritic cat, the one that makes me sneeze every time I visit them.

I smile as the phone clatters, and her voice recedes.

"Okay, I'm back." Her voice is her usual mix of confidence and confidentiality. She always sounds like she's about to tell you something important, secret, meant just for you. "Apparently vandals broke into the Gila Diagnostics testing lab, the one where all the blood vials go. They destroyed a bunch of samples and maybe stole the rest."

"That's creepy. Why?"

"You know what's really weird? And this part wasn't on the news. My brother said that the security cameras were turned off ahead of time. And nothing important was taken. Not even the expensive testing equipment."

"Is Peter supposed to tell you stuff like that?"

"Nope." She laughs. "But he did anyway because it's weird, and he just wants me to be safe with everything going on. The Night Stalker and all. You know the Stalker's taken three women, now, right? And still no sign of them. No bodies."

"Ugh." I shudder. "They're about our age, too. They keep talking about it on the news."

We're quiet for a minute. "Be careful," we both say at the same time. Then we laugh.

"Tell your brother to ask the other cops to put us on their do-not-give-a-speeding-ticket list." I smile. "If he really wants to help."

"Yeah, I don't think they have that." She laughs.

I'm still disturbed by the initial topic. "Who'd break into a lab, leave expensive equipment, and take blood?" I frown.

"I don't know. Halloween is coming up. Maybe they want real blood for a costume party." She snorts.

I'm still uneasy about this topic, but it's more fun to joke than to obsess. "Couldn't the assholes have waited until I got my results? Then I can smear my blood all over their stupid whore faces."

"They are whores," she agrees. "Hey, I have an idea. If they want blood..." she starts to laugh.

I cut in. "They can suck on my fucking tampons!"

She screams with giggles. "You're so gross. And I was going to say that!"

I hear Mani groan in the background. "You guys are disgusting." But she's giggling, too.

"I want to go out tonight. You guys want to meet me at a wine bar or even Starbucks?" I try to dial back the plaintive note in my voice. "We haven't hung out in a while."

"Oh, I can't. I'm so sorry, Bri. Mani and I are going to

dinner at her mom's." She sounds guilty. "Otherwise, I totally would."

"Tell her she can come too," Mani calls.

But I don't want to intrude. Bri is just getting to know her girlfriend's family.

"Actually, I think I'll go out by myself," I tell her.

Suddenly, an image of the man from the parking lot fills my mind, and I almost blink. It's so vivid, I can nearly touch him. In my imagination, he's talking to me. Commanding me to—the vision flickers and fades.

An idea occurs to me. "You know what? I want to try Club Toxic."

"Oooh la la. Fancy." K. whistles. "That's for the super sexy. Of course, that's you."

If I can get in. It's supposed to be so hot."

"Oh my God, you'll get in. With all that sexy red hair and your tiny waist and perfect ass? They'll be begging to chew your tampon, Bri."

She starts laughing so hard she coughs.

I shake my head, but I'm laughing too. "Send me yours, and I'll make them a mix pack."

After I end the call, I pull on my long-sleeve UV turtle-neck and put on the cloth facemask. The special UV glasses. And the gloves. It's still early evening, so there will be a few rays of sun left to avoid. But damned if I'm going to sit here like an outcast. If I put in a good five hard miles, it will calm me down. Running is the one thing that helps reduce my anxiety.

My Nikes pound the pavement. As I pump my arms and work on my form, I let my mind wander. To tonight.

I'll wear high heels and a tight dress. Do my hair and

makeup. Choose a handsome man to pull me close and whisper sexy things into my ear, secrets that will make me forget all about blood work and skin diseases with potential neurological side effects.

I want a night of passion. Maybe even some kinky sex, if I get a good vibe from him and all the signs line up. Because in addition to running, a good night of hot sex is also excellent for stress relief.

The thing is: the man in my daydream, the one who's putting his lips to my neck, is the man I met Monday night, the one in the parking lot. The one who didn't ask my name or want my number and whom I just can't seem to forget.

I know chances are slim I'll ever see him again, especially at the club tonight. But for some reason, I keep thinking of him as I get ready. Just in case.

CHAPTER 4

a^{lain}

"Sire." Martin bows his head briefly and reaches for my hand. "It's been a sick fire while, dude. Yo."

I snort. "No."

It's Friday night, and he's right on time.

"No? Blast it all." He rolls his eyes. "How does one keep up with the language?" He smiles and glances around my entryway, eyes sharp. Assessing.

"Well, it's been a hundred years or so for you. Give yourself time." I slap his back and then pull him in for a one-armed hug.

He blinks at my house and shudders. "Good gracious, the architecture is hideous." He glances around.

"You'll get used to it." I scan the area, too. We're always on alert. Being responsible for your own immortality, every second of every day, means a vampire can't relax. "Come in." I usher him into my house.

We're in the foothills outside the boundaries of

Tucson, in my isolated multimillion-dollar home with a fantastic view of a deep, rugged wash that leads south/southwest and is full of cacti, creosote bushes, and views of the Santa Catalinas. I know it's magnificent during the day because I routinely watch the footage from my security cams. But with my exquisite eyesight, I can see every detail just as well at night.

My territory, the area I own as a vampire, extends out North-West from here towards the outskirts of Phoenix. But I like living here, in the desert close to the Catalina wilderness. My home bumps right up into Lucius Frangelico's territory, and that's fine by me. He's one of the most powerful vampires in the world—living near him gives me extra security, as long as we're on good terms. Which we are, at the moment.

"Martin, did you try out the iPhone I gave you?" I know he didn't.

"I admired the package it came in. I admit I have not yet used the item itself." He gives me a guilty look.

I pause and look at him head-on. "Martin." I tsk and shake my head, partly as a joke but also in genuine frustration. "You need to do this."

He puts up his hands. "All in good time." His brows go up as he passes a wall of priceless art. "After all," he murmurs, "we have so much of it."

"You can only be a historical anachronism if you also stay employed as a period reenactor or a museum curator. Which, as far as I'm aware, you have not accomplished."

I lead him to the back patio, so we can enjoy the night view and the privacy. I've been to every continent, every corner of every country on this spinning ball, and the desert of Tucson fits me best. There's something about the lonely austerity of the desert coupled with the extreme efficiency these plants and animals have developed that soothes my ragged edges. I fit here.

"Well, ahem." He clears his throat and adjusts himself on the patio chair.

I can't tell if his clothes look so ill-fitting because he slept for the past hundred years, but he looks so awkward in his brand jeans and U of A sweatshirt that I want to laugh.

When the patio chair spins, he gives a startled yelp, then shoots me a sheepish grin. "It appears that I don't quite yet understand the 2000's."

"You don't say." I laugh. "I've missed you." He's not just a reminder that I chose a good subject to become immortal; he's also a friend. The polar opposite of Karl.

"Did you, then?" He seems charmed by this. "I suppose I would have missed you as well, had I been aware of the passage of time."

"Ah, I knew you'd emerge eventually. It kept some mystery alive. When will Martin show up?"

"And there is so little novelty now." He sounds melancholy. His profile lit up by the moon, his patrician features sharp and pronounced, he looks every inch the nobleman I found dying in a ditch ages ago, who looked at me, saw my true nature, and begged for my help. I chose to save him based on a sudden instinct that he would be a good and loyal friend.

"Thank you for watching over me." He nods.

I nod. "Any time." The question rises in my chest. "Did it help?"

He doesn't answer for a time. A full minute goes by, but I don't press him because—after all—he's right. We have all the time in the world.

Then he looks right at me, and the expression on his face makes me cold. "No." His voice is low and flat. He coughs. "I almost wished you hadn't watched over me quite so well." He doesn't look at me. "Waking up was a disappointment. And yet I don't have the courage to do anything else."

His words chill me to the core. "You need a hobby. More than a hobby—a passion. Then it will ease." I speak cajolingly, trying not to let the anxiety color my tone. "It works for me."

"I know." He sighs. "I haven't given up, Alain. I'll find my way again."

I turn back to the view. Today the closest cholla has dropped three ears, and the owls are uneasy: There's a coyote nearby, which doesn't scare them per se, but changes the behavior of the rodents. The animals please me. Always on alert, like I am, they are laser focused on their survival. I feel more of a kinship with them than most other beings on any given day.

Yet Martin means more to me than even they do. I don't want to lose him. I have few true friends, and even with the new goals I have in life, I need kinship, companionship, to stay sane. Even though having his friendship and my work sometimes seems like it's not enough —

"One must carry on." He raises his voice and injects a note of cheer. "Shall we have a diversion, then, later this good eve? My body does urge me to find a lady of the night for some enjoyment."

"First, let us talk. I need to update you."

"But my dear Alain. Your voice, as you well know, always brings me cheer. Do tell me the latest."

"It's Karl."

"What has the miscreant done?" He puts his leg down and leans forward, face electrified into interest. A little pleasure, too, I think, to hear ill of Karl.

Martin and Karl never got along, even though I sired them both. And as I came to realize that Karl was and is a weak and selfish vampire, I turned away from Karl, too. The fact that I support Martin and have turned against Karl only makes Karl angrier, but at the same time it strengthens my bond with Martin.

I frown. "He's murdering innocents with no attempt at discretion. In addition, he hinted about some new blood supply. And he's clearly full of an exotic variety." I frown. "I had to ask myself if he was behind the recent disappearances of young women."

"The ones you mentioned the other night?"

"Yes. Three women missing from Tucson. No bodies, no evidence. Just...gone."

"That's not Karl's style, is it? He's not stealthy." Martin raises his brows. "From what I remember." He tilts his head. "He's more of a brute." He snorts. "Violent with no finesse."

I nod. "That's what bothers me. If he's taking the women in Tucson, he must have help. And then there's the business with the break in at the blood bank."

"A what, is that?"

"Ah." I hesitate, trying to figure out how to describe it. "When doctors take blood samples–"

"They do what?" His eyebrows go up into his forehead.

I laugh. "Oh, Martin. We're going to have to do a crash course on what you missed. Yes. There is a safe way to take samples of blood, and new machines can test them for diseases and components. They're stored in little vials."

"Sounds like a lovely way to store a morsel for later." He licks his lips.

"Well, no. Old blood, mixed with the collection medium and preservatives?" I wrinkle my nose. "I suppose one could survive on it in an emergency, but it does have a marked unpleasant flavor."

"It also seems risky, since these buildings, as you explained to me, are heavily guarded?" Martin knows, like every vampire, the importance of staying under the radar. Invisible. Even if he's only catching up to the modern times.

"Yes. So, I don't think he would have taken that blood to drink. But something about it makes me uneasy. Like it's all connected—I just can't figure it out."

"Give it time. You'll figure it out. You always do. I'll help where I can, of course."

"Fuck." I stare off into the distance, tracing the outlines of the mountains against the black of the sky. No human could see the details. I can count every spine on every cactus. Every hair on the desert cottontail below. But I can't read Karl's mind or see even one of the plans brewing in his mind. Linked as we are in certain ways, he's still figured out how to block me from his closest thoughts.

I look at Martin. "He's about to cause trouble. And I'm going to have to deal with it."

"Well, you're no pauper, and neither are you a social outcast. I daresay you can amass your own army, if you need to. You don't have many offspring, but you do have allies."

In fact, I have only two offspring: Karl and Martin. After Karl turned out to be such a disaster, I withheld myself from creating more vampires. I can protect myself with alliances and don't need my own progeny.

"I never wanted to need foot soldiers. Especially not now. In this place." I gesture around the area.

"You're at peace here?" Martin seems genuinely curious. Maybe jealous.

"Well." I breathe out, smell the air. "Closer than I've been in a while. I have purpose, which makes it all easier. Although I guess I'm lonely." I laugh, trying to turn it into a joke. "Not every vampire is lucky enough to find a life-long mate like Lucius Frangelico."

"You want a mate?" He leans forward. "Do tell. Who is she? A shifter? A female vampire?"

I shake my head, sorry I said anything. "I'm exaggerating. There's no one in particular. I just need a one-night stand with a pretty human. My specialty."

"Hmmm." Martin gives me a look. He knows me better than that, but at least he doesn't push. Every vampire who feels the loneliness can sense it in others.

I change the topic back. "There's a fragile balance here with the vampire community and the shifters. Better not to rock the boat."

"Rock the boat?"

"Don't stir the pot."

At his blank look, I append it, "Make trouble. I don't want to anger some of the more established vamps who live in the vicinity. Especially Lucius, the king. He runs the club I like. Toxic. And more than that. He's powerful, a leader of sorts." I pause. "I like him."

"Aha. I see now, my good fellow." He reaches out and slaps my shoulder. His expression, one of mixed sympathy and concern, lets me know that despite his chipper tone, he recognizes the gravity of the situation.

"Perhaps we should leave the discussion of Karl to another time and avail ourselves of the lovely females who await?" His face lights up. "That is, if you feel safe enough to embark on a journey into the physical pleasures."

Karl can wait. My senses tell me that it's important to deal with him, but there is time. I will learn more about his plans, think on it, and determine the appropriate strategy.

One thing you learn over the centuries—if you survive —is that your continued survival hinges predominantly on your intellectual acumen and your ability to think and plan.

Acting rashly can lead to a quick demise.

We're all good at chess, us vampires. Even the stupid ones.

I speak decisively. "We'll go to the club and find women who are acceptable to bring to the lower level of Toxic."

He quirks a brow, so I add: "The main floor is a regular club. We only bring the select chosen below, to the secret BDSM club where the real fun occurs."

"I see." He nods appreciatively. I've already explained to him that the modern word, BDSM, is exactly what he likes in regard to sex, and that he can have both at Club Toxic. Martin and I have much in common. He was definitely a good choice to turn into my offspring.

His smile fades at my next words. "But first, I'm going to show you how to use that iPhone."

Martin groans but acquiesces. He takes the thing out of his pocket, holding it with two fingers, like it's a rotting carcass he pulled from beneath a rock.

I roll my eyes. "You know the importance of fitting into your times, even if it means learning new technology every few decades."

"My dear sir." His voice is haughty. "I daresay I deserve a few days at least to acquaint myself with the trappings of the 2020's." He tosses the phone up, and it glints silver in the moonlight, spinning like an oblong meteorite, before he catches it. Deft, flawless—you have to love vampire reflexes.

I laugh. "True."

But my mind flashes back to the girl. The one I had to mind-bend into leaving, so Karl wouldn't see her.

I want to know what sounds she makes when she comes. I want to stick my tongue into her pussy and taste her juices, her fresh, vital human scent. I want to fuck her so good and hard that she trembles with pleasure and loses all control and begs me for release.

And then I want to nick her neck, at the height of her ecstasy, with my canines, and lick off the rubies of blood that well out, and find my own ecstasy. Find that moment when time stops and my brain shuts off and the only thing that exists is pure pleasure.

I want it so badly that I nearly roar, and my cock goes hard with want.

But she's gone.

And even if she were in front of me, there's something about her that's almost too much. I can't afford to get attached. That never ends well. And I have a feeling that this woman would be difficult to forget after one night.

I adjust myself and shake my head. I'll find another woman, and then another, and another. I'll bury myself in their willing flesh, and before I know it, I'll have forgotten all about the feisty red-head.

She's not for me.

Yet I send out a wish into the atmosphere. An invitation.

Join me. Tonight.

As we approach the club, I slow way down to roll with traffic. There's a line of hopefuls down the block, the young and the beautiful, the rich and the powerful, all praying the bouncers will give them the nod.

"My goodness." Martin peers over. "What a visual feast."

Chatter and perfume and pheromones fill the air, and I scan the line, looking for the one that I'll select. The one I'll bring downstairs and strip and use to my desires.

"Oh, that blond reminds me of a duchess I knew." Martin's voice is eager. "The hair and the haughty eyes. She was a vixen in the sheets." He sounds fond. Then sour.

"But these modern women are scary. What does one even do with them?"

"You treat them with respect, Martin, and go from there. You ask first, never take what isn't offered. Except a little blood, now and then." I wink at him. "Not too much, of course. Never damage them."

But I'm distracted.

I keep thinking about the girl from earlier. None of the lovelies in line, even the shiniest, freshest ones, look the slightest bit appealing. It's almost as if I can smell her in the air —

Suddenly, there she is. The human from earlier. Her hair down and glorious, with curls cascading all down her bare back. Her lips are candy cherry red, the color that makes a man want to bite hard, and suck, and never let go.

"What the…"

I slam on the brakes. She's dressed in a barely-there mini-dress that fits her body so well that I can see every luscious curve. Her legs are long and gleam in the street lights. How does she walk in those fuck-me heels? My dick gets hard immediately.

Did I sense her all the way back in the foothills?

"Well, she is a delight." Martin cranes his neck. Then looks at me, eyes sharp. "You've met her already, yes?" He knows me well.

I idle the car slowly, stopping for a red. "What's she doing here, of all places?"

"Here in Tucson, where she apparently lives? What an astronomical coincidence."

"Smart-ass." I can smell her more strongly now, and

she's just as good as before. Better, because she's pulsing with energy and desire. Need. It's intoxicating.

But I meant it: what the hell is she doing here at Club Toxic? It isn't possible she felt my plea and came because I called her…right?

Martin's voice is wry. "Mayhap, you shall have a busy night."

I scan the road, but of course, there's no street side parking. I head to the Mercado lot, just a minute away. "She's not a fit."

"Then you don't mind if I give her a good tumble?" He's got a faux innocent tone.

"No, you may not, you goddamn animal. Get out."

I park the car and unfold my legs from the Porsche and listen. I can hear at twenty times the distance of an ordinary man even in a crowded concert.

I call to Tiberius, the bouncer on duty, the one whose suits are impeccable, and who prefers his young men built. *"Go get the redhead. Bring her in for me."*

One of the handy things about being undead—with hearing this excellent, we can communicate from farther apart than humans.

"Sure thing, Alain."

"And don't let anyone fucking touch her until I get there."

Maybe she's not right for me, but damned if I'll let another vampire get his hands on her, let alone his fangs. If she chooses anyone at the club tonight, it will be me.

CHAPTER 5

B^{ri} "Excuse me, Miss?" The handsome bouncer inexplicably bypasses the models and comes right up to me. "You can come in."

I glance behind me. "Me?"

"Yes." He's utter perfection in his classy black suit. He's not a huge man, but he gives the impression of restrained power.

"Why me? Not that I'm not excited." I notice a few catty glances and wistful stares and try not to feel like some kind of royalty.

He smiles. "Special invitation from a VIP."

My bubble bursts. "Maybe you mean someone else?"

His voice is patient but firm. "I don't make mistakes. Are you coming?"

"Yes. Of course. Thank you." I follow as quickly as I can in my heels because he's quick.

"Right this way." He gestures as we approach the front.

The building is old, made of adobe, painted white, and

fitted with a thigh-high metal railing in front that outlines the space for a patio. There are no tables, though—just another massive bouncer at the door, all in black, unsmiling. Soft incandescent bulbs are strung up along the upper balustrade, a faux balcony for the second floor, lending the place an air of holiday festivity.

"Have a good time. Welcome to the club." He opens the door to another world.

"Who told you to let me in? Can you point him out?"

But I'm already in, and the door is shut behind me, apparently without needing to pay a cover charge.

Club Toxic, the #1 spot in Tucson.

Music blares from a wicked sound system. The bar is packed, and people are talking, dancing, heads bent together, bodies entwined. The lights are low but perfectly set for the ambience, and the whole place is sexy.

There's a small temporary raised stage in the corner, and I see a band setting up. Someone has a candy red Fender Stratocaster, a tall lean guy with a black ponytail and deep eyes. He looks at me and smiles, and my stomach flips.

He's cute. Is he the one who sent me the invitation? Maybe he saw me in line?

I want to dance. I want to kiss a sexy man tonight. And maybe, if the vibe is right, I'll take him home with me and forget myself in his arms. I look again at the guitarist.

But something whispers in my mind. *No, not that one.*

I frown. Shake my head.

Then, suddenly, my neck tingles, and I feel the urge to turn away from the guitarist, towards the far wall.

And it's then that I see *him*.

· · ·

*A*LAIN

She thinks she's hunting—how cute. She has no idea how out of her depth she is here, at Club Toxic, where the supernatural come to play.

Soon enough, she'll realize she's the prey...and I'm the one who plans to catch her.

Not without a little fight, though, I hope.

As soon as she sees me, her eyes widen, and I can smell the adrenaline flow into her veins. Yeah, she's excited to see me.

I make my way over to her. Her eyes are on me the entire time, her body attentive.

She's even more beautiful than I remember, and I nearly catch my breath as I approach. Her flaming red hair is a mass of perfect curls, and her luscious lips are painted in a beautiful bow. And those green eyes—so large, rimmed with thick black lashes, so expressive, should be immortalized in a painting in the Louvre.

Not to mention her banging body.

"Your car must have made it all the way to town." I signal the bartender and hold up two fingers, point to the bar. *You know the one I want.*

He nods. *Yup.*

"Of course, it did." I can hear her heart speed up, but she keeps her voice casual, as if she could possibly fool me into thinking she doesn't care that I'm here.

I know better.

She stands still although the frenetic beat of the music still thrums through our bodies, resonating at the wavelength of *fuck me.*

"Care for a drink?" I take her elbow, barely touching it.

She sucks in her breath, and her cheeks flush. "Depends what it is."

"It's whatever you want it to be." I pause. "What is it you're looking for here?"

She looks away, and her pulse gets even quicker. "What does anyone want? Pure joy. Eternal bliss. The usual."

Her voice is defiantly flirtatious, but there's a sadness to her, something deep and dark, hidden under the surface. Normally I don't care what emotions humans squirrel away, but I'm curious about this girl.

"What do you want?" She looks up at me, challenge in her eyes.

I put my hand at the small of her back and smile at her tiny gasp. "Exactly the same thing." I guide her to the bar, and it takes just a fingertip of a touch for her to follow my head. Oh, this girl will be fun.

Two glasses of champagne stand tall, rims just touching. The bartender tilts his head. "Enjoy."

"Moet et Chandon. All the way from Epernay." I hand her one of the crystal goblets.

"From France to Tucson. Quite a journey." She raises her glass. "What a tortuous trip, just for a little pleasure."

"Oh, but don't you think that pleasure is enhanced with a little bite of pain?" I check her face.

Yes, there it is: Her pupils dilate, and her blood pulses hard and fast.

"I saw your face when we met. When I spoke of pleasure and pain." I smile. "It's my specialty." Without giving her a chance to respond, maybe keep her a bit off balance,

I tap her glass with mine, a deliberate ping. "To what shall we toast?"

She smiles. "Well, I'm toasting to all my dreams. That they come true." A micro expression flashes across her face. That undertone of alarm, even despair. But it's gone as quickly as it came.

"Then I wish you the same."

"What about your dreams?" Her voice is light. "Shouldn't you save your wish for yourself?"

I lock eyes with her. "I usually get exactly what I want. I don't need to make wishes."

She sips hard and coughs a little. Waves her hand in front of her face. "Excuse me."

She's aroused but off balance, a heady combination—it means that playing her will be even more delightful.

I sip the champagne, savoring the flavor, the bubbles on my tongue. I can hear them pop on her lips, tiny fireworks of carbonation and alcohol. "Remember what I said? This goes well with what you want."

"I remember everything you said." Her voice is low and throaty. She smiles.

My cock gets hard. I murmur something from my old tongue, words I haven't spoken in a hundred years.

She raises her voice to beat the music. "What did you say?"

"I said that we can go somewhere else. There's another level to this club if you're brave enough to find out." I step closer and whisper into her ear, letting my lips brush her lobe.

"W- What kind of place?" She sucks in her breath.

I can smell her body's arousal. I already know her

answer, even before she does.

I hide my smile. "A BDSM club. Downstairs. Secret… and invitation only." I look into her eyes. "I'm inviting you."

She makes a tiny humming noise and shuts her eyes, almost drifting into me. "I don't even know your name."

"Alain. Marchmont. And you?"

"Briana. Shaughnessy. I go by Bri."

I brush a kiss at the base of her jaw. "Sweet Bri. I can give you what you came here for tonight. All the pleasure you can handle…as long as you are willing to play my game."

"Tell me your rules." She narrows her eyes at me. "And I'll tell you mine."

I put my lips back to her ear. "My only requirement is that you do exactly what I say, when I say it. For as long as you enjoy yourself. Yes?"

"You're a dom?"

"Exactly. For one night only." I brush a finger down the side of her face. "You have rules as well?"

She looks away, then back at me. "One night is my rule, too. I don't do relationships. I can leave at any time. If you have any diseases, leave now." She pauses. "And don't call me tomorrow." She sticks up her chin.

Does she even know how perfect she is for me right now?

It's all I can do not to grab her right here and have my way with her on the bar. Among all the civilians. Of course, I have more control than that. Barely.

"Done. Shall we?" I hold out my hand.

She blinks. She's at war with herself, and then she falls

off the edge. She drains her champagne and puts the glass back onto the bar. "Yes."

"Good." I take her hand in mine. "Come."

She follows me across the floor to the coatroom, where I blur the edges of my body as I open the secret door. Nobody's here but the bouncer, another vamp, but I do it just in case. This place must stay a secret from the commoners.

And then I take her downstairs.

CHAPTER 6

Bri

This is exactly what I need. One night with a hot guy before I deal with all of my messy life—the medical concerns and my upcoming visits with Dr. Su, my work projects, everything.

I'd be stupid to refuse this offer. One beautiful night to sustain me.

"If you don't like it, you are free to leave at any time," he murmurs, bending his dark head down to mine. "But I think you'll be begging me to stay."

Just having him so near sets my body aflame. "We'll see." He's probably right, but he's so incredibly cocky. He knows he has me, and that pisses me off. I wanted to be more of a mystery to him. Not easy pickings.

Then my mind is officially blown as he leads me down the dark staircase and opens a narrow door at the bottom... into another world. "How does nobody know this is here?"

"The right people know." He laughs. "It's a BDSM club for the elite."

I'm no stranger to BDSM, and I like kink in my relationships. I've even visited the local BDSM club, but it didn't appeal; I never met anyone special there, and the atmosphere didn't seem inviting.

This club, though, has an entirely different vibe. It's instantly sexy, like someone is whispering into your ear and stroking your body. The people here vibrate with energy, color, brilliance. Heat.

It's full of low gleaming lights, expensive wood and exotic finishes. No expense spared; no replicas. Everything gives the air of being heavy, solid, and quality. Classy.

An immense throne stands haughty in the center of the room, and it seems to me that it's at once ancient, priceless and full of history. Are those real rubies embedded in the inlay? I want to ask what it's used for, but other things grab my attention.

A woman is tied to a perfectly crafted, burnished wooden cross, naked, and a man is lashing her. She cries out, and he steps in, and bends down, putting his head to her neck. Her cries turn from pain to pleasure, and her orgasm rips into the air, making people turn and look.

I put a hand to my mouth. The absolute bliss in her voice and the way he roars out his satisfaction is unreal. It's like romance books come to life, but with some kind of dark edge. She's into blood play, clearly, because when he steps away, there's a red smear on her neck. On his mouth and his hands.

Although I've never been interested, my body reacts with a visceral tug. I want it to be me who had that screaming orgasm—just the way she did—everything she felt –

"Do you like that?" Alain's voice thrums into my ear.

"I—I don't know."

"Don't you?" He smiles.

"I like being tied up." I glance across the room to a spanking bench that gleams in the golden light. "I like that." A slender woman is tied down, ass up, and a man spanks her with a paddle. As her ass grows pink, she begins to make sounds of impending bliss and growing discomfort, both.

My pussy clenches.

"I think we'll start with something similar," Alain murmurs. "Perhaps I'll spank you and tease you, hmmm?" He watches my reaction like a hawk. Smiles when I flush.

"Mmmm…" I lean into him, turn, and let my head fall back onto his shoulder.

He wraps his arms around me from behind. "Will you strip for me, Bri? Let me turn your ass red before I fuck you? Stand in front of me and do what I tell you?"

"Maybe," I whisper. He smells amazing, some cologne I've never smelled before, and his own essence. "If I like what you ask." I might have a spontaneous orgasm just from his voice.

"I'll make sure you do." He runs his hands down my body. "First we'll get another drink."

He's playing me just right, drawing it out. Not pushing. Letting me take this in, at my own pace. It's like he's reading my signals, ones I don't even know I've sent.

It gives me confidence. And makes me needy.

At the bar, a tall man with piercing eyes and a patrician profile takes a glass from the bartender. The glass is baroque looking, heavy and expensive. It's filled with a viscous liquid, and for a second, I think I smell the iron tang of blood in the air. He smiles at Alain and raises his glass. "Cheers."

The red fluid rolls onto his tongue.

"What's he drinking?" I frown. "Is that…?" My voice goes up. It can't be. But it is, and then I see the man's teeth, his canines longer than normal—he's drinking blood.

"Club special. Not for you." Alain looks into my eyes and the room blurs for a second.

A sudden pain splits my skull, and the earth tilts on its axis. I gasp and grab my temples. I'm so disoriented that I stumble and would fall except that Alain grabs me and rights me. I stand up, but I sway.

"Bri, talk to me." He grabs the sides of my face, and his hands cover mine, already on my own head. "Look at me."

I stare into his eyes, and the pain fades, but I'm dizzy as hell.

"Are you all right?" His voice is gentle and fierce at the same time. The words don't make sense yet. For a second the pain returns, and I have no freaking clue where I am. Then it all comes back, like watching a glass window shatter in reverse.

I shake my head. "I'm sorry—what?"

"You were a little shaky there." His hands feel good on my arms. Almost like energy is flowing from him into me.

I like it and don't. It's the kind of thing you need to learn not to rely on.

"I haven't eaten much today. And I had a stressful phone call with my d—this afternoon. I'm okay now." I take a deep breath. "I get migraines sometimes. That felt like one starting. But it went away."

"Good." Alain gestures to the bartender, and suddenly a platter of food appears, like something out of a Renaissance painting: grapes, cheese. I can almost see the brush strokes.

A tall man next to me looks at us, smiles, and wanders off with an ornate glass. There's something familiar about him—but I don't think I've ever seen him before. Strange.

"What was so upsetting about your meeting today?" Alain touches my arm. Soft. And his voice sounds like he actually cares.

For one split second, I want to tell him. Get the feeling he'll understand, sympathize. Console.

Then I remember what life is really like.

I shrug. "I came here to forget about it." I give him a meaningful look.

"Understood." He nods. "I did promise I could help with that." He sounds rueful. Then he leans in and barely brushes my lips with his. "And so much more, my dear."

My body turns molten. "Good."

"You were going to tell me what you want to drink." He smiles.

I blink. "Vodka. Rocks."

He raises a brow. "Just one."

"Why are you in charge of what I drink?"

"Oh, sweet Bri." He has a smug look on his face. "Tonight, I'm in charge of everything you do."

I feel like arguing for the sake of it because sometimes it's fun to be sassy. But the truth is that I want exactly this.

So I sip my vodka and give him my best innocent stare.

"Yes, sir." I run my tongue over my lower lip, a flicker, and smile. "Master."

He practically growls. "Fuck, Bri."

"Isn't that the plan?" I slam the shot down, and the liquor sends fire down my throat, and a syncopated beat later, into my veins and my brain. The world gets warm and pretty, and all the harsh edges fade into themselves, leaving the joy behind.

"Oh, it most definitely is." He smirks. Then he scoops me up into his arms. "But you're going to earn it, baby. The fuck doesn't come for free."

I squeak and laugh in delight, in triumph. This. This fucking moment. I'm euphoric. I kick one foot up and close my eyes, enjoying his strong arms.

He strides across the room to an empty settee and slides me down along his body, and I feel every glorious muscle on the way back to Earth. And his cock. Jesus, he's hard.

"You have a safe word?" He pulls me back against him, so my ass is against his hard cock.

"Do I need one?" I reach back to touch him where I can. Pull at his clothes.

"Most definitely." He breathes a smile into my neck. "Choose well."

His palms cup my breasts through my dress, find the nipples. Pinch. I suck in a breath.

"Red." I bite my lip, hard. "Like blood."

He stiffens behind me. "What an apt choice."

"I'm an apt kind of girl." I grind my buttocks against him. "You'll see."

"I intend to do just that." He spins me around,

suddenly, so I face him, and puts both hands on my shoulders. "You ready?" His smile is dark and dangerous.

"I've been waiting for you to catch up." I roll my eyes and grin. "Thanks for joining the party."

"Take this off." His voice is low. He flicks the strap of my dress with a finger. Steps backs, crosses his arms. "Nice and slow. Eyes on me while you do it." He gives me a challenging stare. "That is, if you're brave enough to do it. If not, I'll have to teach you a good little lesson in private." He glances from me to the room. He's checking me, making sure I like where he's going. Keeping it sexy in case I need an out.

And I do like it.

I move to step out of my shoes, but he shakes his head. "Leave the heels. Listen, Bri." He snaps his fingers. "I'll tell you exactly what to do."

I narrow my eyes at his smug composure, and heat rises in my body. He's arrogant, and I like it. So I slide the dress down and wiggle out of it, carefully letting it pool at my feet as I step out.

Now I'm just in panties and a bra, lacy. Red.

His eyes widen for a split second, and I know he likes what he sees. I exercise and I'm fit, and I'm proud of my body.

"Your turn." I smile.

"Did I tell you to speak?"

"I speak when I choose." I taunt him with my expression.

"Not anymore." He taps my cheek with his hand. "Not unless I specifically ask you to. Or unless you need to say red."

I open my mouth, irritated. Close it because I like the game. Want to see where he's going. Want to feel his hands on me.

"And right now, I'm going to spank you as a reminder to obey."

I blink at him, and my nipples pebble in the air. My body pulses with adrenaline and fear. And desire.

"You see those people?" He points. "You want them to watch us right now?"

I turn my head. Eyes are on us. It's expected; in a club like this, you watch. You are watched. It's all part of the game.

And I don't mind; in fact, it enhances the rush. It's like being famous, for a minute or a second, having people drawn to your drama.

I nod. Smile in anticipation.

"They're going to enjoy this." In a movement so fast I don't register it, he sits on the padded bench beside us and pulls me to his lap. "But not as much as I plan to."

I'm across his hard thighs, ass up, looking at the floor. It's polished hardwood, so shiny it gleams a thousand reflections of the lights refracted in the room.

"You can cry out if you want to." He chuckles. "But I don't want to hear any words."

I swear to God, this lights such a fire in me that if I wasn't wet between the thighs already, I'd soak my panties further.

He taps my ass once with his hand, once again, then spanks. Hard.

I gasp and squirm on his lap. Hold back the "ouch" in my throat.

"Relax." He strokes his hand up and down my thighs. "Lie still."

Under his caress, my body softens, languid, and my muscles unclench.

He spanks me again. Harder than before. The crack echoes around the room, and I wriggle. "Ah-mmm." It's difficult not to say anything, not even, "Ow."

He chuckles. "Good girl. Behave when you're on my lap, Bri."

Now he brings his hand down fast, over and over. Spanks on the roundest part of my ass, and my thighs, and the place where I sit. In less than a minute my skin is on fire, and each new spank pushes my hips into his legs, driving my arousal deeper.

I utter a strangled cry. I want to say "stop" and "ow!" and "Alain!"—but he doesn't want words. In frustration, I grab at his leg and squeeze my nails in hard. Whimper at an especially hard spank, right on the spot that burns the hardest.

His hand feels like a paddle. "Hands down." He slaps over and over. "You want to come? It's not a given. Remember, you're earning an orgasm by behaving for me. If you don't please me, I'll dress you up and send you home, girl."

I yelp and gasp. "Mmmm!" It hurts, and I want him to stop. I want him to keep going. I want him to fuck me. I want to speak.

And because he's my master in this moment, I'm going to let him do exactly what he wants, even if it's making me insane. I'll go through anything to get to the part where he lets me come.

"Feel how wet you are." He pauses and strokes my flaming skin. "Spread your thighs. More. Ah, you're dripping with arousal, aren't you?"

He slides a finger under the gusset of my thong into my pussy.

I immediately clench down. "Gah. Mmm."

He lets his fingers stray to my clit, where he strokes for an agonizingly long moment before pulling away. "I think you like what I'm doing."

I push my hips down into his body, hard.

He laughs. "Too bad you can't speak and tell me what you want. More spanking, is it? Let me oblige."

He commences a rapid attack on my buttocks that has me nearly levitating off his lap. Finally, when I'm just about done, he stops instantly. It's like he read my mind.

"Still," he whispers, and I close my eyes and sink into his body, the pain disappearing as he strokes my ass, over and over, until the burn is manageable, pleasant. Sexy. "That's right." His voice is low and sensuous. "Good girl."

It's like I'm hypnotized, in a trance. I can't tell if it's endorphins, or his voice, or the lights in here, but everything blends into a sensual mix of pleasure, and my whole body hums with enjoyment. Yet the need to come is growing, second by second. I squirm again.

A voice intrudes. "Alain, you have a lovely handful there."

"That I do."

"Care to share?" The new man has a British accent. He's the man from the bar earlier, the tall one next to me. Handsome in his own way, but I'm not a toy to be passed around—

I stiffen up, and Alain's hand on the small of my back grounds me. "No." His voice is flat and firm. "She is mine alone."

"If you change your mind…" The newcomer lingers.

"I won't." Alain flips me, stands, and pulls me into his arms so fast I'm dizzy. "Leave us, please." It's not a request.

I barely have a chance to peek over at the other man, who nods and raises a glass with a rueful smile, before Alain strides over to a curtain and steps into a semi-private alcove. It's dark in here, barely lit by a sconce in the wall that glows red.

"You may speak, Bri. What do you want?"

My voice is hoarse. "I want…" I don't know what to say. "I want to feel your body. Take off your clothes for me."

He laughs. "You think you're in charge here?" The whites of his eyes glint in the dark. I'm barely accustomed to the dimness, but I can make out a chair and a long, padded bench.

"Yeah, I do." My head is still swimming with my emotions and endorphins, and I sway in front of him.

Without a word, he takes my panties in his hands and gently tugs them away from my hips. Then he pulls, and the fabric rips apart, effortlessly. He unwinds the fabric from between my thighs, where it's stuck along my pussy and ass, wet with my arousal. "I don't think you need this anymore."

He tosses it into the black. "You're lovely. If you were mine, I'd keep you this way all the time. Naked and aroused. Begging for my touch."

"I'm not yours. And I'm not begging." Bravado makes me speak.

"Oh, you're not? We'll see."

"I don't beg."

"Not even for your master?" His voice is light, but there's something dark behind it. Something that makes me shiver in anticipation.

I shrug.

"Well, right now, it's only a game for you, isn't it? What if it were something more?"

He moves so fast!—in a second he's got me seated on the bench, and he's kneeling in front of me, between my spread legs. Sucking my nipple. Stroking my thighs. "What if you were bound to me, Bri, and the only way to enjoy pleasure was to do my bidding day and night?"

I moan and grab his hair.

He laughs. "Pull all you want. It isn't going to make me go any faster."

He strokes me again. "Lie down and open for me. Wide."

And I do. Because in the moment, I want him to be my master.

And when I feel his tongue on my clit, his lips brushing along my skin, I cry out, a strangled gasp of pleasure. "Alain!"

He teases me with his mouth. Over and over, bringing me to the brink and then pulling me back. After the third time, my thighs are shaking and sweat beads my forehead. My whole body is damp with effort and arousal.

The dim red lights are so low that details of the alcove are just beyond my reach, like my eyes can't acclimate. It just makes it that much easier to focus on Alain, alone, and what he's doing.

"I want to come. Fuck me, now," I demand, my voice hoarse and needy.

"We do things my way in here," he corrects me, slapping my pussy with his hand. I'm so aroused that it makes a wet sound.

"Ow!" I strain to close my legs, but he holds them open.

"Did I tell you to do that?" He slaps me again, and the pain is like a bright beacon, tugging me every closer to my impending orgasm.

"I'm going to come without you…" I warn.

"Oh no, you're not." He chuckles and pinches my nipple. "Because I forbid it. And you're going to obey me."

He bends down until our lips touch and whispers, "Aren't you?"

"Yes," I moan. I've never been this electrified with need.

"You're going to do every last thing I ask," he says.

"Yes." I arch up my hips.

"Beg me." It's a command, low and harsh.

"Alain, please. Please, I want to come."

"Not yet." He laughs at my frustrated sound and pulls me up to a seated position. "First you're going to show me your obedience."

"No…." I whimper. He was so close. I was so close.

"Kneel." He stands in front of me, legs parted slightly, arms crossed. "There."

a *lain*
Having her immediately get to her knees in front of me, breasts heaving, brow damp with sweat, is the biggest rush I've had in two hundred years. This girl is practically falling apart with desire. And her smell—something about her, I don't even know what—makes me come alive like I haven't in decades.

"I'll do whatever you want." It's hard for her to say the words, but as soon as they come out, she falls into a deeper submission—the thing she's sought from the start.

I've been staying out of her mind, giving myself the chance to know her at a human pace, but some of her thoughts are broadcasting right into my brain. It's like she wants me to read them.

"Anything."

The light is so dim that she can barely see me, this I know. I bend down on one knee and get so close that our lips are nearly touching. Her pupils are wide with the need for light and for me, both.

"Good girl." I say the words into her parted lips.

She closes her eyes and murmurs something.

I stand up again, in front of her. "Unbuckle my belt," I order, widening my stance and crossing my arms.

She does it without question, her fingers hesitant at first on my body, then gaining confidence as she feels her way, figures out the latch and the loops.

"Do you know what you'll be doing next?" I pull the belt from the loops and fold it over, smack it once into my palm.

She gasps.

I laugh. "No, I won't be whipping you with this." I hit my palm again, the crack resounding against the walls of the chamber. "Not yet."

I toss it to the chaise and undress quickly. "But I like the way you think." I get close to her. "And maybe you'll get the belt later, on that pretty ass, depending on how well you do this."

I tap her under the chin with my index finger. "Open. Wide."

She doesn't hesitate a single second.

My cock is so hard it hurts. "Lick." My whisper is guttural, hoarse.

She darts out her pink tongue and lashes it across the tip of my cock, and it feels so fucking good that my thighs tighten up and I growl. "Bri, fuck."

She does it again. "Like this?"

"Yeah, just like that." This part wasn't supposed to be about pleasure but more about control. Establishing my dominance and her submission. But it's turning into more.

I haven't wanted a woman's mouth like this in over a century.

"Hands behind your back." I snap it out. "Legs wider. Good."

She moves quickly to get into the position I want, and the sight of her like that, body contorted at my command, head at my groin, servicing me as I wish, sends a rush of arousal through me that I nearly can't control.

"Suck."

I guide her head with my hand, and her mind with mine. *Relax that throat, girl. Let me in. Deep.*

She won't hear the words, but she'll feel the inspiration to do what she's told.

And she does.

Soon enough, I'm so close to the edge that I could finish in her pretty mouth.

"Nicely done, Bri." I pull away from her warm lips, and she moans a bit, but stays in position, panting. I can see her pussy glistening with need between her parted thighs, and I like the way her breasts stick out with her arms behind her back.

"Up on the chaise, now. Get back into that same position. I like how you look, waiting for my command."

"Yes, Master," she murmurs, crawling her way up, sinuous, damp with sweat and arousal. She assumes the required pose, and she's so fucking beautiful like this that I want to roar and sink my fangs into her soft skin.

"Wait for me. Don't move. I'll know if you do."

I turn my back for a second. I take a deep breath to center myself and get back from the raw edge of desire. I'm the master. Why is it that I feel so out of control?

When I turn back, she's still in position, but she's shifted an inch or so.

"You moved." I narrow my eyes.

"I couldn't help it." She's a little breathless. "I was off balance."

Understandable, forgivable, but also—punishable.

"Next time ensure you're correctly positioned from the start. Ten."

I bend over and grab the belt. "All fours, ass up."

She gulps, and her eyes go wide with panic and desire.

"Faster, unless you want twenty?" I lower my voice. "Or more?"

She's in position in the blink of an eye. "I'm sorry, Master." She wants the ten, and then she wants to fuck. That's fine with me.

"You will be sorry." I make my voice low and growly, and her pussy gets even wetter. I can see and smell how she likes my dominance and how much she wants the belt.

I double it over, raise it up, and spank her hard, right across both cheeks.

"Ow," she moans, twitching her pretty ass.

"Shh." I spank her again, harder, a little lower. "Next time you'll be more precise in your movements."

"Yes, I promise." She can't help yelping as I bring the belt down across her upper thighs.

Even in the darkness, I can see the line of red bloom hard and fast. She'll feel this tomorrow.

"Tell me you like my belt across your ass, teaching you to behave."

"I like it," she manages, then gasps as I bring the belt down again, again, again. "Ow."

"You'll bare your ass any time and any place I command, Bri." I whip her again. Hard.

"Yes, I will! Aaah." She flinches against the pain.

"Raise your ass up to me. Show me you want this."

"It hurts," she whimpers, but she sticks up her hips. "Please, I want you to fuck me."

"Did we get to ten?" I spank her again.

"I don't know." Her voice is raw with need. "Please."

I spank her a few more times, then discard the belt behind me, in the darkness.

"You think you deserve to come?"

"If you wish it, Master."

I don't know how she learned to beg so nicely, but it fucking gets me even harder.

I arrange cushions on the chaise so I can lie back, not fully reclined. "Straddle me, Bri. Hands on my shoulders and don't move them."

I pull her over, help arrange her over my lap, setting her up so her pussy is hovering over my hard cock. "You're going to do some work, now, to finally earn that orgasm."

I use one hand to touch her slit—so soft! So wet! I glide one finger up and down, play her clit a little, then push at her opening to stretch it a bit for me.

I take her narrow hips in my hands. "You want this?"

She nods, moans a little, and I tease her by letting her sit partway down so that the tip of my cock touches the entrance of her pussy. She cries out and tries to sink down, but I hold her firm. Rock her body and mine to tease her clit. "Not yet."

"Oh." She bites her lip and tosses her head back.

I enter the edges of her mind. The urge to orgasm is nearly overtaking her, and I force her to hold it off despite my teasing. I want to push her to the very edge of what she can take.

"You like this?"

I pull her down an inch, and she clenches her muscles down hard, trying to hold herself in place.

I laugh and pull her up, effortlessly.

She whines and wiggles her body, trying to bring her pussy back to my cock.

"Tell me again—who is your master."

I pull her down. I'm long and thick, and as wet as she is, she still has to stretch to take in my full cock.

"Alain, you are. You're my master."

"Ride me, Bri. If you do it nicely, I'll let you come. If you don't, I'll whip your ass again with the belt and send you home to masturbate in your bed."

"I'll do it the way you want!" She's nearly crying with want. She can't come until I let her, and she's going to do whatever it takes to get that orgasm.

I keep a hold on her hips just to steady her but allow her to move as she wants. As she's been commanded.

And fuck, she's good. She squeezes and rocks, and sets a frenetic pace, moving up and down on my cock like a little piston of desire. I know it's work for her because I feel her muscles quiver. I don't care. I want her to wear herself out on my body, be so tired afterwards she can barely walk.

"Keep going." I slap her ass as a motivation and grab her tits. Squeeze them while she goes up and down. Pinch until she whimpers, then ease off on the pressure. "Feel that?" I pull on her tits. "You like a little pain?"

"Yes," she moans, grabbing my hair hard. Tugs.

"How about a little more?" I squeeze harder, then ease off. "Keep moving."

I allow myself to relax into her body and enjoy the pure friction of her tight, delightful pussy, and when she's nearly exhausted herself—before she collapses—I grab her hips again.

"You can come if you let me bite you," I whisper into her ear. Speak it into her mind. "A little blood. You'll love it."

"Yes," she says, her eyelids fluttering. "Just please, please, let me come." She's desperate. Her pussy is surely on fire with need in a way she's probably never felt before.

I pull her closer to me and speak into her wet neck. "Then come. Now."

And as she orgasms on top of me, grinding her body hard, she screams in pleasure.

I allow myself to come, too, and it's the best damn orgasm I've had. Then, at the height of my bliss, I sink my teeth into her neck and suck, letting her essence flow over my tongue and down my throat.

She screams again and orgasms even harder, contorting her body on my cock so hard that I have to grip her with more strength to keep her steady. And as we both come, and come, and I drink her blood, I've never felt closer to another creature in my entire existence.

Bri

THE ORGASM RIPS into me like never before, and I scream. I'm not a screamer, but the power of this feeling is so intense that it can't stay inside me.

I sink my fingernails into Alain's skin, and squeeze my pussy as tightly as I can on his cock, and the universe explodes behind my eyelids and pure pleasure flows through my clit into my veins.

He's biting me, hard, and it feels fucking amazing. I want him to keep doing it because the nerves in my neck seem connected to my clit, and my whole body is lit up like a sparkler, like fire, like a volcano.

My orgasm goes on and on until I can't take it anymore, and then, when it crests, I go dizzy with the pleasure.

I think I pass out a little bit because when I open my eyes again, I'm lying on top of Alain, sweaty and panting, my pussy still sparking with pleasure. I'm so tired I can barely move my limbs. My thighs burn from the effort of riding him, and my ass is sore from the belt. My tits are tender as they press into his chest, and all of it—the pain and the pleasure mixed—is an intoxicating cocktail that makes me burrow into his body.

"Mmmm." I press my cheek to his chest.

His arms go around me, strong. Powerful.

My neck tingles where he bit it and pulses in time with the little contraction in my pussy. "Alain, I can't even."

He chuckles. "Neither can I. Just rest." His voice reverberates in my head. He's inside my head, and he's inside my pussy, still (even though he's not), and I'm inside him —none of this makes sense, but it's like we're one, at this moment.

I don't understand it, but I luxuriate in the sensation. Right now, I feel utterly content and protected. I've never felt this way before.

This time, I definitely fall asleep because when I awaken, there's a soft blanket covering me and a little table next to the chaise with food and water. The water is in that ornate glass, the kind from the bar, and the food is arranged like we're at a 5-star restaurant: little cheeses and toasted bread, fruits. Chocolate.

My muscles are still shaky as I sit up and eat a few things without thinking, just shove them in my mouth. But even as I do, I'm looking around for Alain.

It's still so dim in here that he could be in a corner, maybe, or hiding in the drapes, but I sense that I'm alone.

I sip some of the water and blink. My dress and shoes and purse are here, beside me, and with them—a sense of loss. This night is going to be over.

Of course, all nights end.

I bite my lip and tug the blanket closer around me. "Alain?" Strange, my ass hardly hurts at all. I would have expected to be more sore from our play.

My thighs are still shaky when I stand. I pull aside the curtain of our alcove and peek out into the main floor of the club. Time must have passed because it's quieter. Only a few patrons remain; the tall man from before is at the bar, chin in his hand, looking like the world presses down on his shoulders. A man and woman, naked, grind together and kiss on a settee across the room. But the spanking benches and cross are empty, the wood and leather glistening in the lights. Waiting.

I don't see Alain.

Well, I did tell him one night only. And he agreed.

I get dressed and slide my feet into my heels.

It occurs to me to touch my neck. There's a small bandage there. I frown. Alain bit me, and I liked it. I think he bit hard enough to draw blood–

I told him he could. I remember thinking it, even if I didn't say it. Even begging him to do it.

Suddenly he's back, and the room is warm and inviting again. I didn't realize how much I missed him until he reappeared.

"Bri." He glances at me, and I think maybe his face falls when he sees me dressed.

"Alain." My voice is hoarse, and I clear my throat.

"Sit, please."

Now that we're not having sex, the urge to obey him is no longer as powerful. But I sit anyway because—well, I suppose I just like being in his presence.

He sits beside me, so closely that we touch from hip to shoulder, and wraps an arm around me. "Thank you. That was magnificent."

He seems so full of life, even more than before. His enigmatic smile flashes in the dark. "You are spectacular, dear Bri." He takes my hand and turns it over, then kisses the palm, his lips soft.

I flush. "It was amazing. Yes."

"How do you feel?" He pulls me closer, and I relax into his body.

"I feel–" I think it over. "Good. Really good." It's true.

My body is tired, but I feel energized. Like I've taken more than I gave. Usually after sex, I just feel exhausted. But this time, my fatigue is laced with pleasure and strength.

"I'm glad." He touches my neck at the bandage. "This is all right?"

"Yes."

"It will heal faster than you think. Probably by the time you're home." He carefully takes off the bandage. "See, it's almost done."

I nod.

"I bit you on the other side from your scar." He touches the other side of my neck along the puffy line left over from the surgery. His voice is light. "What's that?"

I turn my neck away from his finger. "It's nothing."

He takes my arm. "And it matches the one I found here and here." He taps just below the other two spots. "Tell me."

"Just a thing." I don't want to think about my life at all right now. I just want to focus on the lingering pleasure. Plus, there's no point in chit chat. "One night only, so don't ask."

"All right. Your first time with blood play?" His voice is low.

"Yes." I slide my hand along his hard thigh. "My first time."

"Then I thank you for the honor." I hear the smile in his voice.

"No big deal." I shrug. "Tons of people do it all the time."

He straightens up. "Bri, it's a very big deal." He shifts

so he can look into my eyes. "Don't do that with anyone else. Here or another place." His face is stern.

I frown. "You're not my master anymore."

He looks away. "Consider it advice, then."

I bite my lip. "I promise, I won't go around asking every construction worker and Starbucks employee to bite my neck."

"You're so sassy." His voice holds humor. Then heat. "If you were mine, I'd whip you again right now for that."

"If you were mine, I'd..." I bite off the rest of the words. Because I was going to say, "If you were mine, I'd let you."

But this man isn't mine. And he can't be. Not with my life the way it is.

Besides, we agreed it was just for one night. He was probably just speaking out of habit.

I have to go." I speak automatically. "If I don't get home before daylight, I melt into ashes." I touch one of the scars on my arm.

His whole body stiffens. "What did you just say?" His voice is cold, commanding.

I flinch. "I mean it's getting late." When his body doesn't relax, I add, "it's a joke, Alain."

Finally, he eases up. "I'm sorry." He shakes his head. "I –" he pauses. "Yes, I must also leave. I'll walk you out."

He doesn't make any mention of phone numbers or next times, and even though this is the way I want it, my heart cracks a little as we walk together up that long, dark flight of stairs into the coat room of the club.

It seems to take only seconds to get to the street, where I summon an Uber.

I shiver, even though it's not that cold.

"Here." He removes his suit jacket and drapes it over my shoulders. "Until your ride arrives." He puts an arm around me too, pulling me close. I nestle into him, fighting the urge to close my eyes and bury myself in his chest.

But he feels so good that I wrap one arm around him. I accidentally stick the other hand into the jacket pocket—and find a pack of cigarettes.

"You know, these will kill you." I say it automatically, holding up the pack before sliding it back into the pocket. Weird. He didn't taste or smell at all like cigarettes.

He laughs immediately, as if I've said something extremely witty.

"'Alain, I'm not kidding."

He stops. "You're quite right," he says, formally. "Thank you for the advice." But there's still a smile in his voice.

Before I can respond, the car pulls up.

"Well, it's been fun." I hoist my purse up on my arm and cross my arms over my chest. The night is heavy with sleep and dark although it holds the tang of dawn in its essence. The street is quiet now, empty of the bustle and life it held hours earlier.

He looks into my eyes. "Bri, thank you. And good-bye." His gaze is unflinching, and suddenly I feel all whirly and giddy and dizzy, like my brain is made of cotton candy spinning so fast it's a blur. Everything that happened tonight compresses into one beautiful spark, which blows up like a firework, filling my vision with golden glitter.

As the glitter glows brighter and brighter, a sharp

headache starts to pierce my skull, like white hot needles. I cry out and put a hand to my head.

Alain says something under his breath, urgent, and whispers something into my ear. Immediately the pain recedes, and just the bright flashes remain, and then they flash out.

I blink. "I don't know what just happened."

"Maybe a migraine aura?" He touches my cheek.

For a second, I can't even think. Did I dance with this man? Surely, we had a drink. But what else?

"Look, here's your Uber."

The car has a pink LYFT sign in the window, and my phone buzzes—it's my driver, who plays the field when it comes to driving apps.

I get in mechanically, even though something is tugging at my brain. I need to ask him something, tell him something—but I get into the back of the car, which is warm and smells like Subway bread. The driver is playing jazz.

I buckle my belt and look up to wave at Alain, but he's already gone.

*a*lain

"So, tell me the progress, Doc." I stare at the screen, examining the charts and data arrayed in columns. I learn fast, but I can't just pick up a double MD/PhD in medicine and experimental genetics on the fly.

My mind flashes back to the phenomenal time I spent with Bri three nights ago–Bri, whom I'm never going to see again.

Bri, whom I should have wiped completely before she left. It's just that she reacted so badly to that first mini-wipe at the bar downstairs and even worse when I tried to wipe her at the end of the night, that I was worried I'd give her brain damage with anything stronger.

And the idea of hurting her was so repellent that I let her get into that cab with just a soft suggestion to keep everything a secret. To forget.

Probably I should have wiped her, though. Fuck.

I still can, if I need to. I could find her —

I force myself to focus on the numbers Dr. Lacey

Albright is showing me. "Are you closer to a final formulation?"

Lacey looks up, her black eyes piercing. "You're not paying attention. I just told you." She taps her mouse to alternate the view on the large screen.

"Sorry." I clear my throat. "I'm here now." I smile, and she shakes her head.

It's just she and I in her office, a private meeting. After hours, of course, when the rest of the medical staff have left this research building and won't see me. They'll never know I'm the one who built this place, was the brainchild behind it all, and that I pay their salaries. That I spend countless hours organizing this place to be the biggest research powerhouse in the world.

Sure, I could wipe them. But why take a chance on messing up the best minds the United States has to offer?

"Latest round of testing on compound X-C37 looks promising with p value coming in at 0.001." She gestures as she goes through pages of data with me. "Based on the rest of the data, we could be ready to petition the FDA for human trials by next spring."

I shift, restless. "Not fast enough."

She gives her trademark tight smile. "Faster than any other drug company in the world, Alain. And with at least triple the initial data. I don't think that's too shabby. First company in the world to even have a drug that might halt demyelination."

I cross one leg over the other and tent my fingers, leaning back in my chair. It smells like new carpet in here, and fresh wood, and the chairs are expensive office versions, plastic and fabric floating on titanium frames.

But I've already built an even better building. "Can we do this fall?"

She purses her lips. "Alain. You hired me to run this."

I put up a hand. "No, you're right. Absolutely. If you have a schedule, I trust you."

"These things can't be rushed." She narrows her eyes. "We're a new company, and there will be extra scrutiny. Relationships to build with lobbyists and senators and donors. It's not just about the medicine."

"But money talks, and I have plenty of it."

"And I'm counting on using that to help me build aforementioned relationships." She smiles. "You know it's one of my skills."

I bow my head. "I do."

We're silent for a minute although I can hear the buzzing of the lights and the beat of Lacey's human heart. At 63, she's strong and powerful, fitter than many people half her age. And yet, so fragile—I spend many hours worrying about her safety and pondering the best ways to inspire her and help her squeeze out as much work as she can during the rest of her productive years on Earth.

"Shall we carry on? Show me the rest of the data." I gesture at her screen.

"First, give me what I want." She stands up and puts her hands on her hips. "I'll need to hire a new lab assistant and an IT tech. Someone to update our internal web site and systems. The usual routine?"

"Do it. I trust you. How is security? Anything…unusual?" Something tells me I need to ask.

"Nothing of note." A muscle twitches in her cheek.

I can tell she's lying. "Lacey?"

She sighs. "Well, the other night there was a man, in the parking lot near the street light. He didn't seem right. He just stood and stared at the building. By the time Owen went out to see about it, he had gone."

"Did he try to get in?" Threaten you?" My senses are on alert.

"No. He was just watching. Do you think it's something to worry about?" She frowns and adjusts her glasses. "Alain, are we in danger here? You know this work is important to me, but so is my family." She gives me a look. "You know how much Deshaun and Tyra mean."

I do know. She has pictures of her cute twin grandkids everywhere and tells me about them often.

"If it's someone from my world, he won't mean you any harm. He's just trying to learn about me."

I don't actually think this is true. Karl is probably reaching the point where he'd harm my endeavors or people I care about just to hurt me. But telling this to Lacey won't help her because there's nothing she can do to protect against a vampire hell-bent on causing harm. I'll set up some secret surveillance to protect her at night while I figure out what's going on.

I keep my voice calm. "Keep any eye out and let me know if he comes back." Try to send her waves of calm energy and positive vibes.

"All right." She clears her throat. I can't tell if she was affected by my mental efforts, or if she's just tabling it, moving on. "Now are you going to watch and pay attention this time?" She gestures to her computer.

I lean forward. "This time, I'll memorize it all."

"Well, then." She pulls up the information and

proceeds to show me her newest creation, a drug that can slow the progress of MS, basically halt it in its steps. And she's working on a drug that can force axons to remyelinate.

This.

This is what I mean when I say that vampires are meant to guide humans, not harm them. With us as the backbone, we can help human development proceed faster than ever before.

I can't do what Lacey does—probably never will, even if I spend a thousand years trying. But I can help her do it.

I need to.

I imagine armies of vampires working under cover, hand in hand with select humans, helping the world advance. Maybe we can even skip generations of work, increase the pace at which we explore space and fight diseases.

Then people like my brother won't need to die in tortured, painful ways.

I'm no longer in the genetic pool, and although I walk this globe, I'm not really alive. More of a parasite than anything useful. And I wasn't lying to Martin—I am lonely. It's so painful that at times I've considered ending things by walking into the sun.

But doing work like this?

It gives me meaning. Hope. And I'll fight to preserve it.

Bri

It's been almost a week since I saw Alain, and I can't stop thinking about him.

My memories are strange, though. It's like they come in little bursts of color, and then I have to struggle really hard to focus on them. Like my mind is actively trying to delete them.

At first, I couldn't even say whether we'd danced. Then it all came back, in a dream—the kinky amazing sex. The things he did, the way he made me feel—it makes me almost regret my one-night-only policy. I want him again.

But I'm not going to see him again; I remember he made that clear, and so did I. One night only. And it's better this way. If I see him again, I'll risk getting too attached, and then it will hurt that much more when he leaves. Or when I do.

Maybe this new consulting job will get him out of my brain.

"Dr. Albright." I put my laptop down on the conference room table, a smooth clean surface. "It's great to see you again." I try not to act like I'm a shy groupie meeting a rock star.

"Briana, thanks for coming in at this late hour." My new boss smiles and takes my hand.

I've read about her in *Scientific American*; she's one of the top researchers in the United States. She's one of the most famous alumna of Howard Medical School, has three PhD's, and even hosts a podcast for young scientists each week—everyone knows who she is these days. And she hired me.

"Evenings are actually better for me." I told her about

my Xeroderma Pigmentosa diagnosis and struggles when I applied for the job.

"I know that." She smiles. "And I'm here at all hours, so it works for me too."

"A fellow night owl." I grin back. I really like Dr. A. She didn't care that I have a skin disease. She only wanted to look at my website work before hiring me.

"Oh, back in medical school, I had to learn to stay up all night. Only way to learn the material. And then when it came to residency…oooh." She shakes her head and smiles. "Well, let's say getting three hours a night was a good one."

"That's so insane." There's a little note of yearning in my voice. "But it was all worth it, right?" I gesture around the room. "Look what you've built."

She nods. "Definitely the sacrifice pays off."

"You know, I wanted to go to med school once." I bite my lip.

"Why didn't you?" She tilts her head. Her eyes are bright and intelligent. Curious.

"Well, my Xeroderma. I was having a lot of issues, and although my grades were good, straight A's in pre-med, I just…it wasn't going to work. I had surgeries. Treatments. It felt too exhausting. I went for my PhD in IT instead."

"You take the MCAT?"

I nod. "I got a 527."

"Bri!" She widens her eyes. "Girl, that's almost a perfect score."

I smile, shy. Then it fades. "It was a while ago, though."

"You know, it's not too late to apply again. Older

students make up a certain percentage of each class." I can almost see the gears moving in her brain.

"For me, it is too late." I answer fast.

"I had a study partner who was a decade older than you." She smiles. "Now she's a cardiologist at Mayo in Scottsdale."

"And it would be too complicated with my condition, especially if it gets worse."

"They make adjustments for disabilities. It's something to consider."

"It would be just too hard." I shake my head. I don't want to think about this because it's a closed chapter. I shouldn't even have brought it up. I know better than this. Life just doesn't let you keep good things, so it's better to give them up first.

"Well, it is harder, the older you get," she acknowledges. "God knows how I even got through my residency." She chuckles, then smiles at me. "But you've found your niche. You're an IT expert."

"Well, I'm glad to be working with you." I smile and brush back my hair. "I'm excited."

"If you can make those changes I texted you, I'd appreciate it. Just come find me when you're done."

"I'm on it." I open my laptop and connect to her secure system using the password she gave me.

Time flies, and by the time I'm done, two hours have disappeared. I'm happy with what I've created, and I'm excited to show the doctor my results.

I head over to her office, but she's not there. Maybe she's chatting with Owen, the security guard in the lobby. She told me they sometimes have coffee in the evenings for half an hour and talk politics when she needs a break from sciencing.

Suddenly the hairs on the back of my neck stand up. I feel odd—like I'm being watched.

Although everything is lit up, and I know the building is locked as always, unease hits me. "Dr. Albright?"

Silence. I glance around me, as my discomfort intensifies.

"Hello?" My heart pounds. I walk softly as I enter the tiled hallway. Overhead lights are bright and cheerful, and it's empty. I take a deep breath: This place is more locked up than Fort Knox. I can't even enter the door that leads to the lab areas: That's for Dr. A. and her researchers only. Fingerprint locks.

I'm being silly.

Garbled voices reach me from the lobby and come into focus as I approach, and I have to admit that I feel a sense of relief to hear Dr. A's feminine voice and Owen's deeper rumble.

"…here again…it's the second time I've seen him lurking around." Dr. A steps, points out the glass front door, then steps closer to Owen and lowers her voice. "Need…keep an eye out…"

"Issues in the area with…." Owen nods.

"I'm just going to make a call." Dr. A pulls out her phone. "Alain?" She heads down the hall, and her voice becomes indistinguishable as she walks.

Alain? I frown. It's an unusual name. What an odd coincidence that she's talking to an Alain, and I met my own Alain just the other night.

Well, not *mine*. It was just the one night. Even if I haven't stopped thinking of him since.

"Hey, Owen." I come up to the guard, curious about what I overheard. "Everything okay?"

Owen nods although he has a strange expression on his face. "Just noticed someone hanging outside the building. Probably a homeless person looking for trash to check. But we just like to stay on top of these things. You know, especially with the stuff going on lately in the news."

"Oh, okay." I glance down after Dr. A, who seems to be having an animated conversation. She waves a hand while she talks. "Isn't our trash locked up?"

Owen chuckles. "That it is. Dr. A. says even our trash is worth protecting. Course, most medical and research facilities do that. Just unlock for the garbage truck."

"So he probably wasn't after the garbage, whoever he was." I peer out the window into the black, but all I can see is the reflection of the lobby, shiny and wide. It's unnerving, thinking that someone might be watching.

"Mmm." Owen bobs his head, noncommittal. Put a hand on his waist, where he keeps a gun.

"So, what was in the news?"

"The Night Stalker?" He tsks at me. Raises his brows. "The three missing girls in Tucson, 'bout your age? Still no sign of them?"

"Oh, yeah." My heart pounds. "Yeah, he's scary."

Owen takes a sip from his silver thermos. The black band on it has his name written in silver Sharpie. Curly handwriting—probably his wife or daughter.

"Three so far. They never turned up." His voice is ominous. "Some freak on the loose. You got a gun?"

"No, I don't."

"Consider it." He pats his holster. "Sometimes the easiest way to keep the peace is to have protection, you know? Anyway, I'll walk you to your car when you go."

"Ah, sure." Normally I'd argue with him, but this conversation is freaking me out.

Dr. A. comes back up the hallway, her low heels clacking on the shiny tiles. "Owen will walk you to your car later." I notice she doesn't ask me. She tells me. And she's winding her hands together, a sign of nerves that she usually never displays.

"He already offered."

"Good, good." She nods to him, as if they've discussed something before. I feel like they're not telling me something. "Did you check the back…"

"It was fine. Like last time." His voice is even. "So I think we're okay."

"Okay. Thanks."

Dr. A.'s face is worried, but she smooths a smile on as she turns to me. "Are you ready to show me results?"

"I am." I hesitate. "Who's Alain?" It's not any of my business, and I know that. But I can't resist.

She starts. "Who?"

"A name you mentioned before?"

When she doesn't answer, I babble. "It's just, you know, I met an Alain the other day. And it's kind of a unique name, so it stood out to me. Sorry if I'm being nosy."

She nods once, slowly. "Let's go over the project, shall we?"

My cheeks get hot. I shouldn't have pried. "Sure, of

course." I hurry back to the conference room and pull up the screen. "I got it all completed. Let me show you."

Later on, after Dr. A. has enthused about my work and given me my next set of projects, I follow Owen, like an obedient puppy, to my car.

Never mind that my car is less than a hundred paces from the well-lit front door, and we're not in some abandoned alley or anything. I mean, the road is right there.

I open the door of my car, but before I get in, Owen touches my arm.

"Hey, wait one sec." He reaches into his pocket and pulls out a silver canister with a black and red sticker, and a keychain with a cable connect on the other end. "Take this."

I reach out automatically. "What is it?"

"Pepper spray. Even if you don't like guns, this could keep you safe."

"Uh…okay." The small bottle is cool in my grip. "I don't think I really need it, but…"

"It's easy. Just twist and spray. It won't come out all aerosol-like. It's more like a laser beam of liquid. You aim for the eyes. Go back and forth, like you're putting out a fire."

"All right."

"Keep it handy." He looks at me. Glances around the lot again. "Just in case."

"I will, but for the record, you're making me sort of freaked out." I hold up the thing.

"Not trying to scare you. Just looking out for you. I have a daughter your age. I'd hope someone would do the same for her."

"Thanks. See you next time, I guess."

"Good night." He waits until I close my door, then heads back to the building. As the door closes behind him, I sigh and start the engine.

It's then that I feel the sensation again, of being watched. What the hell?

Clearly, I'm paranoid from talking to Owen.

The street is yellow-orange with light from the overhead lamps, and the bushes are still in the breezeless air. For the moment, there are no cars, which makes it feel like I'm alone in the world.

Suddenly, a man materializes out of the bushes beside my car, like one second he wasn't there and now he—is. He's tall. Dressed all in black. Stocky. All I see are bright beady eyes, fixed on me.

Then he smiles. Mouths something... I can't make it out. Steps closer.

He says the words again, and this time I hear them in my head. "I'm almost ready for you."

I scream and jerk the wheel and reflexively squeeze the bottle in my hand. I should start the car. I should scream for help. I should dial 911. I should—I look at my phone on the seat for a split second, then back up —

And there's no one there.

The bushes are sparse and empty. The street is desolate. The light flashes from red to green for no one, as there are still no cars. The air is breathless, no leaves move on the tree in the lot, and there's no motion as far as I can see.

"Jesus, fuck, fuck, fuck." I'm shaking. Did I imagine him?

Sweat pops out on my brow. I look over at the building, into the brightly lit lobby, but Owen isn't in sight. I could call him or Dr. A—tell them to come out and …do what?

Look for a man that I saw for one second? Who might not even exist?

Even if he was real, he didn't do anything.

My body is shaky, and it takes me a few seconds to stabilize my grip on the wheel. Actually, I will go back in, or at least call Dr. A. This could be the same man who was lurking before—

Suddenly, my head aches, an immediate explosion of pain. I cry out and grab my temples, and—

I shake my head. Why am I just sitting here? I should be driving home. My head feels like it's full of cotton and water. It's like I can hear whooshing in my ears. I'm dizzy, too. When did I last eat?

There's a fuzzy image of a man in black, but it fades, like a dream receding, and soon it's nearly gone.

CHAPTER 9

𝒶 ^{lain}

"Slash. Come in." I open my door and stand back for the young vampire I've summoned. "You can set up in your usual spot."

Another week has passed, and my concerns about Karl have only grown. Despite my near euphoria about Dr. Albright's progress on our project, I can't fully enjoy it. Not when I know he's lurking around.

I need to handle Karl. Not just because he's endangering humans and other vampires. But because he's endangering my ability to focus on my work, the one thing that gives me meaning.

"Bruh." Slash nods his head and looks around, hoisting his laptop case on his wiry shoulder. "What's up?"

"My good friend Martin is in dire need of a new ID. And a lesson on using social media." I put a hand on Martin's shoulder, as much to introduce him as to bolster his confidence, because he looks sort of green. "He's terrified of technology."

"What's your century?"

Slash goes to the shining dining table that has only ever been used to house his computer during his visits, the one that's polished to a mirror-like sheen and inlaid with hand-carved wood. Made in Indonesia, a one of a kind, it's worth a fortune. And like most of the things in my house, absolutely superfluous.

"The 1800's. But I've been asleep for a century." Martin runs a hand over his hair. "My dear chap, I don't know if this is strictly necessary..."

Slash gives him a dark look. "Do you want to fit into society, so you aren't outed as a supernatural being and killed in a way so gruesome that you can't even contemplate it?"

"Um." Martin clears his throat. Looks at me for help.

But I'm laughing. "Go on, then. He'll hook you up."

"I'm teaching a new class for vamps next month. It's called Social Media 101: You and YouTube. I'll enroll you." Slash slides into one of the wooden chairs, and his hands fly over his keyboard. "Many of us don't actually have a social media account. But it's really critical that you know how to use them, anyway. Otherwise you can't fit in."

Slash was turned in his twenties, and I have no idea how old he is because he won't say. But he's every inch the young millennial. "But first we'll teach you how to use Insta and Twitter. And get you set up with a new driver's license and all that."

"I always think you're the vampire who most fits modern society." I shake my head.

"I agree." Slash gives me a quick grin. He's lean and

94

dresses the way the younger kids—humans—look on TV and movies. He's even wearing some kind of cologne that smells like it came out of a magazine.

After he gets Martin started on a tutorial on his spare laptop–Martin laboriously pushing keys with one clenched index finger as if they're bombs that might explode at any moment–I pull Slash aside for a few minutes and lower my voice.

"I need your help on something else."

"Yeah?" He crosses his arms.

"I need you to help me figure out what Karl's up to. I have this."

I hand him the business card that fell out of Karl's pocket into my hand the last time we met.

Well, business card isn't the right term. It's an index card with some numbers written onto it, scribbled in black pen. And it didn't exactly fall out. I stole it.

"I'm no expert, but that looks like an IP address." I tap the ink.

Slash gives it a glance. "I like to stay, you know, nonpartisan." He blinks rapidly. Doesn't take the card.

"This isn't a whim." I raise my voice, then temper my response. "He's dangerous."

"I stay out of personal stuff between vamps. That's how I survive." Slash looks away, across the room. But he's tapping his foot. I think he knows something, and it's making him uneasy. He may be the Switzerland of vampires, but he's not an asshole.

"What do you know about him?" I step closer.

"Alain. Please. I really don't get in anyone's business." He puts up his hands.

I snarl. "This could be life or death." I look at him, sending him the depth of my concern. Hoping he's receptive to reading the emotion. That he'll care.

He blinks, then clears his throat, and steps back. "Okay. Just this once, I'll get involved. But I don't know much. He offered me some amazing blood to taste."

"What kind of blood?"

"Human blood." Slash gives me a duh look. "From a girl."

"What girl?"

"I don't know. But dude, it was sick. It was, like, the best blood I've had in years." He licks his lips, and I swear, his fangs are ready for action. He looks ravenous just thinking about it. "I've never even had it that good. I can't wait for more..." He trails off.

"More?"

"Well, he said I could have more if I did some work for him."

I cross my arms. "Where did he get it?"

"Do you ask every vamp where they obtain their blood?" His shoulders are high. His chin tight. Like he knows Karl is into something that's completely non-legit, even by vampire standards. I was right—Slash has morals that match mine. He's not as impartial as he seems.

"Not the decent ones, no." I narrow my eyes. "How did he give it to you?"

"In a vial."

"Like from a blood bank?"

"No, it was fresh. Clean. I mean, it came in a glass vial with a cap, like the ones at blood banks. But without the yellow gunk at the bottom. And I could taste the vibrancy.

Full of adrenaline and endorphins, man. This wasn't sick person blood. This was revved up blood." He sort of laughs but stops, seeing my expression.

"What did he ask of you?"

"Nothing. It was a gift for doing some work for him." Slash rubs his face.

"What kind of work?"

"He said we'll meet later this week to go over details. The blood was sort of just a nice doing business with you gift, I guess."

"Or to get you hooked." I groan and turn away, running a hand through my hair. "So you do what he wants without questioning it."

"Do you really think he's doing something danger-ous…" Slash trails off. But I can sense the unease from his mind.

"Yes. I do." I turn back to pierce him with my gaze. "And in a case like this, not taking sides is taking a side… with him." I step closer. "I'd recommend against that." My voice is low. "He's not known for his benevolence. I need to know where he got that blood."

Slash blinks again, rapidly. He lowers his voice. "He could have gotten that blood from anywhere. We all get blood. Lucius Frangelico has fresh blood at Toxic every night. Everyone gets blood." He trails off.

"Lucius gets his blood from willing donors," I snap. "Who are compensated quite nicely for their contributions. This could be something else entirely."

"I did feel that there was something different about Karl," Slash admits. "I mean, vamps are weird and dangerous. Each in their own way. But he's got something else going on lately." He shakes his head. "Even his face."

I think about Karl's ruddy face. Yeah, that was the skin of a vamp full of blood, a plump tick engorged and ready to pop. And chances are, he didn't get that blood anywhere legit.

"So…this." I show Slash the card again.

"I can track it."

"Tell me where it leads. And fast."

"I hope I'm going to get compensated." He sounds glum.

"Knowing you're doing the right thing is its own reward," I chide him. But then I grab the black velvet bag from the counter. "Have I ever let you down?" I roll my eyes and hand him the sack.

When he opens it and finds the polished skull inside, inlaid with diamonds, he whistles, and his face lights up. "The Cleopatra! Where did you even find it?"

"That's my own business." It wasn't easy, is the answer. "But I know that Anton gave you two fainting goats in exchange for his new license, and Andrius gifted you one of the Dead Sea scrolls for a Russian passport, so I had to keep up." I smile. "Since you accept anything but money for your work."

"I can make my own money." He laughs. "I prefer the unusual. It keeps life interesting." For a second, he gets that look—the one that I see all too often on Martin's face. But it passes; I assume he's still young enough, either in actual age or at heart, not to see his forever life as an imprisonment.

"Do it now." I point at the computers. Martin has abandoned his nearly as soon as he started the tutorial.

"Fine. Give me ten minutes." Slash slides up to his laptop and starts working.

I look around and find Martin sitting on the patio, head in his hands. Clearly, he's going to need more time to get used to the digital age.

I find this more funny than I should, given the current situation with Karl, and it makes me laugh out loud.

Martin looks up and glares at me. "Fuck you."

"Perfect intonation. A+." I sit beside him. "It'll come faster than you think."

"Is he helping?" Martin shrugs one shoulder. "With the other thing?"

"Yeah." I pause. "I'm positive Karl's behind the disappearances of the women. I can sense it."

"Because you made him?" Martin's voice holds curiosity. "Is that why you can still sense things about him that others can't?"

I nod. "There's still an odd bond with him."

"Do we have that? What am I thinking right now?" Martin pulls a face.

I laugh again. "You're thinking that you're glad we're friends." I punch his shoulder. *We do have that.*

Absolutely. "Wrong!" But he sinks back into his chair, smiling.

Slash calls over. "The IP address is locked down hard, and it will take me a day to get it figured out. I can do it, though." He likes a challenge.

"Call me when you have it. Don't tell Karl that I'm

asking." I stare at Slash. "But reach out to him and see if you can get more info. Ask him for more of that blood."

"I don't want him to get suspicious." Slash taps his foot rapidly. "I'm an IT guy, not a fucking double oh seven."

"Watch some Bond movies," I snap. "Do it in a non-suspicious way."

"*He's* fun." Martin raises his eyebrows and points to me. "You can see why we're friends, no?"

Slash scowls. Then sighs. He scratches his nose. Mutters, "Better get another skull out of this," and gives me a meaningful look.

I laugh. "Deal."

"Whatever." Slash starts to pack up his gear. "You," he points at Martin, "are hopeless. You're going to need one on one tutoring for, like, a year." He sounds frustrated. "In the meantime, do. Not. Talk. To. Civilians. They will totally tell that you're not legit."

Martin puts a hand to his chest. "You wound me."

"You wound yourself with your horrible skillz." Slash scowls.

"Enough of that." I clear my throat. "I will teach Martin keyboard basics. You just track Karl."

Once Slash is gone, I turn to Martin. I sigh. "Well, that was exciting."

Speaking of exciting: Bri. I can't get her out of my mind. What will it take to forget her? Or to find her again?

CHAPTER 10

B^{ri} I'm tucked into a chair in a lab room, waiting for my blood draw tech. My repeat blood test. After working with Dr. A. last night, I'm still full of the excitement of working with such a renowned researcher. It almost makes me not so scared to be here right now.

It also nearly makes me forget about the odd headaches I've been having lately and the memory issues. I'm terrified they're some new neuro symptom, telling me that my XP is getting worse. I called Dr. Su, and she said it's probably just stress. But I don't like "probably." I want "definitely."

Suddenly, I hear lowered voices in the hall.

"So did they have it?"

"...detective coming in half an hour..."

My interest caught, I get up from the chair and tiptoe to the partially open door to hear better. Through the crack in the doorjamb, I see a woman in a suit and lab coat, probably the lab manager, talking with a coworker.

"Yes, they have a warrant, so we'll give them the information they want."

"And all three did have their blood drawn here?"

The manager puts her hand on the coworker's arm. "I can't tell you the details. Just that we're complying with the warrant. Sharing our records with the police."

"Someone asked me about Margaret Bly on the phone."

"Please keep telling people we never violate HIPAA and don't give out personal information. And keep this confidential. Nobody else needs to know."

Margaret Bly? I know that name.

She's one of the three women who were supposedly taken by the Night Stalker. Does this conversation mean that all three women had their blood drawn here at Gila Diagnostics?

I shudder. What a weird coincidence.

On a whim, I pull out my phone and Google Margaret's name.

I find tons of articles, all copying the same original news story about how she disappeared. How her friends said she complained about a creepy man in black looking through her windows a day before she was gone. How she was smart and friendly and successful.

"Oh no." The part about the man in black makes me shudder.

I remember, at least I think I remember, that I saw a man in black the other night. It's one of those weird memories that cracks and fragments when I try to think about it and comes back and tugs at the corners of my mind when I'm thinking about something else.

For a while, I thought it was just a dream. Or my imagination.

But what if he was real? What if he wants me next, for some unimaginable reason?

What would it mean if all of the missing women were clients here at the blood draw place?

Hmmm. It would definitely be wrong to break into Gila Diagnostics's system and find out. Not that I could do that—I'm a programmer, not a hacker. But my gut tells me I have to follow this.

And I think I know someone who can help.

Later on in the evening, when I'm home with a cotton ball on my vein, held in place by a slice of masking tape, I message my on-line friend Slash.

@Slash: What's up?

In a second, he replies.

@Bri: Hey girl. Working a job. You?

I stare at his avatar, a hand-drawn cartoon picture of a young man with brown hair and glasses. He never posts a real pic and keeps his personal data well hidden. For all I know, he could be a middle-aged woman.

But whoever Slash is, he's wicked funny. Ever since we met on an IT discussion board last year, we've been online friends. Supposedly he lives here in Tucson, too. And from what we joke about, I sense that he is sort of hacky. At least, he's the hackiest person I know.

I've asked Slash before if he wants to meet up for coffee, but he always says no. Still, our online connection is fun.

@Slash: I want to ask you a huge, dangerous favor. #InternetBuddiesRock

@Bri: Intrigued. No promises. What is it?

@Slash: I want to find out if the women taken by the Midnight Stalker had their blood drawn at Gila Diagnostics recently.

@Bri: Oh, is that all? #YouCan'tAffordThat #BitchPlease

@Slash: lol. I can pay up to $25 dollars, haha. #SoWorthTheJailTime

@Bri: Why do you want to know?

@Slash: Just something I heard today. Made me curious.

@Bri? What did you hear?

@Slash: That the police have a warrant to check if all three were patients there. So...can you find out?

@Bri: That's illegal, so absolutely not. #KeepingItLegit

@Slash: aha, got you. #YouCan'tDoIt #Lame #Weak #Loser

@Bri: Not going to tell you how to do your job, but blowjobs go over better than insults. Just saying.

@Slash: Not going to tell you how to enjoy your body, but in-person BJ's are way better than virtual ones. Just saying.

We enjoy dirty banter together, without expectation or commitment. Part of the reason I feel so free to joke like this is precisely because he never does want to meet. It makes it safe.

I assume the conversation is over, but later on, my phone pings with a text. I don't recognize the number. It says, *"Call me."*

The phone buzzes again. *"It's about your request from this afternoon."*

OMG! Is it Slash?

I want to call, but: What if Slash is a weird pervert and by calling him, I open my life up to a stalker? How did he get my phone number? Clearly if he got my phone number, he is a hacker. Fuck! What if he really does want a BJ, and he's gross and old and psycho? What if he steals me and locks me up and…

Another buzz. "I'm not a stalker, and I'm not going to meet you in person, so relax. But I found out something pretty interesting. I promise I'm legit."

I bite my lip. Then I toss caution aside and call. "Hi?" This is Bri?" Might as well meet it head on, whatever this is.

"Hey." Whoever it is, he has a nice timbre to his voice. Very all-American, no accent of any kind. "This is Slash."

"Wow, this is weird. Didn't ever think we'd actually speak in person." So far, so good. No serial killer vibes going on.

"Neither did I." He sounds a little nervous. "But this is a weird situation. So I looked up the thing you asked about _"

"Seriously?" I'm taken aback. "I mean, for real? And so fast?"

He makes a sound. "I'm good at what I do, Bri." He sounds irritated. "Anyway, you were right. All three did have their blood drawn at Gila Diagnostics."

"Oh, wow. That's crazy." I breathe in. "Wow."

"Yup. So, um, why'd you want to know?" His voice is

casual, but I sense something behind it. Like he knows something I don't.

"Well, I was sitting and waiting for a blood draw, and apparently someone from the police station called the office reception woman trying to get information. So it made me curious."

"So you heard a conversation?" He asks it really quickly.

"Yup. Like I texted you."

"What exactly did she say?" He sounds sort of tense.

I try to remember. "I don't know the exact words. She kept saying she couldn't give out information, and she gave her supervisor's name and number. I'm sure they'll get a warrant if they need the info."

"Yeah, she can't bypass HIPAA laws without cause. Anything else?"

"Nope. Why are you so curious?"

He relaxes his voice. "Just like to dig. See what I can find. Like you, I guess." He laughs.

There's a silence.

We both speak at once. I say, "So you called me because –"

And he starts with "So I guess that's all –"

We both break off. "Thanks," I say quickly. Another silence. "I mean, do you want to get coffee sometime?"

"I don't think that's a good idea," he says slowly. "Although I wish I could."

"Uh, okay." I'm not sure what to say to that. "Why is it not a good idea?"

"It just isn't." He sounds sort of sad now.

"I don't care what you look like. I mean, not that you

look weird. Not that there's anything wrong with looking weird." Fuck me. "I'm not asking romantically. Because I'm seeing someone, sort of. I just, as friends…"

"No. And don't try to track my phone because you can't. It's a burner phone. So don't try."

"I wasn't planning to. It's not even my thing." I'm sort of irritated.

"I know. I looked you up."

"Okay, that's officially weird. And not fair, since I don't get to look you up."

"Not in a bad way. Just to make sure it was safe to call you."

"Glad to know I'm safe material." My voice is dry.

"Well, I'll see you online." Again, there's that tone in his voice of regret.

And he's gone, leaving me bemused and a little uneasy.

What should I even do with this information? I can't call the police: "Hey, my hacker friend Slash found out this thing…"

I don't need to. If the police are already calling Gila Diagnostics, they'll come back with a warrant.

But now I can't get rid of a new curl of worry in my gut. Margaret Bly saw a man in black before she disappeared, a creepy man. And as much as I want to convince myself that I imagined the man last week, I know he was real.

CHAPTER 11

*a*lain

Slash is back at my house. It's been a few days since the first time he came over, and I've invited him back to follow up. Martin is on the patio with a glass of whiskey, the doors open to enjoy the night breezes.

"So, guess what I found out." Slash adjusts his glasses. "All three missing humans, the women? They all had their blood drawn at Gila Diagnostics. Their records were destroyed during the break in."

"Excellent work!" I slap his back, full of relief that we're getting somewhere. "How'd you get that information? Not from Karl?"

"Not Karl. I haven't talked to him yet. A contact put me onto it." He opens his laptop. "So I hacked their system and got the information. And I also tracked down that website, finally. You're going to want to see this. Both of you. I postponed my next class to do this for you."

Martin raises his glass and calls over. "The Internet

And You: Don't Fear the Future." He doesn't sound pleased. "I can't say I'm disappointed it's cancelled."

"You." Slash nods toward Martin. "Need to practice logging into the dummy account I made you. It's really not that hard."

Martin rolls his eyes. "The blasted buttons are too miniscule for my fingers." He sips his drink. "I don't understand the odd symbols."

Slash ignores this. "Alain. This is on the dark web. It's that IP address—I unlocked it for you."

I come over and glance at the website. It's black with an intricate skull and crossbones pattern overlaid in a faint gray and reads: "The finest, more delicious blood in the world, fresh harvested, delivered to your door in minutes."

"What the hell? Scroll down."

I read aloud as Martin flashes over, curious to see. "Desire young healthy blood? The best, most exotic flavors in the world? Currently on tap we have three perfect vintiges. All from women in their twenties, all hand-picked to have the best tasting and smelling blood in the world. Supply limited. Auction forthcoming for their L.D.s."

"L.D.s?" I frown.

He shrugs. "That's all it says."

"Contact information?" I lean in.

Slash continues reading the last part. "Want to find us? So find us. You'll now who to talk to…"

"They don't spell very well, whoever it is." I snort.

Slash nods. "It's an abandoned website from the wayback I research periodically on dark web stuff. They thought they deleted it, and they made a mistake. Their mistake was not knowing that I exist." He smiles to himself. "I think I can trace it." He types furiously.

"Well?" I hover over his shoulder.

"Leads to a different IP address here in Arizona." Slash looks up at me. "But from there it gets tricky. It will take me awhile."

"Ok, keep at it."

I say the thing I hoped wasn't true. "Regarding the blood bank break in. I think Karl had someone steal the samples, so he could screen them, find the most delicious blood. Then he tracked down his top leads...and took them. Is using them as blood sources against their will."

"That's horrific." Martin seems appalled. "We all need to feed. But not like that."

Slash shakes his head. "It's insane. We don't treat humans like that. It's just..." he trails off. "I don't have words."

"Karl has worsened over the past century." I frown. "Instead of getting kinder and more mellow, he's allowed cruelty to rule him."

"Why don't you just eliminate him?" Slash raises his eyebrows.

"He has helpers out there, and I can't get rid of him without finding out more, first. If I dispose of him too quickly, it may be like cutting the head off the mythical Hydra. Get rid of one head, and two more grow back stronger."

This is entirely true.

However, I don't add the other, more uncomfortable truth: If I have to kill Karl, it will be proof of my failure as a vampire, my inability to choose good people to turn. I'm trying to remake myself right now with my medical research, and death isn't supposed to be on the agenda. If I can avoid it, I will. Maybe a small part of me still thinks—hopes—that Karl can be saved.

"Well." Slash looks over to Martin, who's listening to our conversation while twirling his iPhone on the smooth tabletop. "I'll see what I can find."

"And so will I." Slash can check the ones and zeroes. I'll be rooting around in the vamp and supernatural underworld, trying to find more details, so I can figure out how to stop Karl…before things get worse.

ALAIN

"Lucius." I bow my head in respect. It's a strange coincidence: I needed to talk to him. Before I reached out, he summoned me to meet at Club Toxic. The Vampire King himself, the most powerful vampire in Tucson and probably the whole United States.

"Alain." He raises a glass and gives me a knowing look. "I hope your ventures are well." We're seated at the bar, our voices low and muffled, so none of the humans or other guests can overhear.

His keen eyes have already noted my urgency, either in my gait or my expression. He's renowned for his reflexes and his skill in reading other beings, human and not.

"My medical facility is on track. It pleases me. Dr. Albright's progress is astounding."

"Good." He nods to the bartender. "Your project

intrigues me. I enjoy hearing the updates as you send them."

"And I appreciate the fact that you help me keep it safe." I smile.

Part of the reason I built the facility just outside of Lucius' range of ownership is that he keeps tabs on what goes on in the vicinity. It's not like he stops caring because something is a half mile outside his territory.

I wanted to be in my own zone, but close to a trusted ally. Plus, there are excellent doctors at the Banner Hospital. The top-notch research nearby at the University of Arizona makes it a slam dunk.

The bartender slides me a glass of Pinot. I lift it to Lucius. "To your health."

He smiles. "A vampire's health is binary. It either is, or it isn't."

"On the surface." I take another sip. "But if you open the onion, there's more to it. I know you agree."

"Care to elucidate?" He sips his whiskey.

"Vampires can rot from the inside out. Metaphorically speaking."

"And I suppose you have a particular vampire in mind?" He takes another sip of his drink.

"Karl."

"Yes." He nods. "Your spawn."

I tense. "We all make mistakes."

"And are required to fix them." He leans in, voice stern. "Karl made a mess last month in Tucson when he murdered that whole family." A beat. "Although I am pleased you fixed it with minimal collateral damage before I needed to involve myself."

I incline my head. "Is this why you wanted to speak with me?"

"He is not allowed permission to hunt on my property. He needs to be stopped." He raises a brow. The implied part is that if he needs to fix my problem, it won't be good for my reputation. Or my standing here in Tucson.

"I have no problem stopping him. But I may need more time."

"Time in which my citizens are terrorized and my vampires put into danger of being found out?" He raises a brow.

"I suspect he's doing something far worse than that recent murder."

Lucius puts his glass down on the bar, a decisive move. "We'll continue this discussion in private."

I follow him to the guarded, locked staircase to his private office upstairs. Seated in his chair behind his massive wooden desk, he looks even more majestic than usual. I wonder at his powers; surely, they're far beyond mine and any vampire I know. It's critical that I convince him to help me.

"Tell me what you mean." He fixes his stare on me.

"Have you noticed Karl's robust qualities of late?" I pause to find the right words. "Like he's full to the seams with energy. With blood. So much of it."

"I have. Go on." Lucius tents his fingers.

"It's unnatural. So it made me wonder why."

"And you found out?" Lucius raises a brow.

"He's got access to a supply of top-notch blood. But it's not…" I hesitate. "Not from a good source." I wince, thinking about what I uncovered just a day ago.

I continue. "There are rumors of a members-only blood store with limited amounts of exquisite blood, all from sexy young women. The blood is full of adrenaline and pain endorphins. Exotic. Delicious beyond compare." I sigh. "And it's true."

"It's not a novel concept." Lucius stares at me. "I have blood at my bar."

"I know you do. Delicious. Scarce. And *ethically sourced*." I emphasize the last words.

"This new blood bar isn't?"

"I believe they are stealing young women and holding them hostage. Draining them over and over again, like blood cows."

There is a silence.

"Possibly torturing them to ensure their blood is full of adrenaline and endorphins. It's bad."

"If that is true," Lucius says, "then it's not sanctioned by me. Or anyone I know. I didn't even give him permission to hunt personally on my territory." He looks fierce.

As the local leader, he controls much of Tucson and has built a fragile alliance with the other supernatural creatures here, especially the wolf shifters. You want to do something in Tucson, you clear it with Lucius. It's how it works.

"We need to shut it down."

"Where is the facility itself?"

"I don't have the exact location. My sources estimate outskirts of Phoenix."

"That's not within my territory."

"It's in mine." I snap it out. "And I must stop him." I take a breath. "But neither you nor I can just kill him and be done with it. Because he has helpers that could continue even if he's gone."

Lucius nods. "He's neither smart enough nor organized enough to do this on his own."

"Exactly." I agree. "He's got allies who will simply move the facility if Karl is killed. I need to get him to reveal the location and his partners, so I can cut this down at the source."

"If his facility is in Phoenix, why is he taking women in Tucson?" Lucius toys with his glass.

I shrug. "My best guess is that he wants to make me look bad because I can't keep him in check. He wishes to make you angry at me. Cast me out. I think he cares as much about hurting me as he does about his actual operations."

Lucius' face is grave. "There are rumors that he has a vendetta against you. And if you leave, he may back off Tucson. Leave the city alone."

I shift in my seat, anxiety pricking at me. "Karl wants you to turn on me. I'm asking you to trust that I can stop him and shut down his venture in Phoenix and his killings here in Tucson."

"I can't risk any more missing women in Tucson. It's too much. It's going to endanger all of us if he continues. I'm not turning on you. I'm telling you how it is."

"I understand. And I'm just asking you to let me take care of it. My way."

Lucius looks across the room, then back at me. "I've learned through experience that you don't begin a battle unless you already know you can win." He stares into my eyes. "Are you ready?"

"I'm working on that." I meet his gaze. "I will get together what I need. I just want to know that you will back me, if I need it."

"I will back you." He speaks slowly. "I will let it be known at this club and within my circles of influence that we side with you."

"Thank you."

"Karl is a fool if he thinks he can manipulate me so easily. And a brash idiot to endanger all of vampires with his plans."

"I agree."

He smiles. "Let us share a drink." He doesn't say anything, but an assistant immediately enters, bringing a silver tray with a bottle and two glasses: Lucius' favorite whiskey, a drink he offers only to those he trusts.

"I saw you at the club the other week with a human." He smiles.

He means Bri. "She was good." Understatement. "But it's nothing."

Lucius tilts his head. "Just good? You were happier than usual. You were even ecstatic." He takes a sip of his drink.

Damn his perceptive nature.

He adds, "Be careful," as if I didn't already know that.

"I haven't stayed around this long by risking things." I sip from my glass and raise it to him. Try to hide my guilt because I didn't even properly wipe her. She will most certainly remember more than I wanted her to keep in her brain.

Lucius is about to respond when his mate, Selene, walks into the room.

She nods to me. "Alain." I see her scent the air, testing me. She's both a shifter and a vampire, making her even more powerful than Lucius. Together, they're an unstoppable force.

"Selene. Greetings." I bow my head to her, showing respect. And admiration.

She's one of the sexiest females I've ever seen, and it's easy to see why she mesmerized the king himself. Her ethereal beauty coupled with her strength make her impossible to ignore. In fact, she's a little frightening.

Apparently having vetted me, she comes right up to Lucius and plants a kiss on his lips, hers red and luscious, and a sudden longing spirals through me.

Not for her—she's taken, and she's not my type, amazing as she is.

No, my desire is directed at Bri.

"One second." Lucius turns away from me to speak to Selene.

As I watch Lucius pull Selene closer and whisper into her ear and see how her face lights up with desire and humor, I wish that I had a female to tug into my body like that. Someone whom I could trust implicitly with my body and my mind—a creature to partner me through the rest of my life. Someone who could turn at least a fraction of my eternity from a drag into a multicolor delight.

Because even though my medical research gives me purpose and pleasure, it doesn't give me the kind of joy that these two obviously share. And despite my powerful friendship with Martin, the relationship with him doesn't complete me.

Sometimes I wonder if I could accomplish more if I

had such a partner, the way Lucius and Selene have each other. But good luck finding someone like that.

"Are you coming to the club tonight?" Lucius turns back to me. "Downstairs?"

"I hope so." But I'm not interested in playing with anyone but Bri.

Fuck one-night stands.

With my mind I try to summon Bri. *Come. Meet me.*

Of course, this isn't one of my main skills—mind-bending humans to my will, at a distance. Only the oldest and most powerful vampires have inklings of this power.

But something about her just clicked. Like we belonged together. Like her brain and mine could meld together so beautifully, just like our bodies. And she did seem quite amenable to my more pleasurable suggestions during sex. Her mind might not be the type that can handle a wipe, but she was more than capable of following my instructions and commands...and loving it.

So I wish it out into the universe because even just one more night with her, even if it's the last time I see her, is something I crave.

CHAPTER 12

B ri

The memories of Alain are stronger tonight. I close my eyes, and his face appears, hovering in my mind. His piercing eyes, his dark hair, his perfect physique. That sexy smile. His touch.

I tilt my head up and breathe out, almost feeling his lips on my neck. My clit tingles with arousal.

Fuck, I've never had such an intense fantasy! It's like he's here.

I frown. The urge to go to Club Toxic is so strong, I want to drop everything and go right now, without bothering with hair and makeup. Just in my old jeans and sweatshirt.

"One night only," I whisper to myself.

But even as I speak, I'm standing up and heading to my closet.

You know what? I am going back to that club. Fuck my one-night rule.

I want Alain, and if he's there, I'm going to have him.

~

"It's me again." I walk right to the front of the line, up to the handsome bouncer who let me in last time.

I'm worried I'll have to explain, convince, but he nods as if I'm expected. "Go right in." He gestures and halfway bows, with a flourish of his arm, a graceful move. "Enjoy."

"I hope so." I say the words under my breath, but the wide smile on his face lets me know he heard.

He's cute…but I'm here for someone else.

Of course, I don't know if Alain will even be at the club tonight. Any night. Yet I feel it in my veins, something pulsing, pulling me in. Like the iron in my blood is being tugged to a true North, an irresistible magnet.

The club is busy, but I don't see Alain. The bar is packed, so I make my way to an empty round table and perch on a tall stool, eyeing the clientele. Tonight, the band isn't playing, and there's nobody with a sexy guitar. Not that I wanted the musician anyway.

I touch one of the scars on my arm, thinking of the way Alain's fingers traced it. Softly. Gently. Like it was something special, not the mark of a freak.

"What can I get you?" A bartender materializes at my elbow, her hair a bright blue, streaked with little flares of pink and gold, like flames of a setting sunset. She's really pretty, almost model-like, but something about her is remote.

I glance at her nametag, but it's obscured by her long hair. Then she moves, and I see a piece of masking tape on the card with a name written in marker: *Blue*.

"A glass of champagne, please. Blue."

"Moet et Chandon?" She smiles at me.

I blink. "How'd you know?"

She hums a little. "You seem like a M and C kind of girl."

She smiles and moves away to another client, weaving through the masses like she's a fish in water, slicing her way without effort. I notice that others watch her, too—she's got such a natural grace.

I look around for Alain, but he's not here. I can tell without looking, somehow—the room doesn't have the vibrant air of expectant joy I felt when I was with him. Still, I keep checking, as if I might have missed him behind a couple. Lurking against the wall. Almost as if by continuing to look, I'll eventually see him.

When she comes back a minute later with my bubbly, Blue leans in. "It's extra delicious tonight."

"Special vintage? Good year?"

"All of the above and then some." She smiles. "We add magic."

"By magic, you don't mean drugs, right? Just checking." I laugh.

"No need for drugs here." She raises a brow. "We make our own high on life."

"I guess me too."

"You guess?" Blue laughs. "Life's short enough. Better do more than guess."

"Amen to that." I raise my glass as she moves to another customer.

Suddenly I get the feeling I'm being watched, but it's not the sexy kind of feeling. It's the unsettling one, the way I felt at work the other night at Dr. A's.

Something tells me to look over at a far corner because I need to know—the people obscure my view, like a brightly colored school of fish in a reef, darting and reforming. Then they part, like curtains before a show, and I see him.

The man by my car. The man who wasn't really there. The hallucination. And I remember everything about him.

He passes something in an underhanded gesture to another man, who disappears into the crowd. Then he locks eyes with me and mouths words, like he did the other night, and this time terror spirals into my gut because I can hear them in my head.

"It's you."

He smiles and lifts up his hand, although it's empty, as if toasting me. Clenches the hand into a fist and loses the smile. Stands up deliberately, staring at me the whole time.

Suddenly he's right next to me--he leans closer to me and sniffs, as if he was a dog, scenting something fascinating on the breeze.

"It's definitely you." He giggles.

I cry out and jump to my feet, rocking the chair and spilling my drink all over my hand, my arm, my clothes. The glass tilts alarmingly, and I feel liquid on my feet, even——

I look up again to chart his progress, to ask for help: He's gone.

And I'm shaking. I can barely put the glass back onto the table, and the sound of it, clink-clink-clink on the surface, is little gunshots into my brain.

What the absolute fuck?

"Are you okay?" Blue is back, a look of concern on her face.

"I'm so sorry, I spilled." I gesture, but I can't stop looking at the spot where the man stood. I get the slightest whiff of garbage and feel like I need to vomit. "I…"

She steps closer. "Don't worry about the spill. God, you're pale. Like you saw a ghost." Her tone is grim, as if she knows a thing or two about ghosts and being followed.

"I saw a man…" I bite my lip. "I don't know. I'm fine." I glance all around, but he's definitely gone. I cross my arms over my chest, all of my happy excitement gone. I feel sick and thick, full of dread. My life looms large in my mind, like seeing an approaching car out of control in a rear-view mirror.

"I'll bring you another glass. On the house. And have someone wipe this up." She gives me a sympathetic smile. "And I'll tell someone about the creep."

"Thanks."

Before she reaches the bar, she turns to the door, and I see her whisper something to the friendly bouncer.

I get back onto the chair and take a deep breath.

This is all wrong. This night was supposed to be another refuge for me. Now it's turning into a panic. I realize that my plan to come here and find Alain was ill-conceived and stupid. You can't materialize people when you want them. You can't make life twist the way you want it to go. All you can do is hang the fuck on and try not to fall out of the roller coaster.

I drain my new glass of champagne in a long gulp, the liquid bubbling a dull burn at the start of my throat, but the punch of the alcohol doesn't give me a happy high.

As I put the glass down, the bouncer is beside me. "Did someone bother you? One of the bartenders told me you were upset."

"Well, it was—a weird man." I shudder.

"That doesn't sound good. Who was he?"

"I don't know. Some guy I didn't recognize."

"Did he touch you?" His voice is like gravel.

"No. He just…he just looked at me. And—I think he smelled me." I shudder again, thinking of those gleaming eyes. "It was gross. And he whispered that it was me. But I don't know him."

"What did he look like?" His voice is surprisingly tense.

"I don't know." I'm frustrated with my own lack of information. "He was dressed in black. Tall. Stocky." I bite my lip. "Little beady eyes." I raise my hands. "I know that's not much, but—he was just creepy. Really horrible little smile." I hesitate.

"We don't tolerate anyone bothering our clients. I'll take care of this."

"But he's already gone." I hope.

"Just wait one second, okay?" He nods at me, then he turns away and mouths something into his headset.

I almost want to cry with relief that he's doing something about it. Truthfully, I'm more unsettled now than I've been in a long time.

I wait next to him, tuning things out, until I hear the word "Alain." It's like an electric shock down my spine. It's like Alain is everywhere except in front of me. Is this the same Alain, my Alain? Why does everyone know his name?

"Did you say Alain?"

"Isn't that who you're here for?" His smile is a little smug. Although still concerned.

I frown. "Why would you assume that?" A beat. "Yes." I stick up my chin. "Actually, I was looking for him, yes."

"Well, he's on his way. Wait for him." It's an order, and I can tell, but one I don't mind obeying. Because I feel like Alain is the only one right now—for some odd reason—who can help me feel better.

He hovers his hand over my shoulder. He doesn't touch, but the nearness makes me feel warm and comforted, somehow. Like he's a protector. Like the creepy man can't get to me now. "And I'll keep an eye out for any weirdos."

And then my world swerves in a new direction because Alain is here.

ALAIN

There she is, my Bri.

Standing beside Tiberius, she's anxious and worried. I can see it in her stance and smell it coming off her skin. I'm ready to snarl and toss aside anyone who's bothered her.

The worst part is that I think it's my fault.

The man who hassled her? It was obviously Karl, from what Tiberius told me.

But for now, I come up to Bri and take her hands without asking, and she gives them, as if it's what she wanted to do all along.

"You're here." Her fingers tremble: she wants me. The emotion surges out from her and wraps around me like a hug. She wanted me to come. Just like I wanted to see her again, too.

"You okay?" I search her face.

"I am." She smiles although it's a bit shaky and doesn't fill up her face. She's not, but dammit, I'm going to make sure she gets there.

"Good." I don't let go of her hands. I don't want to.

She doesn't either, and we stand there for a long second, like an old-fashioned couple about to start a dance at a Victorian ball.

"Come with me." I step closer. Look into her eyes. Not mind-bending her, just hoping, showing her how much I want her. "I can make you feel better."

She doesn't say, where? She doesn't hesitate. She just looks up at me and nods. "Okay." She lets out a breath, a little sigh. "Okay."

I put my arm around her shoulder and communicate to Tiberius. *"If he comes back, let me know immediately."*

"Sure thing. I've notified Lucius and the others."

"How did he get in? Nobody saw him?"

"Guess not. We'll look harder, now that we know he's still around."

She follows me to my car.

I start the engine and check the backup camera out of 'acting human' habit, even though my senses can tell me if anything is behind me or in my vicinity. "Tiberius said the man didn't touch you?" I clench the steering wheel so hard I feel it begin to bow under the pressure, and I ease up. "Didn't hurt you?"

"No. But he smelled me." She shudders.

Yes, definitely Karl—and clearly, I need to keep a closer eye on Bri from now on. Set up security for her as well as Dr. A.

My unease is strong, but I push it back because right now I need to focus on helping Bri feel better.

"He was probably just a random creep." I make my voice convincing. "But the security team—if he comes back? They'll take care of him."

"All right." She gives me a tentative smile. "Thanks."

"We can salvage this night." I stop at a red light and look right at her. When our eyes meet, the spark grows hot between us. I sense her worry recede as her attraction to me blooms. "You came to the club for a reason, right?"

She ducks her head and smiles. Turns pink. "Maybe."

"Well, so did I." I quirk a brow. "And I have a feeling it was the same reason."

"Maybe it was." She smiles more broadly this time.

"So we shouldn't let a random asshole ruin our grand plans."

She laughs. Then looks at me, her gaze serious. "Are we going to your house?"

"Would you prefer to go to yours?" I touch her leg. Relax.

She sinks into the seat just a bit. "I don't actually care, as long as I'm with you." She seems surprised at her bold words, but smiles.

"And I feel the same way," I murmur. "One night wasn't enough, Bri, was it?"

She makes a little noise. "I suppose it wasn't." I can't read her tone. She's still melancholy, perhaps because of the encounter tonight or possibly because things between us are getting more complicated than either of us intended.

But fuck intentions. Right now, I just want to be with her.

"Rules," I merge onto the road, "are an interesting thing. Because if you make them, you're allowed to break them whenever you want."

"Come what may," she says. "Come hell or high water, we can break our rules." She smiles and shakes her head.

"The high water wouldn't be so bad. Didn't Noah build a pretty good ark?"

I glance at her, and she laughs. "That he did. Just forgot the unicorns, that sloppy asshole."

Now it's my turn to bark out a chuckle. "Shame."

"Now the hell part, that would be more of an issue." She bites her lip and looks out the window.

"Sure, but we can deal with that too."

"Can we?" She looks over at me, serious. Like she really needs to know.

"I'll do my best." There's a rough determination in my voice, and she starts. It's like she knows we're talking about something else, something deeper than a joke. "And I'm not in the habit of failing."

"Sometimes things can't be controlled." She tightens her hand into a fist.

"But on the other hand, often they can." I reach over and take her fist, and she unfurls it like a rose opening at dawn. I hold her fingers in mine, enjoying the feel of her smooth skin. Her warmth.

"Hmm." She's non-committal. Looks out the window,

then over at me. "Why did you really come to the club?" Her tone is plaintive. She needs reassurance.

"What I said before. I came for you."

She flushes, and her lashes flutter. "I came for you, too." Then she mutters, "Guess I couldn't control that."

"Speaking of control," I'm determined to get her into a lighter mood, "you want to give it up to me again tonight?" I slide her a glance.

She flushes and smiles. Yeah, she does.

"Maybe. We'll see." She's going to make me work for it.

Luckily, it's the kind of job I like best.

CHAPTER 13

Bri

"Wow, this is nice." I glance around the entryway of his home.

Understatement. It's modern, luxurious, with every amenity. Full of art that looks many notches above expensive. I can tell without asking that the carpet is Persian, the statue isn't a replica, and the closest Monet on the wall probably exchanged hands at Christie's for over a million. And the location—poised majestically on a huge plot of land right by the mountains, no neighbors in sight. The desert all his.

A strange look passes over his face, almost frustration. Instead of being pleased with the praise, he looks weary. Does he not like compliments?

"I feel like I'm about to walk on the ceiling of the Sistine Chapel. Should I take off my shoes?"

"I hope you'll take off more than that," he murmurs. "In time." He runs one finger down my cheek. Barely touching, but it sets off all kinds of tingles on my skin. "But first let's have a drink."

He smiles and offers me his hand, a move that's sweet and strangely intimate. "And for now, if you don't mind, I prefer the heels on your sexy legs. Like last time." He looks me up and down, then locks eyes with me. He's teasing me, testing me: Will I obey him? It's a command, even if it's cloaked in a lovely compliment.

"Then they stay on. And I'd love a drink." It turns out I will obey.

My face gets hot, but it's a warmth of expectation, the rise of impending pleasure getting my blood hot. I want him to get dark and dirty and dominant with me.

"Good girl." He bends over and brushes his lips over my neck, in the spot where he bit me last time. He nips softly, and I whimper without meaning to, my legs going weak with desire.

He laughs. "Come." He tugs my hand once.

"Are you going to limit me to one beverage again?" I follow his lead to the kitchen, a vast expanse of granite and stainless steel and a bowl of green apples shining under dozens of twinkling lights. "Like at the club?"

He lets me go, takes a bottle of wine from a rack and deftly twists a corkscrew. "I don't think I'll need to." He pours, and the red wine glimmers like liquid rubies.

We drift closer together, our bodies nearly touching as we stand with our goblets. My skin wants to be on his. I crave his hands, his mouth.

I step closer.

"That's right." He smiles into my eyes. I can feel the heat from his body. I feel like he's saying "that's right" not just about his comment but about the way I want to touch him. Is he reading my mind?

"Oh?" I raise my glass when he does, and the rims touch, letting out the softest chime of crystal on crystal.

"Mmm." He sips his wine and smiles. "You'll not want to waste your time when there are sweeter pleasures to be had."

"You're quite sure of yourself." I tip up the glass and let the wine touch my tongue. It's fruity and warm, with undertones of currant and leather. I close my eyes and savor the way the alcohol hits my bloodstream with the indescribable burst of intoxication.

"Maybe I'm sure of you." He takes another sip of wine and looks at me.

"You don't even know me." But I'm charmed, infatuated. There's something about him I just—*like*. Even if it's as of yet unwarranted.

"Let's remedy that." He puts down his glass. Takes mine, too, and sets it on the counter beside his. So precisely that the glasses touch. "Let me get to know you."

He runs his index finger over my shoulder, down my arm. Rests at my inner wrist, above my pulse. "I think you like that idea."

"I might." In truth, my heart races at his touch. "But I want to talk for a few minutes. Tell me something about yourself."

He tilts his head. "I like red wine and fast cars."

"I already know that. Tell me something deeper. More important." I mimic what he did, letting my fingers rest at his clavicle, feeling his body through his crisp dress shirt. Then I run my entire palm down his arm, slowly, feeling the muscles with my fingers as I go. As if I were blind, learning him by touch.

"Like what?"

I glance around the kitchen. There's one object on the counter that doesn't match the rest of the décor. It's a plain stone, larger than my fist. Rough. It doesn't look like a priceless gem or a fossil. "What's the story with that? There must be something fascinating about it."

He tenses up for just a second. "Someone special gave it to me."

"Who?"

"You *are* chatty for a woman who said one night only and don't call." But his voice is soft, open. He puts one hand on my waist. Before I can agree or refute, he continues. "When I was young, my brother and I found that once while exploring. We thought it might be the start of the ruins of an old castle."

"Was it?" My tone is light, but suddenly I sense that he's remembering something melancholy.

"It was the beginning of something." He has a faraway look in his eyes. "But not a castle. He—died. Very young."

"Oh, I'm so sorry." I touch his hand. "The rock is a memory, then?"

"Can an inanimate object ever truly be a memory?" He's not mocking me. It's like he's asking the question of the universe. "But I kept it. I always will, I suppose."

"I keep things, too."

"Do you?" He pulls me closer, just a bit. "Such as?"

"Well, pictures. Photographs of my parents. They died last year. I still miss them."

"Now I'm sorry." He touches the back of my head, and

I lean into his body, resting myself against his solid form. He's strong and powerful, and I feel comforted in his arms.

"Thank you. It's hard. I…okay, this isn't what I wanted to talk about." I wipe my eye, even though there's no tear. "The pain of losing people never goes away, does it?"

He shakes his head. "No matter how much time passes." His voice is somber. "But at least the memories stay." He touches my face, then lowers his voice. "You tell me something. What were you worried about the night we fucked?"

I shrug. "You really want to know?"

"Yes." He doesn't look away.

"Well, okay, then. If you insist." This is when I usually lose them…might as well get it over with.

I take a breath. "I have an incurable disease that's getting worse. It's called XP. Xeroderma Pigmentosa. Any tiny bit of UV light makes my skin blister and bleed. This past year, I had skin cancer removed three times. That's the scar you asked about." I touch my neck.

He touches it too. "I'm sorry." His voice is sincere.

"Yeah." I stiffen up as he runs his fingers over the length of the incisions.

"Does it hurt?" He removes his hand.

"No." I shake my head. "Not anymore. But I have to cover up completely when I go in the sun, these days. UV shirt and hoodie, full face mask, sunglasses. There's a plastic face protector I could get. Dr. Su says—well, you're probably not interested." I swallow.

"That's why you said you'd turn to ash at daybreak." His face is alert.

I nod. "Joking makes it easier to bear, sometimes. You

have no idea, Alain. How hard it is to avoid the sun at all costs."

He smiles, but it looks sad. "It must be difficult."

"It's impossible! It's like I'm not even human anymore!" My voice goes up, then I catch myself. "Sorry, I'm getting worked up. This is why you shouldn't have asked. Most men don't even want to deal with it. It's hard to date someone who's on permanent night shift."

I try to smile, but it comes out a bit wobbly. "Not that we're dating. I don't mean that. This is just a one-time thing. Two time. Whatever." I force myself to stop babbling.

Please, please don't dismiss me.

"I would never dismiss you for such a thing." His voice is hoarse.

I start, both at the passion, and the way he used the exact word in my mind. My eyes widen.

"I mean," he blinks and adds, quickly, "you're worth more than that. It would be a foolish man who let you go for that."

"Thank you." I'm touched.

"Thank you for trusting me with your truth." He sounds oddly formal. Almost guilty, even, which is weird.

"Well, the truth shall set you free," I say although I've forgotten the author of the quote. "Right?"

"Sometimes it can do the opposite. You have to choose your confidantes well." He runs a finger down my face. "In this case, you got it right. You can trust me." He rests his hand on my cheek.

"Well, you can trust me, too." I smile at him. Put a hand on top of his hand. It's a very tender moment, especially compared to how we met. What we did last time we were together, on a night that was supposed to be a one and done.

He puts both hands on each side of my face. "Any more questions…for now?" He raises a brow.

I whisper. "No."

"Then may I suggest we move to the bedroom?" He leans in so his lips barely brush mine. "And share some more secrets?"

Our breaths mingle, and my head swims.

"Okay." I'm still whispering. There's something hypnotic about his eyes. I feel drugged in a mystical way, like I've been in a room of incense and meditation and people chanting o*hm* for hours. "I'd like that."

"Yes, you will." He takes my hand in his like before, and I marvel at how strong he is. His fingers are long, and his hand engulfs mine. I can see his power, and it warms my heart to see how softly he's guiding me. And how rough he might be in just a few minutes, when he uses that hand to punish my ass.

I suck in a small breath, thinking about it. He laughs. "That's right," he murmurs. "I will do that."

I blink. "How did you…"

"Oh, I can guess what you want." He's casual, confident.

I don't know how he keeps getting into my head. It's not natural.

Don't worry. I won't hurt you. I'll only do it to help make it better for you –

I shake my head. "Alain?" Did he speak out loud?

"Come."

His room is full of dark wood and dim lights. The bed seems like a display model, full of a perfect burgundy cover and tons of throw pillows. I can't shake the feeling that it's not been used; it looks too—artistic. Like it's here just to look at, like so many of the other items in his home.

But I forget that when he closes the door behind us with a quiet but solid click.

"Alone at last," he says, his voice light.

"We were alone before."

"Alone with intent." He smiles. "Take off your dress."

"Just like that?" I raise my eyebrows.

"Yes." He sits on a straight-backed chair at the side of the room and crosses one ankle over the other knee. Undoes his tie. "You know the rules, don't you?"

"But the rules changed. We said one night, and yet here we are."

I step closer to the chair and reach back to undo my zipper.

"Mmm, and I'm glad about that." He tosses his tie to the ground beside the chair and undoes the first button on his shirt. "The other rules are the same. You do what I say, when I say it. Or suffer the consequences." He drawls it out, emphasizing the word *suffer*, which is enough to make my pussy wetter than before.

"Unless I say red." I slide the dress off my shoulders, smiling at the way his pupils dilate and his body tenses.

"The only things you'll be saying are *Alain* and *please*." He unbuttons one cuff and slowly rolls the sleeve up, folding it over carefully several times.

My eyes widen as his powerful forearm is revealed. "Maybe you'll be saying please to me."

I let the dress slide down my body, wiggling my hips to tug it lower. When it pools at the floor and I step out of it, in just a bra and a thong, his eyes glitter with desire. I feel the power of my own sexuality, and the resulting exhilaration is even more intoxicating than wine.

"What do you want, Bri?" His eyes are so powerful. So deep.

"What we did last time. Like that, again." I swallow.

"Okay." He smiles. "What else?"

"Surprise me." I undo my bra and toss it over to where he dropped his tie. "Like what you see? Want to do any begging?" I giggle and step closer. Fuck, I want him so badly.

I'm expecting him to come back immediately with some kind of dommy, snarky reply, but the look in his eyes —so surprisingly tender—has me doing a double take.

Then he shakes his head and gestures with his finger. "You are being extremely insolent, my dear. I'm afraid I'm going to have to punish you."

CHAPTER 14

*B**ri*

He gives me that wicked smile, the one that sends spires of arousal all the way from my nipples to my clit.

"Oooh, big surprise." I raise my eyebrows and sashay closer. "Never would I have expected those words to come out of your ….aaah!"

I shriek out in surprise as he reaches out, lightning fast, and grabs me. In less than a second, I'm over his lap, ass up, arms and legs dangling down. I'm laughing and startled and turned on all at the same time.

Just like in the club, I recognize that this is the moment I love: When it all starts. The beginning of the game. It's exhilarating.

There's nothing in the world like it—when you're about to start a delicious scene, with all the sexy possibilities in the world in front of you. I'm addicted to this feeling.

"Once again," he murmurs, "you act like this is just a

game." He slides his hand over my ass, stroking. Then my thighs. "Just for some light fun. But imagine if I owned you?" He runs his fingers over my waist, then down my legs. Up. "Completely? And obeying me was locked into your very psyche?"

"Mmm..." I moan. His words touch a part of me that has long been dormant. To be honest, I sort of feel like I'm already there.

"Think how much you'd love serving me, doing my bidding." He strokes my inner thighs, and I part my legs just a bit to give him access, in case he wants to touch. "And rest assured, your punishments for any transgressions would be far more severe than anything you've felt so far." He taps my ass once, a light slap.

I moan again. "Alain, God, I could come just if you do that again," I murmur.

He laughs. "No, you won't. You're going to wait for permission, like last time. No matter how long it takes. Promise me."

"Okay, I promise." I wiggle my body, sending little sparks to my clit.

"Not like that. Call me Master. Promise you won't come until I give permission." His voice is suddenly colder. Stern.

I speak immediately. "Alain. Master. I won't come until you grant me permission." And with the words, it's like something locks into my mind with an audible click. I can almost feel the power I've given him surrounding me. And it turns me on even more.

"Good." He sounds satisfied. Pleased. "If you come too soon, I'll give you a dozen with the cane and make you stand in the corner before giving you another few to follow up, Bri."

I suck in my breath. "That's mean!" I blink rapidly. "I wouldn't like that."

I might, though.

It turns me on to think about bending over, exposing my ass. Alain standing there, dominant and strong, flexing a supple, wicked cane in his hand. Then having him raise it up and bring it down hard across my buttocks…ooooh.

I press my thighs together at the thought. Would I like it? I might.

"Yes, you probably would like it. But I think you'd like other things better," he murmurs. "The cane would be a deterrent. To train you out of bad behavior. To teach you what not to do, so you could better serve me."

With that, he spanks my ass, hard.

"Ow." It feels good, and I like it.

"Oh, that was nothing. You just wait." He spanks me again. "This time you can talk all you want, sweet girl. But I won't stop until I think you've had enough. And –"

He cuts me off as I start to say something—"And if you mouth off, I'll only spank you longer. Harder."

I whimper in need, then yelp as his hand comes down again and again. He's spanking hard right off the bat, and it hurts. There's no warm up, no time to acclimate to the sensation. Just his solid palm, over and over until my ass burns.

"Alain, stop!" I wiggle in vain, trying to pull myself away from his grip.

"Oh, baby, you've got a ways to go," he chides me, and continues his assault on my bottom. "And are you supposed to tell me to stop, hmm?" He spanks harder, which I didn't think was possible, until I squeal out my response.

"No! I'm not. I'm sorry. I'm sorry."

"Master," he reminds me, delivering some especially hard slaps to my thighs.

"Ow. Master! I'm sorry, Master."

"Say it like you mean it." His voice is firm, determined. Cool.

My mind swims, and it feels like I'm reeling, falling, and he's going to catch me. But if he does, he'll own me…completely.

And I let myself go. "Master," I whisper, raising my ass up a fraction. "I'm sorry."

"Good." Did he say it, or I am imagining it in my mind? His voice fills my consciousness. His scent envelops me. All I can do is focus on his hand, spanking my ass.

It burns, it stings, but he's in charge—and letting him decide when I'm done is such a turn on that I really do think I could come. A few more hard spanks, ones that allow me to push my hips down into his thighs –

"Bri, are you allowed to do that?" He stops spanking. But it's like he wants to tease me harder because he inserts his finger under the string of my panties and tugs, forcing the fabric to pull at my clit. As the sensation intensifies my need, the arousal grows more powerful.

"I'm…" I pant a little bit. "Oh, Alain…." I can't even find words. The sting on my ass is exquisite and mixed with the pleasure starting to burn in my belly, I just want more of everything.

"I think we'll do just one with the cane as a lesson." He moves fluidly, sliding me into his arms. Strides to the bed and deposits me carefully before I can process what's happening.

Before I know it, he's got me arranged lying on my stomach, with a pillow under my hips, my legs spread slightly. Arms in front of me. He carefully slides the panties down my thighs. "Ah, completely naked," he drawls, "and all for me. I like you this way."

"Alain." I close my eyes and see swirls of color. My whole body sparks with pleasure.

"I think I'll tie your hands," he muses aloud. "Even though you're quite obedient, I want to make sure you know that you're mine tonight. That I'll do what I want with you."

He steps away and comes back with the tie he tossed aside earlier. "Hands together." He laces the fabric around both of my wrists and knots it expertly. So fast. "You could get out of this," he murmurs, bending down, one hand on my burning ass, the other holding my hair in one hand. He kisses my neck. "But you won't. Because you want to be my prisoner."

"Yes," I moan. His hand on my ass is torture—I want him to stroke away the burn. Maybe to spank more. Definitely I want his fingers between my thighs instead of atop my buttocks, if I had a choice.

He slaps me once. Chuckles. "I like you tied up. I should do this every night."

I want you to. Did I say it or think it?

My stomach flips at the thought. I never plan to see lovers more than once these days, since I gave up on relationships. Here we are for a second time, and already I'm dreaming of a future?

But when he comes back with the cane, all I can focus on is the present moment.

He shows it to me, a long, thin bamboo rod. Flexes it. "This can be used like silk, or it can do serious damage."

I shudder. *Well, I did say to surprise me.*

He touches my shoulder. "I won't damage you. But this will hurt, my dear. Think about whether or not you'd really like a dozen, next time you're inclined to disobey."

He swishes the cane through the air behind me, and I flinch, expecting to feel it on my ass.

But it was just a practice run. He does it again. "Using a cane takes skill, you know. I'm a master. Perhaps I'll accustom you to its bite and turn you into as much of an aficionado as I am."

I make an incoherent noise and wiggle. I'm dying with anticipation.

"Oh, no moving," he chides. "Part of taking the cane is learning to be still for it. Accept the punishment."

"But I…" My heart beats so rapidly that I think I'll pass out.

"Tell me you want this, Bri. Ask your master for the cane."

I feel new moisture between my thighs even as pangs of fear and adrenaline flow through my body. Because in this moment, he is my master. I'll do whatever he asks.

"Master, please. I want the cane."

"By all means, let me indulge you." His voice holds humor and a burr of arousal.

Then I hear the swish and crack of the cane. For a split

second there's no sensation. Then I scream out loud because I swear, he's put a bar of furnace-hot steel across my ass. I swear it's burning. I'm dying.

"Ow, ouch, oh my God." I wriggle furiously, tugging at the tie. "Fuck!"

He pushes my shoulder, firm but gentle. "That was one. Do you want another?"

I settle down immediately, eyes going wide. "No."

He rubs my ass, and murmurs something, and the fire subsides just enough to be bearable. "So maybe you wish to avoid more strokes with the cane, yes?"

"Yes, no more cane, please. Alain. Master." I'm babbling.

"Good." He swishes it once again, then tosses it aside. "Keep in mind I can always fetch it again, if necessary. If I need to correct you. Do you understand?"

"Yes, I'll be good, I promise." I whimper and then sigh in relief as he strokes my ass again. I pull at the tie, but it doesn't yield. Knowing I've willingly given myself over to him to do with as he pleases has turned me into a ball of need. Just sensation.

He's still fully dressed while I'm naked, but now he stands and pulls off his shirt. His pants. Eventually he's naked, and although I'm tied up on my stomach, my burning ass still elevated on the pillow, I can turn my head to see him.

And he's phenomenal.

Last time the club was so dark that I barely got to examine his body.

Tonight, the room is bright enough, so I can see every muscle, every plane. And that glorious, hard long cock. It's thick and firm…and huge. I know, because I felt it last time. Seeing it, though, is even more arousing.

"Last time, you rode me. Today, I'll do the work. Up for just a second." He taps my ass, and I lift my hips up, then he gently pulls the pillow out from under me, running his hands down my body as he arranges me anew.

His touch is expert, soft. Practiced. "Stay still while I touch you," he whispers. His fingers stroke away the pain from the cane, tracing the welt he left behind until instead of hurting, I swear it blazes with sweetness. He ducks his hand between my legs for a quick second, stroking along my pussy until he finds my clit.

I gasp and push into his hand. "Alain."

"Look at you wearing the mark of my cane." He strokes my ass, then my clit, alternating until I'm dying with the need to come. "I fucking love it. God, how you'd look with a dozen or more stripes on your ass. Feeling it the next day and thinking of me every single moment. Maybe you'll learn to love the cane after all, hmmm?"

"If you make me feel like this afterwards, I just might." I open my legs wider, hoping to entice him.

"I'll always make you feel like this." His words are rough, like he means it. He softens his tone. "All night long."

He kisses the curve of my waist, glides his hands over the sides of my breasts.

I exhale and lift up, hoping he'll slide his hands under and play with my nipples, but instead he strokes my hips, both sides. "So pretty." His voice is low, and I can barely hear him, but the emotion comes through. Raw. Needy. "You are so fucking beautiful."

I hum in response, closing my eyes.

"Turn over for me." His voice is low, hoarse. He helps me flip over and arranges my hands—still tied, over my head. My hair is all wild, cascading down my shoulders, and he strokes it out of my face. "Look at you." He smiles. His eyes are dark and mysterious. "My captive."

Now he touches my breasts, tweaking the nipples softly, grazing them with just the tips of his fingernails until I squirm and cry out in pleasure. "Alain!"

He's kneeling over me, hands on mine, pushing them into the pillows. His body is so close. "Mine," he whispers.

"Maybe you're my captive, too." I spread my thighs. "And I don't even need bonds."

I say it as a joke, but when he doesn't respond—at least not with words. There's something in his eyes, something fierce and powerful. And although he says nothing, a small smile plays on his lips.

Finally, he speaks. "We'll see." And then he bends down and takes my lips with his, and I lose all sense of time.

His mouth on my tits, sucking, biting until I cry out, then licking until I squeal with pleasure. His hands, warm —on my shoulders. My belly.

"I'm going to bite you again," he says. I think. The words reverberate in my skull, echoing softy.

"Mmm…" I close my eyes and shift my body.

Then I feel his teeth on my inner thigh. I gasp and cry out, but the sharp pain turns to immediate pleasure as he sucks over the wound. It's like a tiny orgasm on that patch of skin. It's unbelievably hot, and my clit throbs with need. "Alain." My voice is hoarse.

I hit my tied hands on the pillow above me. "Please."

"Not yet." He kisses his way up my body. "I need to taste you." Then his tongue is on my clit and I'm transported.

"God, oh God, I'm going to come," I beg him.

"No. Not until I give permission." He slaps my breast, not hard, but sharp. Once. Again. "Wait for it."

"Yes, Master." My body backs off, even though it's painful. I've never had to hold off an orgasm with such difficulty. I'm breathing hard. Sweating. "Fuck, fuck, fuck."

He licks along my pussy lips, then thrusts his tongue into my pussy. I moan and wiggle as the sensation grows. I'm helpless under his touch.

Just when I think I'm about to come, he pulls away. "You want to come, Bri?"

"Yes." I'm almost in tears.

"Ask for it, then."

"Please let me come. I'll do whatever you want."

With that, he spreads my thighs and thrusts his iron-hard cock deep into my pussy.

I lift up my legs, and he grabs me by the calves, pulling me toward and up as he pumps me. His cock is all I crave in the world right now. My existence is my body and his, his cock in my pussy, every stroke bringing me closer to release.

"You'll let me bite you and spank you and punish you when I want," he demands.

"Yes, everything you want, please," I beg.

He pauses, and I cry out in irritation and dismay, but

when I feel his lips on my neck, I know he's going to bite me there again.

Strange thoughts flow through my mind because bites on the neck are usually—I mean, I know it's just folklore and mythology and all, but it's so typically—but of course that's not real, but it's just—and what was with the blood in the bar?

Images flash in my mind and then spark like fireworks when his teeth sink into my skin. Alain in black. Alain's face, lit up, against the night sky. Alain dressed in historical clothes, like he's in a painting from the 1800's. Alain and me in the club, as if I'm hovering above, watching him fuck me. Alain's friend drinking a glass of blood. Alain's long sharp teeth, driving into my body.

The needle sharp pain gives way, once again, to a second of numbness and then that growing warmth and pleasure.

I don't know what the fuck is going on, and I don't care. The pleasure is too great.

Now he's pumping me again, his cock even thicker and stronger than before, his body powerful. I'm buzzing, high above the world, my mind spinning in ecstasy, better than anything.

Better than everything.

And when I come, a second later, the feeling is so exquisite that I cry out garbled sounds and clench my whole body as the unbelievably beautiful sensation rolls over me and through me with such force that I almost pass out.

lain

When I bite her for the second time, I suck hard, taking more blood than I maybe should. But she's so fucking delicious.

The taste of her blood mixes with the exquisite flavor of her pussy, and I roar out my pleasure.

When I come, my whole world goes pure white and then black, and the orgasm takes me to bliss. I allow myself to revel in the sensation.

Jesus fucking Christ. I haven't had a fuck this good in two hundred years.

A few minutes later, she's nearly passed out, relaxing in my arms, and I'm still high on her blood and the sex. My whole body is pervaded with vigor and power, and when I look at her face, I feel a surprising sensation: I want her. Still.

Usually, sex is about getting blood, and the orgasm is a nice extra. Like mixing the necessary and the nice-to-have and getting a great combo. It's about the immediate gratification, and then I just want the woman to leave.

Not with Bri. In fact, I don't want this to be the last night, either. I want her again tonight.

Maybe every night.

And it's not just for the blood, although I must admit that something about her essence has given me more energy than I've got from a human in decades.

I sigh and run a hand over my face. There can be no lasting romantic relationship between humans and vampires, and it is folly to even dream of it.

Yet here I am.

Bri stirs in my arms, and her eyelids flicker. She speaks without opening her eyes. "That was amazing." Her voice is dreamy, drugged. When I bit her, my saliva entered her bloodstream and added to her euphoria.

She's figuring things out; I saw it in her face. Read it in her mind. If she gets any more ideas, I'll have to wipe her harder, even if it's risky.

Fuck. If I have to do a longer, more complex wipe, it would really mess her up. Maybe it's because she's a redhead? I read a study claiming that redheads are genetically more susceptible to pain, although God knows there's no scientific study about how they respond to vampire-induced brain cleanses.

I sigh. I hate the idea of her forgetting even a second of the time we spent together. I'm going to have a very difficult decision to make later on.

But for now, I just want to enjoy her presence. Pretend the rest of my troubles don't exist. Because when I'm with her, I get those feelings I've always sought and never found: Peace. Relaxation. Joy.

I turn to her and kiss her awake. "Hey, beautiful. You ready for round two?"

～

Bri

The night passes in bursts of pleasure, and after some time, I'm so sated with sex and Alain that I'm barely coherent. Everything is good and bright and beautiful.

I lie on the bed, drowsing, half-watching him put away things we used: A crop. A paddle. Leather cuffs. I smell our sex in the air, and I like it. The sheet covering me is as soft as air and keeps me the perfect temperature.

"That was perfect." And it was.

"Agreed." He comes back and slides in beside me, taking me in his arms.

I snuggle up close and put my hand on him, wanting to touch as much of him as possible. "So what do you do?"

"Besides give you the best fuck of your life?" He smiles.

I hit his chest. "Brag much? What if I have other, better men?"

"Do you?" His voice is guarded.

I bite my lip. "Well, no. I don't. What about you? Other women?"

"No."

Relief floods my body. It's just another one-night stand, but God help me, I already feel so possessive of him. I think I'd want to scratch out the eyeballs of any woman who so much as kissed him.

He laughs. "I bet you would."

"I…"

"I mean, I bet you would like another round." He sounds smug.

"Eh. We'll see." Of course, I do. But I'm not going to be the needy one and beg for something I probably won't get. I know how life works.

"So did you get your blood tests back?" He touches my arm.

"Still waiting." But it's sweet that he asked. That he cares.

"Is it hard to wait?" He looks at my face.

"It's torture. But I stay busy, you know, with my web design work." I nod, to emphasize how in control of it I am. Try not to indicate how much I needed this night with him to push away the fears and doubts. To chase away the panic. "What do you do?"

"I'm in finance."

"What kind? Banking?"

"I manage investment portfolios. Stocks. Options."

"Things I know nothing about."

"Most people don't. That's why I do pretty well." He smiles. "I can help them with it."

"Well, if you need a new website." I wiggle my eyebrow. "You know who to call."

He smiles. "I have a guy for that already."

"You strike me as the kind of man who has a guy for everything." I think about the Porsche, the casual way he took charge at the club, his whole demeanor. His house of treasures. Clearly a multi-millionaire.

He looks away for a second. "You can't hire people for everything."

"Like real friendship. Or true love."

"Exactly." He sounds sad.

Is someone like him lonely? It hardly seems likely—he could have anyone he wanted.

I touch his arm. "I read an article about how some people in Japan hire fake families to pretend to love them. Fake wives, fake children. It was an article a while back, in the *New Yorker*."

"I read that."

"Didn't it seem creepy?"

"It seemed tragic." He's thoughtful. "And entirely inevitable. When people can't get what they want naturally, they try to get it any way they can. Even if it's not sustainable."

"Not that a guy like you would ever be in that position." I laugh.

"I suppose nobody who does that ever thought they'd be in that position." He sighs and takes my face into his hands. "But the good thing here is that neither of us are faking this."

He smiles and traces a finger over my lips. "When you cry out my name and beg me to come, I know you really want it." His smile deepens into something wicked and bold. "Isn't that right?"

It is right.

And so is the rest of the night, until we lie together, finally exhausted.

"It will be dawn soon." His voice is low. "Shall I get you home to avoid the sun?" He pauses. "You can stay here during the day, but I must leave. I have business." He looks away.

I sit up, the experience slowly pulling away. A tide, inevitable. Sad. "I should go home. Yes."

He touches my face. "I'll let you get dressed. Come in the kitchen when you're ready, Bri."

I find my clothes and put them on, not wanting day to come. I wish this night could last forever, so I could just live in the moment, in the joy of being with him. I don't want the troubles that the day will bring.

When I enter the kitchen, he's got his hands in his pockets and he's staring out through huge plate glass windows that look like they can slide open to expose the patio, like a lanai in Hawaii.

"I'm ready." I come up to his elbow, and he pulls me to him, close, and I swivel to press up against him. I wrap my arms around his body and squeeze, as if I can hold him to me this way. Make the night last longer.

He strokes my hair, then sighs. "My car is still in front."

"All right." I grab my purse.

He opens the front door. The air is cool and moist with night, and smells like the desert; creosote and cactus flowers. The moon is bright, and the stars are flung on the tapestry of the sky like diamonds.

"If you want." I blurt it out before I can second guess myself. "Want to meet at the club again next Friday?"

My heart starts to pound.

He hesitates, and the silence grows thick and awful.

"You know, never mind." I try to laugh. "I'm sorry, sometimes I just say things that I don't mean –"

"Yes." He cuts me off. Looks into my eyes. "Next week." I swear there's emotion in his eyes, like he wants me above all else. I can almost hear him saying it in my head.

"Okay!" My voice trembles a little with emotion. I think about taking his hand and grabbing a bottle of champagne. How nice it would be to sit on a mountain and watch the sun come up together, maybe wrapped in a blanket, me lying in his arms.

He frowns and looks away, as if he can see my thoughts and doesn't like them. I remember skin cancer and blisters and bite my lip.

I've already asked life for too much. I shouldn't be so greedy.

"Well, I'll take that lift home," I say, going for levity. Things feel awkward now, even though we've spent another exotic, passionate night together.

"Of course." He guides me to his Porsche, and as we glide through the pre-dawn streets, nearly empty, lit up just for us, I feel like we're in a dream…and I never want to wake up.

CHAPTER 16

Bri

"So, you going to come out with us this Friday?" K. sorts through a rack of vintage T's. "Dinner, then movie, and it's the new one you wanted to see. Pick you up at seven?"

"I can't." I pull out a pink T-shirt with a huge picture of Julio Iglesias screened onto the front, the graphic cracked in places but still vibrant. "This is so bad it's good."

K. flips the tag. "Not for $85, it's not." She snorts.

"Come on, you know you love it." I hold it up to her body. "Try it on."

We're in Generation Cool, a funky retro resale shop on 4th Ave. It's fun to come here in the evenings, when people are strolling, to check out the eclectic shops and cafes.

"So why can't you come?" K. pushes Julio into my arms and extricates an original Gucci shirt that's about 8 sizes to large for her small frame. "This one is even more. Jesus." She shakes her head.

"I have plans." It's been a few days since my last tryst with Alain, and he's all I can think about. My body aches for him, and I can't wait for Friday…when I get to have him again. The rest of my life seems dull and bland compared to the exquisite moments I spend with him.

"Oh?" K. raises her brow. "With the guy again?" I feel like there's a little tone of something in her voice.

I ignore the vibe. "Yes, with the guy. Alain." Just saying his name makes me smile, a little sly grin. "Friday is kind of our night." It's been three Fridays so far, each one better than the last.

"When are we going to meet him?" K. puts the Gucci back and turns to look at me.

"Well." But I don't answer.

"And why doesn't he have social media? You know what I think of people who have zero digital footprint."

She steps closer to me to allow egress for the girl on rollerskates and bright pink hair, who zooms into the propped-open door in shorts so tight they could be paint. A photographer follows close behind, snapping shots as she poses. The worker behind the counter, who gives off random whiffs of faded 420, does not seem bothered in the slightest—apparently this place is cool with pics.

"You think they're psycho weirdos. I know." I make a face.

"Why don't you have even one picture?"

I laugh a little. "He's really rich, I think. Into finance. Likes his privacy. Kind of old school. Does it matter?"

"Yeah, because I need to see if he's cute enough for

you, duh." She rolls her eyes. "Seriously, though. Who under the age of eighty-two isn't online? I mean, my grandma's got Facebook, and she's 90."

I shrug. "Well, he's about ten years older. And he told me he's just not into social media. Some people aren't."

The truth is, I find it a little odd, too. But when I'm with him, I'm so caught up in the sex and the attraction, the magic of it all, that I don't care. "Look. You've been bugging me forever to find a guy and have some fun. Now that I did, you're on me about that?"

"So." K takes a breath, and I get the horrible feeling that she's about to say something I don't like. "Are you dating him then, for real?"

I wrap my arms around myself. "No, definitely not." I try to keep a note of disappointment out of my voice because after all, this is the way I like things. Simple. With an end date. An easy out.

"Uh, okay." She makes a face. "Just seems like you're pretty into him, though."

"Listen, it's new," I say. "Too soon for a label. Besides. You know how I feel about long-term relationships."

"I know." K reaches out and pats my arm. "That's part of the reason I'm worried. You're getting so wrapped up in him. I don't want you to get hurt if it, you know, ends like your last boyfriends." She winces as she says it.

"Oh, that's sweet." I look at her face, so earnest and kind, and feel a rush of affection. Dear K, my best friend in the world. "What would I do without you?"

"You'd be really sad," she says immediately. We both laugh.

"Alain is…really awesome." The word is lame

compared to his essence, but I can't think of a better one. "And once I figure things out, I'll introduce you. I mean, if we even see each other again. We might not. I don't even know."

The thing is, I feel like Alain is temporary, an apparition. Like I'm asleep, having an amazing dream, and if I try to pin him down, poof!—like smoke, he'll disappear. So I have to sidle up to him, enjoy him for what he is. Not ask for more because I can't possibly live with less. I'm addicted hard.

"You've been different lately." K looks away from me toward a shelf of vintage Ninja Turtle figures. She picks one up and turns it in her hand.

"I am? How?"

"I don't know." She pauses. "Maybe happier. Like you're more... energetic. But a little bit frantic, too."

"It's the hot sex." I laugh, but she doesn't.

She continues, "I'm glad you're happy. Just, take care of yourself."

"Don't I always?"

We drop the topic and continue on to the Chocolate Iguana, whose brownies—in my opinion—are almost as good as sex.

Later, though, I think about her words.

I've always felt distant from life, as if I'm watching it instead of living it. Ever since my disease was diagnosed and I had to spend less time in the sun, I felt as if I'd retreated from the world.

It's been years now, and as time goes by, it feels more and more like everyone else is in a movie, and I'm watching. And the distance from me to the screen is growing.

Being with Alain punched through the screen and dragged me into the essence of life. For the first time in forever, I feel vigorously, enjoyably alive. If that reads as frantic, well, who cares?

I like it.

I don't know how this will end. All I know is that I want to seize it now, while I still can.

CHAPTER 17

Bri

"Ready to go home?" Alain smiles at me, that gorgeous smile, the one that makes me go weak.

"I suppose." I grin back. I'm getting more comfortable with our arrangement. He gave me his cell phone number and took mine, which feels like a huge commitment. We still have no formal title, but after another night together, our bond seems so strong. When I'm with him, I feel like he's perfect for me. I know I can't count on this lasting; my relationships never do...but maybe this time things will be different. Even if they're not, I don't ever care.

"Let me get the door for you." He smiles as I hit the button to unlock my car doors.

The evening air is cool, like usual, and I hear a night bird call. He touches the driver side door of my car, then puts his hand onto my shoulder for a second. "One kiss before you get in."

His lips touch mine. It's perfect for a split second, and then it all goes wrong.

I smell the scent of rotting garbage and hear a hiss. My eyes fly open, and I see the man in black pop into view. I swear, he materializes out of nothing.

His voice is a sinuous hiss. "357A-19. We're ready for you now."

He reaches out to grab my arm, and I scream, clutch onto Alain. I know without a doubt that this man is worse than cancer. Any future is better than one in which he takes me.

But he's strong and so fast! How can a person move like that? I twist away and try to run, but he's there like I went nowhere, his fingers digging into my arm. "So perfect that you're here with Alain. Like a wrapped gift, just for me." He giggles.

I scream and push, pull, but he's got me. "You'll be my best blood source yet. And the perfect LD," he whispers.

Suddenly Alain is between us, moving so fast he's just a blur. He's literally flying, his whole body off the ground. His eyes glow, and his teeth are long, sharp. He hisses and roars, and the man in black cries out.

The two of them lift off the ground, blurring so fast I can't see who is who. They hiss and howl, attack and dive.

Alain attacks again and again, and the man stumbles. Falters. Finally, he flashes out of my sight like he was erased. Like magic.

I'm crying, shaking. I can't think. I've fallen to the ground because I feel gravel on my knees. Hard, cutting. The air is chilly, and I know I've gone insane.

"It's all right, Bri. He's gone. He's gone."

Alain scoops me up, effortlessly. Grabs me and heads back into his house, slamming the door behind him.

"You're safe in here, okay? He can't come in here. Not unless he's invited."

"I can't—I don't –" My teeth chatter and I can't speak. "I don't understand."

I remember how the man almost got me, and I scream.

"It's okay. Bri, you're safe." Alain's voice is soothing.

But I keep screaming, and my whole body trembles for a long time. Finally, when I sink back into his embrace, I'm able to ask the question into his shoulder.

"Who was that? And who are you?"

I don't want to know the answers. But I need them.

He takes my hands, which are cold. Ice.

"I need you to listen with an open mind." His eyes are piercing, and my mind swims, just like at the club, just like when we were fucking.

Images flash and disappear: Sex. The man drinking blood. Alain's teeth, long and sharp. Alain flying, fighting the way no human can. Alain in my head. Telling me what to do. The man by my car.

All the fragmented memories come together in one impossible whole.

"You're a vampire," I say, before he can open his mouth.

It's insane. It's not possible because vampires don't exist. And yet, when I see his face, I know it's the truth.

"Yes." His voice is calm, but his body is tense. "I am."

I can't accept it, even though I know it's right. "Okay. I've gone crazy. I need to call Dr. Su and get some new meds. Oh my God." I try to stand up. "Where's my phone? Please take me home." I'm babbling. I want this to be a bad dream.

"Bri." His voice holds a command, and I sink back to the couch. "That was Karl. He's a vampire, an evil one. We think he's taking the women in Tucson. He's dangerous. I can't let you go home, or he'll kill you." The words are flat but hit like bullets. "Vampires are out all night and sleep at dawn, while the sun is out. The sun kills us almost instantly. Daytime is the only time you're safe from him."

Panic wells up, and I think I'm going to lose it.

Alain grabs me tight. "Easy," he whispers into my ear. His hands are tight and firm on my arms. "You're not going to lose anything. Calm. Follow my voice."

Without second-guessing it, I allow myself to fall into the deep well of his aura. Alice down the rabbit hole, falling, falling. Then—I catch on something. It's like he's caught me, inside my head, preventing me from freaking out.

"You're safe right now. It's all right." His voice is a beacon, guiding me back to my confidence.

"Okay." My voice is small, but no longer holds a quiver. "I'm all right."

"Yes, you are." He's smiling, even at this strange moment. "Oh, sweet Bri." He sighs. Then his voice is focused again. "What exactly did he say to you?"

"He said, *we're ready for you now*. And that my blood would be perfect. And a number. Like a tracking ID." I blink.

"A number? What number?"

"I don't know. Like a tracking ID."

"What ID? From where?"

"I don't know." I draw back at the look in his face. "I'm not lying."

He softens his features. "I know you're not. But it's important. I need you to think."

"I'm trying!" My voice comes out a whine and a tremor at the same time.

He sighs, as if frustrated, but his voice—when he speaks again, is softer. "Bri, I'm sorry. I know this is strange and terrifying. I was so focused on fighting him that I couldn't use my skills to hear everything around me. Please try to remember."

"Okay. I'm focusing." I roll my eyes at him.

His eyes narrow, and I know what he's thinking—and for one split second, my mind darts to sex and spanking—before flashing back to the present.

"Oh my God. I think I know what that is."

"Tell me." Alain holds my shoulders and looks into my eyes.

"It's my Gila Diagnostics blood draw ID. That's the number I always see on my results page."

"Oh, no." Alain's voice lowers. "You get your blood drawn there?" He takes my shoulders, like he's upset. "Bri?"

"Well, yes." I'm taken aback. "That's my usual place."

"Fuck." He mutters something else I can't hear.

But I need to tell him what else I know. "And all three of the missing women in Tucson? They had their blood drawn at Gila Diagnostics, too."

"How do you know that?" Alain's eyes are dark, his voice sharp. But he's not surprised. It's like he already knew that information. He's just surprised that I know, too.

"Uh, a friend found out for me. A hacker friend."

When he keeps staring at me, face almost ferocious, I

swallow. "Alain? It's…I mean, I have a friend online. His name is Slash, okay?"

"Oh, *fuck*." Alain gets up and shakes his head. "Did you say Slash?"

"Yes?" I raise a brow. "Why? Do you know him?"

Alain barks out a small laugh. "Apparently, it's a small world, Bri."

He grabs his phone. "Slash. Get over here. Now." He slides the phone back into his pocket. "Bri, I have a very short window of time to get some things done before I need to rest. And you need to stay here."

"Uh, okay." I blink at him. "But I should go home for my –"

"You're not going home for anything." He crosses his arms. "Karl is out there, and if you leave the boundaries of my home, he can take you."

"But he can't come in?"

"No."

"Okay. Good. But I need my medications, and my laptop, and..."

"Fuck." He scowls. Grabs his phone again. "Some-one's going to get it for you. Does he have permission to enter your home?"

"Um, sure, but without the keys–"

"Just give him permission." He narrows his eyes and holds the phone to my ear. "You've met him; it's Tiberius. The bouncer at the club."

"I should say what?" I blink." I can't keep up with what's happening."

"Hello." The voice on the phone is comforting. I can imagine Tiberius' perfectly styled hair and impeccable suit. "I see Alain found you. Tell me I can enter your home?"

"Fine. Enter away." I wave my hand and scowl at Alain. "The address is–"

"I'm already inside. Meds are these, inside the cabinet? The blue bag?"

"Yes, but how did you–"

"Got the laptop, too. Need anything else?"

"I…" I turn to Alain. "How is he already at my house?"

"We move quickly." His voice is dry. He takes the phone from my hand.

"So, Tiberius is a vampire too?" My voice rises.

"Yes." But he's distracted, typing something on his phone. His whole body vibrates with a strange energy that seems part anger, part concern.

"Of course, he is. And I assume everyone else I've met lately is a vampire?" I cough. "People at the club?"

"Some of them. Yes. One second." He lowers his voice and turns away. I can only catch snippets of his words.

"Jesus." I shake my head. "This is insane."

I stand up and pace, back and forth on the Persian rug. Glance at his wall, at the Monet, the Mondrian, and what looks like a Picasso. "Where in the fresh hell did I land?" I murmur.

I think about calling K.

I can't call K. What would I tell her? If she even believed me, I'd probably endanger her, too.

And for the first time, I realize that my life as I know it is over.

At least I'm with Alain.

And that thought gives me far more comfort than you'd think it should.

∼

"ALAIN? I'M HERE." It's a voice from the door.

"Come in, Slash. Don't panic, but I have a human here. Bri." Alain is at the door in a split second. It's unnerving to see him move so fast!—but even as I blink, I realize that I recognize the newcomer's voice. It's "my" Slash, hacker Slash—the one who called me.

"Bri?" Slash does a double take, as he steps in with a trendy laptop bag slung over one shoulder. "From online?" He looks like a real-life version of his avatar: Short brown hair, sort of messy, wire-rim glasses, slender. Typical Gen-X clothing. Chucks.

"Slash, from online?" I'm as dumbfounded as he is. "You know Alain?"

"Uh-huh." Slash looks at me like he's trying to figure something out. "How do you know Alain?" He frowns. Looks at Alain, me, back to Alain. His shoulders seem stiff.

Before I can answer—confused about why Slash was so friendly online to me and now is so cold, Alain cuts in.

"I'm not pleased with you." Alain glowers at Slash. "Why in the holy hell would you be sharing information with her," he gestures at me, "and leaving me out of the loop?"

"What are you talking about?"

"The three women all had their blood drawn at Gila

Diagnostics?" Alain's voice rises. "How did it not occur to tell me that Bri was your contact?"

Slash shakes his head. His face looks pale, like he's tired. "Alain, how would I have any idea that you know Bri?"

Alain growls. "She's in danger."

Slash looks uncertain. "Alain, I don't normally tell contacts about each other. It's my privacy rules?"

I clear my throat. "My friend K. said that the security cameras were turned off before the break in at Gila Diagnostics. Maybe you should see if you can find out who did that. Can you find that information online?"

"How did your friend know this?" Slash sounds dubious.

"Her brother is a lieutenant. He told her."

"Slash, can you check it out?" Alain's voice isn't a question. It's more of a command.

"If there's an event log, I might be able to trace the information to an employee ID." Slash's voice is somber.

"It's my fault," Alain says, under his breath.

I shoot a glance at Slash, but he's setting up his computer and logging in.

"How would it be your fault?" I venture.

"Because..." Alain starts.

"She knows about you, and you're telling her even more?" Slash sounds ominous. "You know you're going to have to wipe –"

Alain cuts him off. "It's my fault, Bri, because I made him. I made Karl into a vampire. Now that he's turned on me, he wishes to destroy everything I care about."

"But he had my blood draw ID. He already wanted me." I put a hand to my mouth.

"It will give him extra pleasure to hurt you because it also hurts me." Alain shakes his head. "Perhaps in worse ways than he originally planned."

"I still don't understand. I have so many more questions."

Alain turns back to me. "I will answer them, in time. Can you be patient?"

But it's not really a question. He's telling me I have to wait.

And as I glance at the window, too, where the dark is barely, imperceptibly lightening, fear spikes my heart. What disaster is the new day going to bring?

ALAIN

Tiberius drops off Bri's things, and we confer briefly, as I tell him what I need, and he tells me what he saw: Nothing. No signs of Karl. After his attack on Bri, Karl completely disappeared.

But I know he'll be back. Any thoughts or hopes I had of saving Karl—ridiculous! I curse myself for the weakness of allowing myself to even consider it. If I'd ended Karl earlier, when he was less powerful, this attack would never have happened. His whole sick blood bank idea would not even exist.

I have to face the fact that I fucked up royally by imagining I had the power to make things work out the way I hoped— and this mistake can never be corrected without force.

In this case, violence needs violence. And I'll have to deliver in order to protect everything I care about.

Bri is drowsing on the couch, but it's an uneasy sleep. She twitches and moans, and her eyelids flutter as if she's about to awake. Her shoulders are tense even as she dreams, and I am positive this is no relaxing slumber.

"What are you going to do about her?" Slash tilts his head toward her.

"That's my business."

"It's all of our business now." Slash is young and brash for being so new. But he's not exactly wrong. "We don't tell humans about us except in rare cases. Already too many know."

"Consider this one of the exceptions."

"Are you going to wipe her?" He fixes his gaze on me.

I look away. "She doesn't wipe well. It would hurt her."

"How many times have you even been together?" His voice goes up. "Are you, like, dating?"

"That's not your business," I snarl. "Besides, you called her on the phone? You're her friend online? You're as bad as I am."

"Not even close," he retorts. "She didn't know a thing about me being a vampire. I was just her hacker friend, finding information." But he looks guilty as fuck. I know he wants companionship as badly as I do. He knows he slipped up, too.

I guess Bri is just intoxicating to both of us, in different ways.

"She can be trusted." I know this is true, even though I've only known her a short time. But I feel it in my gut. My heart.

"Well, if you're sure." He sounds wry. Then shakes his head. "I guess I shouldn't have called her." A second goes by. "But I felt the same. Like I could trust her."

"She's in it now, anyway," I add.

We both look at her in her uneasy sleep.

He says: "I liked her, you know. We're friends online." He sounds defensive. "She's really smart and funny."

"How can you be friends with humans online? That doesn't even make sense." Is it strange that I'm a little jealous?

It sounds like Slash has a little crush on her himself. Does she have more in common with Slash than with me? I'm not a newb like Martin, but I don't spend any social time on social media. To me, it's more of a research tool. I know how to look at other people's accounts, of course. I don't need accounts, and if I had them, I'd need to worry about keeping them legit and updated.

He shrugs. "It's the only way I can have any friends my original age. Don't knock it."

I don't tell him that it matters very little whether he finds his human *friends* on-line or at the bar or at the bottom of a fucking well: They're all going to die and leave him, and soon enough he'll stop trying and save himself the pain.

I want to tell him to get over his stupid crush already.

A lesson I apparently haven't learned yet myself.

Bri moans again.

"I wish she could rest." I stand over Bri, then crouch down, silent. Gently touch my hands to her forehead. *Rest.*

She doesn't respond, so I push deeper into her mind. She let me in while we were having sex, but I feel guilty going in while she's asleep, even less able to push me away. Something I've never really cared about too much with most humans. But Bri, she's already an exception. Like Dr. A., I already care about Bri so deeply that it rivals my affection for Martin...and that's saying a lot.

Rest easy.

She sighs, a deep tremulous breath, then her body stills, and her shoulders soften.

She and I really do have a strange connection. I can't do this with Dr. A. Can't really communicate things with humans like this. It's only with Bri.

"Speaking of sleep." Slash stands up. "It's about time." He looks from me to Bri then back again. Sighs. "Wow. That's going to be...wow." He gathers up his things. "I'll be back when it's dark."

"Be careful. If he knows you're helping me, you're in danger, too."

"I know how to take care of myself." Slash gives me a salute and disappears.

I stand by Bri, torn. I need to go to my lair downstairs and rest until nightfall. I also need her to stay here, safe. And I need to feed.

The night being what it was, I haven't gotten the chance for fresh blood. I have a pitcher of reserve in my fridge, and a hundred bags in my lair freezer as emergency stock, but who wants that, when the best quality stuff is right in front of you?

"I'm sorry to do this," I whisper into her ear, knowing she can't hear me. I'm not saying it into her mind, either. I guess the apology is just for me. Or maybe I'm not that sorry.

I bend down and dip my fangs into her neck, her soft white skin, let them go deeper than I ever have. Her fresh blood bursts onto my tongue, and I almost cry out with the pleasure of her taste. When I've taken enough, I lick the wound shut and enter her mind—this time strong. Masterful.

"Sleep until I come for you," I order her. But it's a soft order, one that she needs to accept.

She seems to mull it over for a second in her subconscious, questioning whether it's a valid command...

"Because I am your master. You promised you'd do as I say. Remember?" I flash her images of our lovemaking. Her begging. Her promises.

Oh, I know she only meant it for the moment...but I hope it's enough to let her agree to this, for now.

And thankfully, she does. She sighs, then goes into an even deeper sleep than she was before, her breath soft and even.

I cover her with a woven blanket and drop a kiss on her forehead. Then, on a second thought, I pick her up and put her into my bed. She'll be more comfortable there than on the couch.

Karl needs to rest himself, so there's no chance he'll be back before nightfall, and anyway, my home is protected with multiple alarms and locks. Bulletproof glass, steel frame construction and doors—it's impenetrable to most attacks. So even if Karl sends human allies, they won't get in.

I hate to leave her, but the torpor tugs at me. I stumble down to my basement lair, using eye and voice recognition to open my bunker vault, the safe that houses me while I rest away from the sun.

I drop into unconsciousness faster than usual, tired from the events of the day. The last thought before I go under is of Bri.

CHAPTER 18

Bri

I awaken as if pushing upward from underwater. I'm in a deeper sleep than I've ever had, and it's terrifying to see the light refracting and moving above me, miles above me, and my lungs about to burst–

I sit straight up and gasp, then pant. I'm in Alain's bed, alone.

The events of the previous hours come back, and with it, the tumult of emotions: Fear. Exhilaration. Lust. Terror.

"Alain?" There's no answer, and I feel alone.

I find the attached bathroom and use it. There's a brand new toothbrush and a tube of toothpaste, expensive French soap and soft plush towels, and I use them too. The mirror is spotless, not a single water mark; it could be a window.

The girl looking back at me is a wraith with pale skin, bags under her eyes, unkempt hair.

There's a brush, seemingly brand new, so I use that as well. At least now the wraith doesn't look 100 percent homeless. Small wins.

I hear a rustle from the other room, the main room where I fell asleep across from priceless art, while vampires conspired in undertones.

"Alain?" I pad out on socked feet, and peer in. "Oh, it's you. Slash. And—you. I've seen you before."

The other man is tall and darkly handsome. He's the one from the bar.

"Ow." I put a hand to my forehead. It's like a light flashing off and on; the image of him drinking a glass of red fluid. I force my mind to focus, and the image stops shattering itself, hovers for a second, and stays. "I remember you. You were drinking a glass of blood. At Club Toxic. And later you asked…" I flush. "Uh, something." I'm not about to say, in front of Slash, that Martin asked to share while Alain was spanking me.

He starts. "How do you remember that?" He clears his throat. "I apologize sincerely for the, ah, other thing. I won't ask again."

"Who are you?" I counter, fighting a flush.

"I'm…" he breaks off, smiles, but it seems sad. "I'm Martin. A friend of Alain's."

"I'm Bri." I frown. Still feeling twinges from the way the memory twanged and moved in my mind.

Martin gazes at me. "If you're hungry, there are human provisions in the—that. The immense silver storage compartment. It's cold."

"You mean the fridge?" I raise my brows.

"See for yourself." He regards the refrigerator with a look of awe. "It's miraculous."

"Where are you even from?" Because I'm starving and Alain isn't around and because this is the most surreal thing that's ever happened to me, I follow his direction.

I open the door and blink—the main shelf is filled with a magazine-worthy chocolate cake, macarons in a fancy plastic box, at least fifteen jars of caviar, French cheeses with ribbons and exotic wrappers, and an extremely large piece of what is probably Serrano ham. The other item, a pitcher of something red—I'm assuming blood, doesn't appeal.

"The better question is *when* he's from," Slash says. He's typing as he talks, and his face takes on a slight blue glow from the screen of his laptop.

"What do you mean?" I glance at him around the fridge door, then reach for the cake. I'm going to channel my inner Marie Antoinette and have a shit-ton of this deliciousness. I think I deserve it, you know?

"He's old, Bri. And then he napped for a century and just woke up, so he's like, a time traveler." He raises one hand to do air quotes on the word *napped*.

"Are you that old, too?" I stare at Slash, fascinated.

"No." He doesn't elaborate. Keeps his head down, looking at his screen.

"About my brain. My memories." I'm not about to give up on that topic. I place the cake onto the shiny granite countertop and look in the closest drawer for a knife and fork. "What's going on there?"

Neither of them answers.

Then I feel him from behind me—Alain. I turn to look at him, fork in hand. "Hi."

I feel strange in his presence. Like we're linked more deeply than before, in a way I don't understand.

"Bri." His gaze is possessive and warm as it travels over me, and the little smile that hovers on his lips tells me that he's feeling the same instant attraction. He's just as handsome as the first time I met him, and God help me, if those other two weren't here right now, I'd jump him.

"We need to talk. You need to explain." My words tumble out. "All of this."

"Ah, we'll give you some privacy. Call us when you want us back." Slash gestures to Martin. "Come on." The two of them exchange a look like they're not too happy about this and blur away; to where, I don't know. But I can tell we're alone.

"Now please. Tell me. About you. About what—how you are this way." I stare at Alain.

"I'm a vampire." He sighs. "I'm three hundred years old. I have some immortal friends and an enemy. Karl came at you last night. He wants to ruin me and is willing to destroy Tucson's vampire community and kill countless humans to do it. He's also out of control with his lust for blood and power, and if he's not stopped, he'll wreak havoc."

"Oh." I process this. "Okay."

"The thing with Karl? I made him. I turned him, a century ago. So I have an unusual bond with him. I made Martin, too, but he and I have a positive bond. We're allies. Karl is an enemy. I…should never have turned him. It was a bad choice. I hoped I could rehabilitate him, convince him to be different, but it was ineffective. I've learned since then, but at this point, it's either me or Karl. One of us needs to die. And it's not going to be me. And I swear I won't let him harm you, either."

He looks at me. Waiting.

"Where were you from?" I shake my head. I have so many questions, so I'll ask these now and circle back to the danger. The attack.

"Europe." He has a far-away look on his face. "France. My family was wealthy, but money couldn't pay for health, and three of my younger siblings died in infancy. The one who survived apart from me, my brother, it was just the two of us."

He has a fond look on his face. "He was sick, too, though. He had what today is called ALS or something much like it. His muscles stopped working."

"You searched for the castle with him?"

He nods. "Yes. We thought maybe there was a buried treasure. I had dreams of finding a cure for him."

"Like, what kind of cure?"

He sighs. "We didn't know much about the body, about healing. I was hoping for magic. An amulet." He shakes his head. "instead, we dug up a vampire. A sleeping vampire, in his lair. He wasn't well protected by any means."

My eyes widen. "And then?"

"It was my fault. I was the one who woke him. He was angry. Hungry. He..." His voice breaks for a second. "He killed my brother in front of me. Drained his blood and tossed the body aside. Said that was a favor for both of us —me, because I was still alive. My brother, because it spared him a death far more gruesome."

I go silent, waiting for him to continue. "Sated, he toyed with me. Said he could keep me in his lair and save me for a meal, later. Kill me next time he had hunger. But I was clever, in my desperation. I saw that he had nothing, no clothes, no real protection, so I bartered with him. Said I'd bring him what he needed if he spared me. Said I'd get him money, clothes, whatever he wanted. Said he had no better chance for his long-term prosperity without being caught."

"And he said yes?"

"He did. So I made a pact with my brother's killer." His voice is low and full of pain. "I brought him jewelry and valuables from my family home, so he could sell them and accumulate wealth. I gave him clothing from my father's collection. Horses. Everything he wanted. And he fed on me, too, regularly, although not enough to take my life." He shudders.

"Your family didn't notice the missing things?"

"Of course, they did. Servants were blamed. Fired." He shakes his head. "One jailed. Died in jail." His jaw clenches. "And I said nothing to save him."

I don't know what to say. His story is horrifying. Fascinating. I'm distressed and eager to hear more at the same time.

"He was ruthless. He exploited me until it became natural to me, too. And when I was older, stronger, he decided to turn me into one of his own. To serve him."

"So you got turned into a vampire against your will?" My voice trembles.

He's silent for a moment. "It wasn't against my will. I said yes. You have to really want it. Beg for it, even."

"But you're..." I hesitate. "You're not a bad person now. Right?" I raise my brows. The truth is that I know nothing about him apart from the fact that he's good in bed, and we have a bond. But I sense it; he's hard but not evil. Please, I beg silently in my mind. Please.

He looks away. "For many years I did things—I don't know if one can atone for such deeds. All I know is I'm trying."

"'Did you kill people?"

He nods. "Yes." He has a bleak expression. "I did."

"Why?"

"Because my master bade me do it. For his nourishment. For his protection. And sometimes for his pleasure. And I was beholden to him, until I was able to break free from his control." He swallows. "And yet I still continued to kill for a time, for my own anger and my own pleasure. I killed so many humans I lost count. And eventually, I killed my master, too."

"Alain!" I stand up, horrified.

"I'm not going to hurt you." He puts up a hand. "That life is behind me. I've evolved."

"That's not the point!" I step back. "You—you're a murderer!" I put a hand to my mouth. Nausea roils in my gut.

"Not anymore." He steps forward, and I back up again. "In fact, I do the opp-"

I don't let him finish. "How could you—be with me? Without telling me? You let me have sex with you, and you've killed people for pleasure?" I think I'm going to vomit. I have to focus to hold it back. "When were you planning to tell me this?"

I think about Alain as a young man—vampire. Killing people with the same look of glee, perhaps, that I saw on Karl's face as he attacked.

"I…was never going to tell you. I was going to wipe your mind." He says it quietly. "Let you go on your way, after our one night together."

"Wipe my mind?"

"It's a thing we can do, vampires. We can erase certain memories. In most people. You, though…" he shakes his head. "You reacted so badly to it. I knew if I had to do a longer, more serious wipe, it could cause brain damage."

"You were going to brain damage me?" I can't comprehend this.

"No!" He roars it. Then repeats it quietly. "No. When I saw it didn't work, I decided I wasn't going to wipe you. Not again. I swear it. I will never wipe a memory from you again without your permission."

"But you tried it?"

"Two times. Once at the bar, then after we fucked the first night. When you got into the cab. But never again. My promise is my word."

"So that's why I've been having weird headaches and my memory is all messed up?" I put a hand to my head. "I think maybe Karl did it once too. Because after I saw him the first time, I got a horrible headache and forgot him for a while. And the memories are shaky."

He nods. "It's your memories fighting to come back. Your brain doesn't like being wiped."

I'm as horrified as I've ever been. My heart pounds so fast I think it might burst. "Get away from me!" A tear of despair rolls down my cheek. "Alain, I let you control me. I trusted you."

"And you still can." He holds out a hand. "I'm different, now, Bri. I'm not that vampire anymore, the one who killed. That was right after I was turned. My mind broke, and it took time to regain control of myself. I tried to tell you, I've set up a foundation to research and cure illnesses."

"You're a killer! And you were going to erase my memories. And I let you take control of me...and... How the hell do you have the right to even do that? Who the fuck do you think you are?"

I'm so enraged that I want to scream, to break things: his things. I want to put a knife through his art. I want to— I want to get the hell out of here.

I look to the door, the windows. It's night again —"How did I sleep all day? I need to go home. Please!"

"I went into your mind. I encouraged you to sleep, so you could rest and not awaken while I was torpid. I have to sleep while the sun is out. All vampires do. The sun kills us."

I laugh without humor. "I guess we have that in common." Even though I'm angry beyond words, the fact that we do have that in common warms my heart in a strange way because I rarely find anyone who understands my situation.

I cross my arms and shiver although I'm not cold. "You have to let me go home."

"I can't do that." His voice is low and firm. "Hate me if you want, Bri, but you're not leaving here."

"Oh, yes I am." I march to the door and grab the handle. "And if you come after me, so help me God..."

I twist and turn, but the knob won't turn. The door is solid. "Why won't it open?" I yank and pull. "Alain, you can't keep me captive." I run to the sliding doors off the kitchen, but those, too, refuse to move. I pull at a window. "Alain, let me out!"

"No."

"Then I'll break my way out!" I grab the closest thing, a metal bowl, and hurl it at the sliding door. It hits with a low thung and bounces off, barely missing me as it careens past me to hit the floor and shudder to a stop.

"Bri, stop that. You can't get out, so don't try. You'll hurt yourself."

"I'll do whatever the fuck I want! Fuck you!" I scream. I reach for the next closest item, a little brass sculpture that looks expensive. It's heavy. I throw it as hard as I can at the door and wail.

"That's enough." Alain is at my side in a flash, and the statue is back on the door. He wraps me in his arms. "I told you to stop."

"And I told you I won't!" I'm frantic now, out of my mind with fear and desperation.

"You're going to obey me," he snarls and locks eyes with me. "Now. Or else."

"Or else what? You'll kill me?"

"I said I will never harm you, Bri, and I mean it. But I'm not opposed to spanking some sense into you." He gives me a little smile that doesn't reach his eyes. "If that's what you need to settle down."

"You can go fuck yourself. I'm not going to settle down."

"All right, then. Spanking it is."

"Alain, no! I'm not into it right now!" I punch at him as hard as I can.

"Yeah, fight me," he whispers into my ear. "Fight me,

baby. See if you can get away. Wear yourself out punching."

"Let! Me! Go!" I rush him, kicking, trying to scratch.

He grabs my forearms, effortlessly, holding me in place. Locking me with his eyes, his mind as well.

Stop.

The voice echoes in my mind. His voice, and I can hear it even though he's not talking –

I go still, eyes widening.

"You see?" He touches my face. "You still trust me."

I narrow my eyes.

"You wouldn't have given me control unless you trusted me," he murmurs. "Because your heart told you I was a safe bet. Your instincts were right. I may have a dark past, but you can trust the Alain who exists here, today."

"You lied to me." I try to pull away from him, still enraged.

"Everyone lies." His voice is hard. "But not all for the same reason. I lied to protect you not to hurt you."

"But you hurt me anyway."

"And you are going to hurt me, too."

"Oh, because I won't fuck a murderer?" I hiss.

He shakes his head. "You're going to fuck me, Bri." His eyes are sad. "You'll hurt me another way."

"You are one manipulative bastard, and I want to go."

But his eyes are working the usual magic on me, melting my inhibitions, turning my body to languorous honey. Raising the desire. Tamping down the inhibitions.

"You see?" he murmurs. "All it takes is one look from me, and you're going to obey your master."

One tear rolls down my cheek. "You're not my

master." But he is. Somehow, I don't know how, he already is.

He smiles. "Are you sure?" He leans in, so our lips are almost touching. "Go, then." He speaks into my mouth. "If you don't want to fuck me, step back."

He waits. The heat from his body rises to meet mine, our temperatures mingling, encouraging each other to rise higher. I feel the air around us charged with electricity. My skin crackles.

"If you think I'm such an evil monster, you are free to move."

But I won't move. I don't want to anymore.

All I can think about is his mouth, and his hands, and his cock. About how his body feels on mine, and in me. How I crave his control. And how I do trust him still, despite what he just told me—horrible, awful things that should make me turn away from him forever.

God help me, I still want him.

I need him. My sunless, ageless vampire, my worst relationship choice yet--I need him.

"But if you stay, you're going to obey me," he whispers, his lips touching mine, so softly, but the passion explodes at that brief touch. "And you're going to love every second of it. And you're going to trust me."

I look into his eyes for a second. Another. Maybe an hour.

I don't know how much time passes before I say to him: "Yes."

ALAIN

She's so angry, she could breathe fire. And she's not wrong to hate me. I lied to her, and I've done terrible things. Stupid things, too. But she still wants me. And fuck me, but I'm going to make her scream for her pleasure tonight.

She's riled up with her passion, and her endorphins are flooding her body. I can already tell that her pain threshold is going to be much higher than normal. Plus, she still has my venom in her body from when I fed on her last night. Together, that will make her tolerance equal to the rougher games I like to play.

She likes them, too.

When I command her to strip, she does it. I spank her hard, until she cries out, until she's so wet, she's dripping with need.

"Say it," I whisper to her, stroking her clit with my finger.

"No." She moans and pushes her hips upward.

I bite her nipple just hard enough to make her catch her breath. "Then no orgasm for you."

She closes her eyes and smiles. "You always give me an orgasm."

She's right. I'd never actually withhold her pleasure, and she knows it. She's as much my master as I am hers.

That thought is troubling because I'm used to being the one in complete control—not just of myself but also of those around me.

With Bri, I'm off balance.

"Maybe not," I threaten her. "Maybe I'll spank you again and make you wait until morning."

But I can't resist her luscious body.

I grab her and pin her hands above her head. Her breasts heave as she breathes hard and looks up at me through her eyelashes. "Fuck me, Alain." Her lips are so red. She smells of sex and her delicious, fresh blood.

I can't resist.

"Say what I want," I murmur, letting my cock brush against her cleft.

She whimpers and contorts, trying to feel more of my body, but I hold her down.

Finally, she gives in. "Master," she whispers. "Please."

"Ah, there it is." I drive my cock into her, hard.

"Yes, God," she mutters. "Alain."

I pump her hard. "You're mine, Bri. Mine." My voice is fierce.

She grabs me and digs her nails into my skin, cries out. "Always," she says, and then her body clenches in pleasure.

I come, too, as much from her promise as from her body. If only I could have her for always, savor this pleasure with her every night.

It's a hollow dream, but I grasp it with all of my might and cry out my pleasure, our voices mixing together, and we collapse into a tangle of sweaty limbs and satisfaction.

CHAPTER 19

B^{*ri*} "Good evening." Slash eyes me from over his laptop screen. His eyes are inscrutable, but I hear censure in his tone. "Alain's not up yet."

"I see that." I grab the cake from the fridge and supplement with a chunk of brie. I'm a little worried that maybe Slash and Martin heard me and Alain having sex the previous night. I hope they didn't. "We're going to have to get some vegetables in here or else my arteries will congeal."

"Tiberius will bring more food…for you." Slash is still examining me. He mutters, "Since you're so needy."

That hurts. "What's with the attitude? I thought we were friends." I place my gourmet meal onto the shiny counter and fetch a new fork.

"It takes more than a few online exchanges to be a real friend." His voice is cold. "And I'm busy." A beat goes by. "And you were quite loud in there."

Shit, he did hear.

"Well, excuse me for existing. So sorry." I take a large bite of cake. "Do you not eat food?"

I chew mechanically, trying to pretend I don't care that he's being an asshole and that I'm not embarrassed. It's one thing to scene in a club where people want to watch and hear. It's another entirely to be overheard by people who had no such desire.

"We don't need to."

"But you can?"

"If we want, for the taste." He's not looking at me. "That's why Alain has that stuff—it's probably his favorites. If you don't mind, I'm not the Vampire Manual, Bri."

"Whatever." But I'm sad. Slash and I weren't besties, but we were friends, online. He was just as much fun as my online friend Foxfire, who even met me for happy hour and was a pretty kick-ass chick.

And while I know you can't always translate internet buds into IRL bonds, I didn't think Slash was a total douche.

I eat a large portion of cake, then wander to the sliding door in the kitchen and press my face up against the glass to look outside, but even so, the reflection from the indoor lights makes it hard to see.

"I'm still locked up? Like a prisoner?" I try the door, but it won't open for me.

Slash doesn't answer.

My phone is still missing; I don't know where Alain put it. Even though we had fantastic sex last night, I'm more confused than ever.

"Fuck." Slash pushes his laptop lid down. "Fuck, fuck,

fuck. Ugh." He gets up and runs his hands through his hair, messing it up further.

"Stuck on something?" I narrow my eyes at him. Glad he's upset. Still hurt at his words.

He doesn't reply but paces back and forth, hands on top of his head, sort of stretching and walking at once.

"Probably, it's your attitude," I offer. "When someone's in an asshole mood, it's much harder to concentrate."

He gives out a deep sigh. "Bri, look, I'm sorry to take it out on you. It's just—having humans know about us, it's a liability. It doesn't end well."

"For whom?"

"For everyone involved." He shoots me a dark look. "I mean, what do you think is going to happen here? Really?"

"Really? Fuck you. Right now, I'm just still trying to figure out if this is actually happening, or if I'm going insane. Or maybe stuck in a nightmare. I was attacked yesterday by a flying crazed vampire, and today I'm locked up with more vampires, and..." I shake my head. "I haven't worked out the ten-year plan yet, Slash."

"Well, let's play it out." He crosses his arms and stands, looking at me. "You like Alain. I get it. But he's never going to age, and you are. So if he doesn't get tired of you, you have, what, ten years together, tops, before it gets weird? Maybe fifteen? I mean, if you're even still alive by then. Or he is."

A cold feeling settles in my bones. "Why wouldn't he be?"

"Because probably you'll give up his location. What human can resist talking about a vampire? Writing about it? Making money off of it? Or even accidentally telling a friend?" He shakes his head. "It endangers us all."

"I wouldn't do that."

But I think about how hard it would be to keep such a secret from even my best friend. I couldn't even tell K.? How could I exist without talking about things with K.? And could K. resist telling Mani? And Mani tells everything to her mom. Who in turn has a gaggle of old ladies at bridge…and so on.

I tune back in to hear, "And if other vampires know you know? Let's say, I trust you. Alain trusts you. But other vampires don't…you could be in danger. They might want to eliminate a liability. And I'm not just talking Karl. Maybe they'll think you and Alain are both liabilities. Get rid of you both."

I shudder and wrap my arms around myself.

"And maybe you're thinking you could turn into a vampire yourself. But it's not that easy. Or that fun."

"I didn't ask for that." I step backwards.

"You didn't need to. I can see it in your face," he says. "We all can. Every human thinks about it." He pauses. "We know because we were you, once." He turns away.

I bite my lip. "Look, Slash. I promise I'm not going to tell anyone about you all. Not one person." Although my heart cracks a little, thinking about how this will put a wedge in my friendship with K.

"And I have to live with that flimsy little paper promise?" He snaps. "That's my security from you? God, Bri. It's excruciating!" His voice goes up into a shout, then he sinks to the couch and buries his head in his hands.

Is he crying?

"Slash?" I lower my voice and approach, tentative. "Are you...okay?" I hover a hand over his shoulder, pull it back.

"I'm sorry." His voice is low. "But you have no idea how hard this is."

"What do you mean?" I'm taken aback. "You're immortal, and you're complaining about it? Should I bring you a little cheese for that wine?" I point to the fridge. "Many fine choices there."

"This. Being this." He looks at me, and the raw anguish in his face makes my eyes widen. "Being immortal but fragile. One ray of sun will melt me into dust."

He snaps his fingers. "Nobody can be trusted, not even other vampires. Not even the one who made you. Always looking over your shoulder. Rebuilding your persona again and again and again, every decade, every year. Fucking endless starting over and over. It's exhausting."

There are dark circles under his eyes. "And I'm not even....I'm young, for a vampire." He laughs without humor. "You think it's going to be so amazing. And then it's...this."

"But you seem so happy." I sit beside him. "Usually." My anger is gone, replaced with a strange sort of sympathy. Whether he's overdramatic or not, he's clearly suffering. And I suddenly realize that being immortal comes with its own host of problems...maybe worse than human dilemmas.

"It's an act." He looks down at his jeans.

"Does every vampire feel this way? Does Alain?" It makes my heart crack to think Alain might live with such dread, too. Even if I'm so angry I could punch him, I still care deeply.

He shrugs. "From what I understand, we all go through it periodically. Some handle it better than others."

"I'm sorry. But, I mean, my life isn't super easy right now, either, okay? I could be dead in five years. I have a disease, Slash. It's not just that crazy creep who tried to kill me. And I don't know…"

I shake my head. "What the future holds. People leave me, too. My parents died. I can't manage a normal relationship like my friends. I'm always at the doctor. Human life is so short and fragile. I didn't go to med school in college, and now I never can. Things don't usually work out for me. You should be grateful you have so much time to accomplish your goals."

"That's the problem for us." He shakes his head. "It's too much time. When you have infinite tomorrows, there's no motivation. It's hard to keep going, sometimes."

He reaches out without looking and takes my hand. "For what it's worth, I did consider you a friend. That's why I'm so angry at you. Because I had fun talking to you online. Because chatting with you made me forget the difficulties for a while. Because you made me like you the way I used to like my—ah, ahem, *sister*, and you're going to leave. And you're in danger. And I can't fix it."

He sort of coughs on the word *sister,* and suddenly I understand: Slash *likes* me. Has a crush on me, maybe. He's jealous. He didn't like me as a sister at all but something far more. And I'm with Alain.

"Oh, Slash. Look, I…"

"No, I get it. You're with Alain. I can see the bond you

already have." He sighs. "I guess I just. Never mind. I do want to be your friend, all right?"

There's nothing to say about the fact that he wanted me, so I just nod. I squeeze his fingers. "So…you're sorry? *Buddy.*"

He smiles. "I'm sorry. Buddy."

"Okay."

And we sit there, holding hands for a minute, until Alain enters.

At first, I think he'll be angry, or jealous, but he just looks sort of sad.

Then I figure he maybe heard the whole conversation or that Slash told him in some kind of weird telecommunicative way. Because he just gives a sort of small smile.

"Maybe Bri can help you with your issue," is all he says.

Slash nods. "Want to take a look?" He lets go of my hand and stands up. "I'm having a tough time with a piece of code I need to analyze my data."

"Sure, I can take a look." We go over to the table, and he flips up the laptop. "Here."

He shows me what he's working on, and I run through ideas in my mind. It feels so fucking good to focus on something technical. Already I feel our old camaraderie return, the way we joked together online. I have a feeling that Slash will adjust fast to being my bro.

Alain comes over with my laptop and phone. "Here." He gives me a look. "Please use them wisely. Don't tell anyone about us." I know he means, *vampires.*

"Thank you."

He touches my shoulder. "You're welcome."

Now that I know Alain is a vampire, Slash's words keep running through my mind. "If he doesn't get tired of you." "Ten years tops, if he's even alive by then."

And I add my own commentary: *If I'm even alive by then*.

I mean, I was never thinking of ten years with Alain. I wasn't even planning on ten *weeks*. It started with a one-night stand, for God's sake.

Plus, Alain is a murderer and a rogue. Even if he's supposedly "reformed" now, does that matter to me? Should it matter?

I try to push the thoughts of my head. Focus on the programming for now because it will keep me sane.

But even with all my anger at Alain for lying to me, for being something I wish he wasn't, for having the past he does—I still desire him with every fiber of my being. And even if it's a total folly, I wish we could have some kind of future together.

～

Bri

This time Alain doesn't make me sleep when he does. "I need to rest soon," he says. "Are you going to stay awake?" He looks toward the window.

"Do you have black-out blinds?"

He shakes his head. "Yes. They're on a light-sensing timer. They'll descend at the first ray of light."

"Oh." I take a breath. "Wow. Mine are manual. And I have my UV face shield and my long-sleeve UV shirt, so I guess I'll be all right with all of it."

He regards me with a steady look. "I'll have Tiberius bring clothes for you, and anything else from your home that you want. Food." He looks toward the fridge, frowns. "I'm sorry I didn't have a variety. I'm not used to feeding humans. If you make a list, we'll get it."

I smile. "You sure have a refined palate."

He looks a little embarrassed. "We exist on blood, and only eat food for pure pleasure. Those are the things I like."

"I commend you on the cake. The caviar is a little overkill."

He laughs, but his face tells me he feels the tension between us—my anxiety.

"How long am I going to be here?" I look down at my jeans then back up at him.

"As long as it takes. You can work from here, right?"

I nod. "Yes."

"Do you need to see any clients in the near future in person?"

I shake my head. "Nope. I don't need to see anyone." Then a tear rolls down my cheek. "Sorry." I wipe it away.

He sits in a kitchen chair beside me. "What's wrong?"

This makes me laugh. "Really?" I sigh. "Okay, you know what? When I think about my life, it's actually amazing how little time I spend with other people. I work mostly online. I don't go out during the day. Sometimes I hang out with K. and Mani at night."

"And that upsets you?"

"I don't know. It just makes me feel so...disconnected, I guess." I shake my head. "Like I'm not part of life like other people are."

"Well, I'm not human anymore. But from what I've observed, there's no normal."

"Sure, but my disease makes it harder to fit in."

"It also gives you insight into life."

I look at him. "But is it worth it?"

He shrugs. "Sounds like the same question Slash was asking himself."

I breathe out. "Do you feel like he does? Like life is scary?"

He tilts his head. "I don't like to talk about that."

I just look at him.

His eyes burn. He says, "Then I'll tell you this. I've never said these words aloud, before." He pauses. "There's a constant pit of despair tugging me closer, with a powerful gravitational force. I have to work hard every moment to keep myself upright, so I don't fall in." He clears his throat. "Some days it's harder than others. And some vampires fall into it and never get out. Like Karl."

"Does every vampire start out...killing?" I don't even know the questions I want to ask.

"Usually. The blood lust is a powerful urge. As we age and mature, we can temper it down. Control it. Develop our powers. You're born as a wild animal and need to tame yourself."

"Wow."

"Yeah."

He adds: "If you're created by a powerful vampire, they can help you adapt without resorting to violence. Teach you how to control yourself from the beginning. Most haven't done that. Even if you try to help your offspring, you sometimes fail. Like I did, with Karl."

"I see." I bite my lip.

"No, you don't. Not really." His voice is hard. "It's like being suddenly and completely addicted to meth and crack cocaine and alcohol at the same time, at a level that's a thousand times higher than any addict has ever faced. And you have to tame that and hold it back. You have no idea."

He stands up, takes a breath. I can almost see him calming himself back down. "And I'm glad you don't. It's not a good way to live."

"But you said you do good things now. Right? Tell me." I reach out my hand: An apology, maybe. Or at least a bridge.

He sits back down and takes my hand. I feel the tingles of attraction immediately. With Slash, it was a grasp of friendship. With Alain, it's like I'm giving over my entire body to him.

"I started a foundation with expert medical doctors to work on cutting edge research into diseases like ALS and MS. They're working fast to come up with novel techniques to reduce symptoms. Look for a cure. For prevention."

"Wait. Do you mean...Dr. Albright?" My voice goes up. "The one I work for?" I don't wait for an answer. "She's the expert in the news working on MS research. She mentioned an Alain when I was there one night. It was you, wasn't it?"

"Ah, yes." He clears his throat. "Lacey Albright."

"I knew it!" I congratulate myself. "It's not a common name. At the time, I wondered." But I'm confused. "You do finance, right? Are you also a doctor or something?"

He shakes his head. "I'm no doctor, and I can't do

what she does. I created the foundation and the labs specifically to work on research into those areas."

"Why?"

His voice gains an eager note. "I can help accelerate the work and carry it forward. With my support, then humans can work faster than before, and we can come up with cures. It's the thing I live for." Now I see the spark in his eye. "It almost makes all of that other stuff I mentioned —the depression, the loneliness—worth it. Because I have this incredible goal."

"So you do trust some humans? Or is Dr. A. a vampire, too?" A surge of curiosity and jealousy flows through me, even as my heart warms to hear his story. Dr. A. didn't seem like a vampire. But then again, neither did Alain, when I first met him.

"She's fully human, and she's the only doctor who knows the truth about me."

"She's amazing." I bite my lip.

"Yes." He's gesturing now, completely into his topic. "Bri, with her running the medical research facility, and me bringing her state of the art equipment and resources, it's untold what we can accomplish!" His face sobers. "And I can't have anything detract from that goal. Like Karl."

I shudder, thinking of Karl's face. His eyes.

But I don't want to talk about Karl.

"What changed you?" I turn to look into his face. "From a killer to a rescuer."

"I don't know." He has a distant look in his eye. "Time, maybe. Learning more about the world. The older I get and the more in control of myself, the more I see that I have a duty to help humans. That maybe it's been my goal all along. That I am duty bound to use my skills and talents to help the world advance. I can still be part of the human race, in a different way."

"Do other vampires feel the same way?"

"Some, maybe. Others, no. We're all at different places in our journey."

"What Slash said…about you and me. About our future…"

He sighs. "He shouldn't have opened his mouth. Little bastard."

"But it's true, isn't it? We get along right now. But I'm going to get older, hopefully." I laugh a little. "Someday, God willing, I'll be an old lady." I feel tears in my eyes. "I'd be like your Grandmother." The thought is horrifying and ridiculous at once.

"Stop."

"But it's true. We have an expiration date, no matter what happens."

"Mmm."

"Have you ever been tempted to turn someone into a vampire? For a girlfriend or wife? I don't know what you'd call it." My heart speeds up. I don't necessarily want to be a vampire…but something inside my heart hopes he'll say, *yes. You.*

"No." His answer is immediate. "It's too risky. Many humans die in the process. Even if they survive the transition, a large number become enemies because they never get over the shock, the anger, the difficulty of being immortal. They blame the one who turned them. I would never risk it."

He adds, "Besides, it would only be a distraction. I have my work right now. That's all I need." His voice is vehement, as if he believes what he's saying 100%.

The disappointment that wells up in me is crushing, but I fight to hide it. "So that's why you wanted just one night."

"Yeah." His voice is bleak. "And why I wipe women's minds after we're together. There's no point in anything more for either of us."

"That must be so sad." I speak without thinking. "Never having a solid future. Even though you have an infinite one."

He touches my cheek. He looks into my eyes. "Being with you, Bri. It's the most pleasure I've had in—" he pauses. "A long time."

I touch his face too. "Me too."

"And I don't want this to end, yet." His voice is low. "Because I care about you. Being with you gives me joy."

"Me too." My eyes are misty with emotion and my voice quivers. "Me too."

He holds me gently. Neither of us speak.

And although no promises are made and no vows exchanged, I swear it feels as if we're committing to each other. Because the thing I see in his eyes behind the talk of impermanence feels like it's bound to last forever.

CHAPTER 20

*B*ri

A few days have passed. Strange chunks of time. I'm living in a vampire's home, hanging out with other vampires, and the whole time, my life is in danger.

In some ways, I've never been happier. Being with Alain—even with the danger, even with his disturbing past and the fact that he's immortal—completes me in a way I've never known. Every minute we spend together, I feel like we just belong with each other. The sex is off the charts phenomenal. Even after our fight—or maybe especially after our fight.

Even though he flat out said he'd never consider turning another human immortal, I swear he cares about me in a way he can't even elucidate. Like there's something there in his eyes, a deepness that goes beyond our differences.

Unfortunately, the situation with Karl is getting dire. The police have not been able to find the missing women. Knowing what we know—that they're probably being used as a living blood bank, makes it critical that we find them immediately…before it's too late.

And being the only mortal one in the house makes me an outsider. Not to mention a security risk.

Alain is on the phone with Tiberius. "No, out of the question. Absolutely not. She stays here, where she's safest."

I know they're talking about letting me go back to my own apartment and having a vampire guard stand inside my door to prevent any other vampires from trying to get in.

"No, she can't do that. She needs to stay completely under the radar."

It's been a constant topic of discussion lately: How to keep me safe. Away from Karl. It seems to take as much time as the actual hunt for Karl, which makes me feel very guilty.

Every evening, Martin and Slash join Alain for long discussions, after which one or two of them disappear for hours scouting.

Tonight, I hover at the edge of the kitchen, listening. They're sitting at that fancy inlaid table in the dining area, and Slash has his laptop open.

"Okay, so I got the person who turned off the security cams at the Gila Diagnostics. It's a Wallace Grainger. Says he's thirty-two years old, lives on the South side. Got his home address." Slash points to the screen.

Alain leans over to look. "Print it out. And his ID photo."

Slash nods and the printer hums.

Martin grabs the papers. He's become better at technology over the past few days, in my opinion. At least compared to where he started. He even texted me a text message the other day. It was all caps, but still—a real text. It said, "HI BRI." I told him I was really proud. He rolled his eyes but then said, "really?" and gave me a little excited smile. I feel like we're friends, now. Just like I am with Slash, whom I told he should be teaching at a university. I think he liked the idea; he said "huh," and got a sort of small smile on his face. I helped him figure out his code error the other night, and he told me I was one of the smartest humans he knows, which I understand to be a great compliment.

I even sort of consider Slash and Martin like family. It took no time at all to achieve a level of comfort with them that I rarely get with other people.

For example, they're so much better than my aunt and uncle, around whom I feel stiff and awkward. They're judgmental of K...and have nothing to talk about other than the price of gas and the evilness of the opposite political party. I may have blood bonds to them, but the emotional bonds are non-existent.

"Can I see?" I come closer to look. "I don't know him."

I didn't expect to, but you always wonder. It's a picture of a stocky, unsmiling Caucasian man with thinning brown hair. "He looks kind of mean, although that's maybe not fair to say."

"Well, he's certainly no angel." Slash pulls up another screen. "He routinely clocks a full twelve -hour shift, but his car leaves the lot every day at noon. He's scamming the system somehow."

I eye the address. "Hey, that's not far from Mani's house." At Alain's curious look, I add, "You know, my best friend's girlfriend?"

He nods "yes" and looks away. I think he feels guilty because he told me not to talk to K. about any of this, and he also knows she's the only person I can talk to.

"I miss her." My voice is more wistful than intended. She's already suspicious of my extended absence—we usually hang out frequently, and I've had to make excuse after excuse. Every time I talk to her, she asks if I'm okay.

"I hope you remember you can't tell her about any of this." Alain sounds stern.

"My memory isn't that bad. At least, when someone's not tampering with it." It's a joke…sort of. I've forgiven him for trying to wipe me, since he promised never to do it again. But apparently some hurt lingers because my voice is sharper than I meant.

"Excuse me?" Alain's voice is cool.

"Well, if I don't get to see her soon, it's not long before she'll send out her brother or something. The cop?" I give him a look.

"I would encourage you to prevent that." Alain doesn't raise his voice further, but he sounds tense. "This is the best place for you right now."

"I wasn't denying that. And I can't prevent other people from doing what they want."

"You keep mentioning her."

"Well, she's important to me. Family. K. is like the sister I never had."

"You don't want us to have to wipe her and her family,

right? You know that's a risk." He arches a brow. "I wouldn't want to do it, but if I had to…"

I suck in my breath. "Are you implying that I'm going to tell her about you?" I'm irritated. "I thought you trusted me."

Slash makes an uh-oh face, looking from me to Alain. "Um, so back to the topic? It's going to be day soon." He gestures to the windows. "What do you want to do, Alain?"

Alain has the patio door open; he's peering out into the sky. I can smell the fresh desert air and take a deep breath.

"We can go tomorrow night and find him." Alain's brisk as he turns to look at us all. "Make him tell us everything he knows about Karl and the women. It's possible they just paid him off to turn off the alarm. But perhaps he's part of the scheme. Tonight, we need to meet again to review data and plan."

"I could go." I step closer and touch Alain's arm. A breeze from the mountains lilts over and caresses us.

"Go where?" All three of them stop and look at me.

I blink. "To Wallace's house today, when you sleep. During the day, to save time. Just to check it out. Or I could ask K. to get her brother the cop–"

"No!" Alain's voice is so sharp I take a step back, startled. He closes the patio door shut so hard it nearly vibrates —but I notice he forgets to set the special lock, the one he still won't teach me to undo.

He speaks in a normal voice, but the urgency is still there. "I forbid you to leave, Bri. It's too dangerous."

"But all vampires are sleeping during the day. It would be fine for me to just drive by and check it out."

"If Wallace is involved, he could have lookouts with guns. Or you could tip him off that someone is investigating. And the last thing we need is the police right now to scare him away." Alain sends a stern look.

"Well, I was just offering to help. I mean, I feel sort of useless sitting here doing nothing." I gesture around the house. "And stir crazy."

"The best way you can help is to stay safe." Alain's tone is flat. "Let us do this. We know how vampires work."

His voice is firm, but I think I see fear in his eyes underneath the sternness, and concern.

Martin uses a gentler tone. "We just want you to be safe, Bri, like Alain said. We know how much you care about this and want to help find the missing women. Just because Wallace is not a vampire doesn't mean he's not a threat to you."

I don't reply.

Alain comes to me and lowers his voice. "Bri, I'm sorry I raised my voice, but it's my job to protect you. You're vulnerable, and I won't have you harmed. Okay?"

He touches my cheek. His eyes burn with passion and those other emotions, the ones he won't speak aloud.

I nod. "Okay."

But I'm still frustrated by his attitude. I'm not weak. I'm not completely helpless. I hate that he thinks of me as a zero in terms of my ability to help.

"Be safe." He kisses me, a quick but tender touch to my lips.

"You too."

When he disappears to his lair, and Martin and Slash have darted off to their own safe spots, I'm unsettled as I sit alone in the living room that morning with the blackout shades drawn.

Our differences, the ones that I have been trying so hard to forget, loom large in my mind.

Being with Alain has consumed me entirely. Physically, he's magic. Being with him is spellbinding—when it's just us.

But when we talk about vampire wars and death and blood sources, I recognize how utterly different our lives are. How incompatible. And it's becoming clear that as much as he desires my body and enjoys my company, he thinks of me as completely useless when it comes to anything else.

I don't know how long we're going to last together.

But I force myself to think about something else. Because regardless of what I know to be true, I still desire him. So I'm just going to pretend things are fine…as long as I can.

I NAP FOR A FEW HOURS, apparently, because when I get up, it's almost evening. My schedule is erratic; I stay awake with the vampires, but my body still wants to be awake during the day, too. I'm constantly tired and unsure of what day or time it is.

I sit for a few minutes, listening to the utter silence of the house, then pick up the papers that Slash printed out. Look again at the man's face. His address. Slash has written something below it in pen: *"gets drinks every evening at the Rusted Nail Saloon."*

I'm filled with the burning desire to show them that I am useful. I can do critical things, even if I'm human. Plus, I'm sick thinking about the missing women: If there's a chance to help them, I want to be part of it.

I remember that Alain never locked the patio door. Although the blackout blinds have rolled down, I can push them out of the way—and I can leave if I want to. And sure, I agreed not to go to Wallace's house address—but I never said anything about the bar, so technically I'm not breaking a promise.

Having made up my mind, I put on my UV garments and my face mask and grab a jacket and hat, so I can disguise myself at the bar. Luckily Tiberius brought over the entire contents of my closet, in an insanely short amount of time, so I have every garment I could possibly need.

My car is still parked outside, as it has been since the night of Karl's attack. It starts easily, even with its myriad mechanical foibles, and soon I'm on the way, my phone's GPS guiding me.

I'm excited as I drive through Alain's secluded, hilly area to the more densely populated center of Tucson, but my enthusiasm fades as I head into the Grant/Alvernon area, and plummets as I pull up to the Rusty Nail.

It's not a very pretty place. For one, it looks really run down, and not in a rustic faux-old-timey way that means rich millennials are stuffing the tables. It seems like it's ready to be condemned. Also, there are five motorcycles out front, which means I'm probably not going to fit in.

Well, fuck. I might as well check it out.

When I walk in, I expect to stand out instantly, but nobody cares that I arrived.

The place seems remarkably empty for all the bikes out front; there's just a bartender in his 60's watching a soccer game on a grainy TV. One man sits at the bar, far end, slouched into his drink. Dirty clothes. Baggy pants, jacket, hat. Staring at nothing like it's a full-time job.

For once my excess amount of clothing seems appropriate and also a good way to hide. I stuff as much of my hair as I can into the back of my jacket and wipe a wisp of it out of my face. Pull the hoodie up.

The bartender doesn't come up to me, so I wait for a minute. Finally, I ask. "Can I have a beer?"

He turns around, slowly. Examines me. "You want a what?"

"Corona."

Another pause. I almost think he's going to tell me to leave. "Yeah. Sure." He shrugs. Pops a top and puts it down in front of me. "Eight fifty."

Jesus, for one beer? But I pull a ten from my purse and slide it over the battered wood bar top, which is sticky in places and lacks varnish in others. "Thanks."

He grunts.

I grab a stool and slouch down like the man at the end of the bar. If anyone comes in, I'll look like just another worn-out drunk, losing myself in my own existence.

But nobody else comes. It's quiet, except for the shouts from the TV. I'm pretty sure it's got to be a re-run game.

I check my phone. I don't like this place at all. It has a

horrible vibe, and the neighborhood is sketchy at best. I'll give it five more minutes–

And then a man comes in. He glances at me but doesn't seem to see me. He's walking fast and gives off a nervous energy.

My heart pounds with excitement because it's him— the man from the picture! Wallace. The one who turned off the alarms at Gila Diagnostics.

I casually sink lower into myself and put my head onto my arms, nose to nose with my drink. Hopefully he won't care that I don't belong here.

I feel his gaze on my back, but he slides into the seat next to the drunk at the end of the bar. "Roy."

The bartender slides him a shot glass without asking— Patrón. At least the liquor comes from a Patrón bottle. Who knows what's really in there, or whether it's been watered down; a place like this, I assume, wouldn't be past that. At least I saw him open my beer bottle, so I figure that's legit.

"Mac in today?" Wallace asks.

"Nope." The bartender turns away. "Just the crowd in back." He gestures to a closed door at the back of the room.

"He been in yesterday?"

"Nope."

"Well, what the fuck." Wallace makes a disgusted noise.

The bartender turns up the volume on the game. Wallace pulls out his phone and taps. "Mac. Give me a call back. We gotta get the stuff. Fuck, man. Call me when you get this."

Wallace's agitation seems to grow. He taps his foot against the floor, drums his fingers on the bar. He downs his drink, gestures for another. And a third.

Pulls out his phone to call the same person. "Mac, fuck it. Where are you? You know how serious this is. The LD's are his big thing. Dude, call me back."

He tosses the phone down. "Shit, man, he was supposed to meet me here."

The bartender shrugs. "Last time I saw him was a few days ago." He seems utterly unconcerned with Wallace's situation.

But I couldn't be more amped up. LD's? I've heard that word before. Karl said it to me when he tried to take me. "You'll be my best LD yet."

What does it mean?

Wallace calls his friend again. "He's coming tonight, and if we don't have the special blood draw stuff for the LD's he'll be beyond pissed." He sounds almost desperate. "You gotta fucking call me back, man. We don't want to leave him hanging."

He tosses some bills onto the counter. "Call me if he comes in."

The bartender grunts.

Wallace grabs his phone and strides out. He stops for half a second to glance at me, but he keeps going.

I hear a car roar off and let out a deep sigh. I haven't taken a single sip of my beer.

I slide off the stool and head out the door, eager to get back and share my news with Alain and the others.

lain

"You did *what*?"

Bri was gone when I woke up, and I panicked. Then five minutes later, she waltzed up, all wrapped up in a baggy sweatshirt and her tight jeans, and knocked on the fucking door like she was a pizza delivery guy. I could have had a heart attack, if I were capable of it.

Bri shrinks back a little bit. "I went to the bar. And I found him." Her voice is defensive, and she sticks up her chin. Her defiance is adorable. If this weren't so serious, I would have a lot of fun punishing her. "And guess what? He said he needs to get the stuff for the LD's."

"The LD's?" I frown. I'm still cold inside, thinking about what would have happened to her if Wallace decided she was a risk. It makes me ill.

She nods. "He said they need to get stuff ready, or they'll be in trouble. Probably from Karl. You were right. He's definitely more into this than just shutting off a security camera."

I want to kiss her and spank her. Maybe both. "Bri," I say sternly. "You promised me you wouldn't go anywhere."

She flushes. "Well, you were sleeping, and it seemed like a decent plan. And nothing bad happened!" She steps forward and puts her hand on my arm. "Except I got you information."

It's hard to stay mad at her when she's obviously so proud of herself. "Did he say what the LD's were?"

She shakes her head. "It has something to do with blood. I'm sure of it." Her voice is excited again. "He called his friend and left a message about needing to get blood draw stuff for the LD's. Special blood draw stuff. It's definitely for the missing women."

It's excellent information, but I can't process it. I'm still hung up on what could've happened to her. "You could have been hurt." It feels like something is ripping inside my chest. I haven't felt this way about a human in a hundred years. I don't understand my own emotions.

"I was careful. It was fine."

"It wasn't fine. You're lucky nothing happened." I pin her with a hard stare. "You're mortal. Completely fragile, and you think you're a warrior." These humans! They have no idea.

Although...my little mortal's not entirely weak. She deals with her XP and her complicated life. It's just... physically, she's like spun glass. She needs to be more careful. Fuck!

I already spend so much time worrying about Dr. A's health that it's driving me insane, and I don't even lo— care about her the way I do about Bri. It's going to tear me up inside to deal with this from Bri every day. Keeping her safe could easily become an obsession. And I certainly can't do it if she plans on disobeying me and sneaking out whenever she pleases.

"Instead of lecturing me, why don't you call your friends and get them started on the new information?" She looks away from me, acting like she doesn't care. But I can hear her heart beat faster. Maybe she wants me to punish her.

"I've already sent messages to Martin and Slash. You're lucky they're on the way, or else I'd spank you so good and hard you'd be sore all day tomorrow." Bringing sex into it makes it easier to handle.

Her pupils dilate. She definitely likes the idea. Too bad we don't have the time.

"I heard you've been quite a busy young lady." Martin gives Bri a side-eye glance as he walks in.

She doesn't smile. "Wallace implied that he and his friend were supposed to meet Karl tonight. So if you follow Wallace, you can find Karl."

"Did he say Karl's name specifically?" I take her face in both hands and look into her eyes. "Think."

She blinks. "No. But I'm sure he must have meant Karl. He talked about LD's, like Karl did. Said they were supposed to get blood draw stuff tonight, or they'd be dead. What else could it be?"

"I have to say it, Bri did a good job." Slash smiles.

I let go of Bri and frown at him. "Do not encourage her. She endangered herself," I emphasize. "To get some information that isn't critical. We were going to follow him anyway eventually."

"But not tonight," Bri argues. "You weren't going to do it tonight. Now you know it's critical to do it right this moment. And the sooner you find Karl, the sooner you can find the women."

Martin claps his hands together. "Let's make a plan."

But I can't focus. I keep thinking about Bri. How awful this situation is, how much danger she's in, and how it's all my fault, putting her into a situation like this where she's over her head. Where she could have been hurt.

As much as I care about Bri, it's becoming clear that this relationship, whatever it is with her, may be impossible. If she gets hurt or worse because of me, I'll never forgive myself. And she deserves better from life. I just need to figure out what to do about this.

Alain

WE'RE outside Wallace's house, hidden as only vampires can do, Martin and I, nestled into an overgrown mesquite tree patch outside the adobe side wall, facing a window that shows a glimpse of Wallace's messy living room. Slash is back with Bri. Every time I think about what she did, I get so upset that I can't concentrate.

"Alain. Alain?" Martin pokes me. "You need to focus."

"Sorry." I shake my head.

"You were a little rough on her." He sounds reproachful. I know he's come to think of her as a friend, as does

Slash. Maybe even part of our ragged, odd vampire family. But she's not. She's mortal.

"She needs to understand." I clench one fist. "She has no idea how much danger she's in. She thinks she's helping, I get it. But she doesn't have the skills."

"She seems pretty resourceful for a human." His voice is neutral. "She seems to have a way of getting information, right?"

"Yes, she does. It's impressive. But you know what could have happened." I bristle.

"Easy, friend." He laughs. "I'm on your side. We're all on the same side." He pauses. "Although I agree she took risks. She should have cleared it with you first. But maybe if you took the time to—"

A car engine roars and headlights flash. "Shh. It's Wallace."

The man is high as a fucking satellite; we can see it as soon as he exits the vehicle. Smell it rolling off his body, along with the acrid odor of sweat and fear. It's done nothing to calm his nerves. His hand shakes on his phone, and it takes him three tries to get his key in the door.

"Let's go. Do your thing."

We blur up to the front door, and I find him, ease into his mind. It's a rattly cluster fuck of a mess, and his thoughts and memories whir like butterflies. He's so frantic that I can't latch onto anything in particular. Plus, I'm still rattled at Bri, which makes it hard to focus.

I take a breath. *Let us in. You want to let us in.*

I sense his surprise, then his suspicion. "Need my fucking gun," he mutters. "Fucking prick."

"He's not amenable." I shoot a glance at Martin.

"Can you see any of his memories?"

I shut my eyes. "You try, too."

"I can't do it like you can. Not unless it's someone with whom I'm particularly close. Physically or emotionally."

I take a deep breath. Get flashes of memories.

Karl's red face. A meeting with Karl. Karl hissing instructions. Boxes of glass vials and gauze and IV bags. Cash. Trading things with Karl. Fear. He needs to provide larger blood collection vials. Specialty size. Not standard. Didn't get them from Mac yet.

No sightings of the women. He knows about them, though.

"He's deep into it." I peer harder. "He knows about the women."

LDs. It creeps him out. He wishes he'd never gotten into this, but it's too late. He wishes he'd never met Karl. Who steals blood? And auctions off the last drops of it like it's a special prize?

"I got it. Martin. LD stands for Last Drop. He's going to kill the women and auction off their last drops of blood. Bri was right that it had to do with their blood." I say it proudly. "She's smart."

Then I shake my head. Yeah, so she's feisty and intelligent. She's also going to get herself killed if I keep her in the inner circle like I have.

Then I'm horrified. The very idea of draining women and selling their last drops of blood is an unholy mess— it's already hard enough for the vampire community in general to keep such desires tamped down well enough to prevent massive human bloodshed. If this scheme happens, it will only open the door to more and worse atrocities. And it certainly won't help us stay under the radar as an extra-human species. I wish more than ever that I'd killed Karl ages ago. I'm going to right that the very second I can.

"God." Martin seems stunned. "Does he already have buyers lined up?"

I try to get more memories from Wallace.

Suddenly, instead of Wallace's mind, I find myself in Bri's. I see a memory of the two of us fucking. It's so vivid that my cock gets hard. What the hell? I see her care for me and her concern.

I force myself back. How did I connect with her from so far away and so powerfully? I frown. Now that I'm thinking of her, the worry about her wells up again.

I shake my head. "Yes. But Wallace doesn't know who they are. Just that they exist."

Wallace is on the phone again. "Mac, Jesus Christ, man." He wipes sweat from his brow. "Where are you?"

"Sounds to me like his friend decided to disappear," whispers Martin. "Can't say as I blame him."

Then the phone rings. Wallace grabs it and checks the number. His face gets white.

"H-hello?"

The other speaker—I can hear the voice—is Karl.

"Meet me at the spot at ten. Bring the supplies." He hisses the words.

"Uh, I thought you weren't doing the LD auction until later this week?" Wallace's attempt to sound casual is pathetic. "Maybe tomorrow instead?"

"Do I need to help you remember who you work for?"

Karl's voice is cold. "Do I need to find another supplier, one who actually has the skills to provide what I ask?"

"Wait! I have information for you." Wallace twitches and sweats. "Give me another chance."

"What is it?"

"A girl. You said to watch for a girl. There was one in the bar."

"What kind of girl?"

"I don't know. She had a shit ton of clothes on. I seen red hair though, like you said."

Bri! They're talking about Bri. Fuck.

"What did she do?" Karl's voice is eager. I try to latch onto the sound and follow it. For a second, I think I have a sense of trees, but then—like before—Bri's memories pop into my mind. One of us arguing.

I shake my head and curse, and the signal is gone. "Damn it. I can't trace him. It's too difficult, just from a voice on the phone."

I focus again on the conversation happening inside the dingy, ramshackle house.

"I don't know! I left first, and she didn't follow. So we're safe."

"Of course, we are." Karl's voice is smooth and unctuous now.

"And I just need one more day to get you the stuff. Just one day." Wallace sounds desperately hopeful.

"Oh, don't you worry about time. It's all fine." Karl's voice is soothing.

"Okay, man. I swear, one more day, I'll get it. I promise you." Wallace babbles and swipes at the sweat on his brow.

"Just come to the spot, even without the equipment. I have a new assignment for you."

"Okay, man, I'll be right there." Wallace sounds relieved. Almost happy. "And don't worry about the girl."

"Oh, I'm far from worried." Karl chuckles. "I promise you that. She'll be taken care of."

I shake my head. I'm going to have to really try to make Bri understand. Lock her down if needed. I absolutely cannot let Karl get to her --

Something is pushing at my mind.

It's Bri again. But not like she's trying to communicate with me—more like she's panicky. Worried.

I try to focus on the emotion, but it fades. I turn back to Wallace. I'm the only one who can do this right now, but I need to be sure Bri is okay.

"Listen." I grab Martin's arm. "I keep getting this… feeling. Can you go back to my house and check on Slash and Bri?"

"Why not just call them?" Martin touches his phone.

I try, but there's no answer.

"Fuck, I need eyes on them. Maybe I should go. You stay here." I look around.

"No, you're the better one to stay. Keep trying to get into his thoughts. I can't do it like you do." Martin peers out of the mess of mesquites. "I'll go check on her."

"Thank you. Hurry."

Alone, I quiet my mind and try to get into Wallace's memories again. Like before, they're agitated and blurry, like a TV with too much static.

Suddenly Martin calls my phone. "Alain, Bri is gone." His voice is rushed. "Slash said he opened the patio door to let her look at nature, and she went out for a few minutes. When he went out to check on her, she was gone."

"Fuck!" I almost drop my phone. "Can't he find her? Follow her?"

"He said she's not in the area. He checked."

In the house, Wallace is pacing, and then he suddenly decides to leave. Grabs his car keys and heads out the front door. It's my chance to follow him. Have him lead me to Karl, so I can surprise my enemy and overpower him, make him tell me everything I need to know. Surprise him, then kill him.

But I hesitate. "I'm coming back. I need to help find her."

"What about Wallace?"

"Fuck Wallace." I'm already heading back to my house, as fast as I can. "We'll check on him later." It's awful because following Wallace is our best chance to find Karl. But I can't leave Bri alone out there, somewhere. I need to help her.

I get there in no time, but it's still taking too long. "Where did she go?"

"I don't know!" Slash's face is pale, his eyes wide. "I'm so sorry, I had no idea she'd–"

I rush up to her things, her laptop. Papers. "What's this? It's an address."

"I don't know." Slash looks at it. "She must have jotted that down before she left."

"Let's go. And you better hope we're not too late."

CHAPTER 22

Bri

I sit next to the sliding glass door with the lights off, trying to look for an owl. Alain told me they frequent the area, but I can't see one from here. "Slash?" I turn to him.

For a second, he doesn't respond, which means that he must be so crazy into his programming right now that he's almost turned off some of his vampire perceptiveness. He absolutely also hates the idea of being tasked as a babysitter, and sometimes—I have to be honest—he seems less focused on safety than the more mature vampires. Like, way less. Almost like he's not even paying attention.

"Slash?" I come up and poke his shoulder.

"Yeah?" He's busy with his computer, so intent on the screen that he seems part person, part machine.

"Okay if I go out to check on the wildlife?" I roll my eyes. "I won't go far."

He looks at me hard, as if trying to see if I'm lying. "Okay, but just stay on the patio and leave the door open.

Otherwise Alain will kill me." He looks at me again, as if checking my face, my mind. He can't seem to get in like Alain, but I know he can sense deception.

"I just want to see the owls." I shrug.

"Fine." He does something fast with his hands and the lock clicks.

"Thanks."

But Slash is already buried in his work. He doesn't seem to hear.

I slide open the door and breathe in the air. For a few minutes, it's peaceful, even if I don't see any wildlife at all.

Suddenly my phone buzzes with a text from K. I smile, and then breathe hard, horrified.

Because it reads: *"Mani in car accident, in hospital. Please come, I need you."*

"Oh my God!" I gasp. I turn to the house and look toward Slash, a hand on my mouth—then, unsure if I should tell him, I immediately call K.

Her voice is garbled and sounds strange. It's a bad connection or something. "Oh my God, Bri, a drunk driver hit her at an intersection. Oh my God. Oh my God." She's hyperventilating.

"Is she okay? What's happening?" I try to keep my voice calm, but I'm ready to panic, too.

"I think she's okay. She talked to me on the phone, but her arm is broken. They're taking her to…" the phone goes staticky all of a sudden, and her voice glitches in and out. "But...don't know…can you…my phone battery dying..."

"K.?" My voice goes up. "K? I can't hear you?"

Nothing.

I hang up and try again, but it rings and rings and doesn't even go to voicemail. Fuck!

My heart is pounding. I open my mouth to call to Slash. *Help me. Help me get to K.*

But what if he won't?

Alain was clear that I'm not to leave the house under any circumstances. Maybe this wouldn't qualify as something important enough to leave. And I do understand the danger that lurks. But it seems like Karl is busy with his blood auction activities, and this is K.!

I try calling again, and suddenly I get another text from her.

"Sorry my phone died, calling from a nurses phone. Need you to stop at Annies house. I left so fast I forgot my purse and get my bag because it has my and Mani insurance info in it please bring to Banner hospital." And she includes an address.

K. mentions Annie, her senior citizen "adoptee," often. Annie is an octogenarian who apparently makes really good scones even though she's half blind. It's part of K.'s volunteer work to help lonely seniors get companionship.

I make up my mind. I have to go to K. I think I'll be safe enough if I go quietly.

I look back toward Slash, who's not even in view anymore. I know he sometimes likes to pace Alain's front room, shuffling his feet on the carpet while he thinks. I send him a silent apology as I reenter the house, grab my purse, and go back out the patio.

It's the work of seconds to make it around front. I look around carefully, even stop and listen, but everything is quiet. Feels safe. I don't have that icky feeling I got before

Karl attacked, and I have confidence that I'm alone out here.

I just need to get out fast before Slash starts paying full attention and realizes I'm gone.

I keep looking around as I get into my car and drive, but there's nothing unusual as I make my way from the hills desert area closer to Tucson. It seems to take forever, and I'm anxious the whole way.

"Finally!" I pull up to the house whose address I plugged into my GPS.

I get out of the car and run up to the door, knocking, then ringing the bell. "Annie?" I say it loudly because I know she's partially deaf. The neighborhood is dilapidated, like K. has often described. She sometimes brings Annie groceries to help her get by—

"Annie!" I knock louder, so hard my knuckles hurt. "It's K.'s friend, Bri!" Hello!?"

But it doesn't look right. It's completely dark, no lights on at all. And as I blink and look around me, I recognize that this house seems not just quiet but abandoned.

There's a messy pile of mail on a broken chair by the front door, as well as dust and some leaves. The top envelope is thick and looks important. It's got a real estate label on it. But that doesn't help me now.

"Annie?" I nearly shout it, even as a horrible recognition starts to dawn: I'm at the wrong place.

A dog barks somewhere in the distance. I can hear the muffled roar of traffic although this street is empty as a tomb. "Hello?"

My voice falters. Shit, the GPS probably messed up, like it does once in a while–

And suddenly I smell the scent of garbage and feel the horrible prickle on the back of my neck. I know I'm not alone.

"You're right on time."

I whirl around and my eyes go wide with shock because standing right behind me—so close I can see every detail of his terrible eyes—is Karl.

"I see you got my text." He giggles.

I step back and put up my hands. My voice is high and scratchy. "Where's Annie?"

But I already know what's happening. He set me up. Annie isn't here.

Somehow, he tricked me—shit! I should have trusted that tiny feeling I had! I don't even know how he did it...all I need to do now is get out of here.

He giggles again. "Did you like how I disguised my voice when I called you? It's a new skill I've been practicing."

He clears his throat and smiles. When he speaks, my blood runs cold because it's K.'s voice—almost. "Oh, Bri, I need you! come help me!" He giggles so hard he almost doubles over. "Your Alain," he hisses the word, his eyes narrowing, "Isn't the only one with friends who can do research. I found out all kinds of things about you and your...friends. And I have a buddy who's good at phones."

He mimics K. to say the next thing: "And it was so easy to get you here."

Now that I hear him in person, not over the phone, I note the tiny hint of menace in the tone. It's not quite K., even though it's K. On the phone, I just assumed she sounded a little weird because of the connection and her stress.

"Where's K. and Mani? if you hurt them… " I try to make my voice menacing.

"I'm sure they're fine." He waves a hand. "Although who can tell, with you mortals? Always doing foolish things." He doesn't come towards me. It's like he knows I can't get away, so he's letting me run. A cat with a mouse.

"Help!" I scream. "Help!"

But there's no one around.

I glance at my car. Is there time to run to it?

"No, there is not." He has a faux apologetic tone. "I wasn't sure if you'd come alone or with Alain. Either would have worked for me. This way doesn't work for you much, though."

And then his hand is on me, cold and claw-like. "Your time has run out, little sweetblood." He turns his head. "Bring it."

A man steps forward from the gloom of the overgrown mesquite trees—it's Wallace.

I scream and twist. "Let me go!"

"She's a handful." Wallace's eyes are wide and red-rimmed, and his movements jerky. He has rope. Tape. Jesus, they're going to take me somewhere–

I push and pull, but Karl holds me effortlessly.

"Alain!" I scream. "Help!"

"It's just you and me, lovely. Well, you and my friend here, for the moment. I'll come later." Karl shoves me hard toward Wallace, then stands back, like he's going to enjoy a Broadway show. Even crosses his arms and laughs. "Tie her up and take her to the house. She will be my number four."

Wallace smells like onions and dirt, and he's strong. But he's human, and I might have a chance. I grapple with him, knee him in the groin. Hard.

He screams but doesn't let go of me although his grip weakens and slides on my arms.

Karl laughs like a banshee. "Oh, ho ho ho! Oh, your face! Get her!" He sounds positively gleeful.

I kick Wallace's shin. Try to extricate one arm, so I can go for his eyes. But he's too strong. And I don't know the right moves.

"Oh, this is priceless." Karl's face flashes up, full of delight. "What a show."

Wallace grunts and grabs my neck in a headlock.

"Ow!" The pain is excruciating.

"Careful, we need her whole," cautions Karl. "Not too much damage." His tone is a sudden hiss, a threat, full of evil. "Yet."

"A little help?" pants Wallace. "She's fucking fighting me. And you're just standing there!"

"Prove your worth," says Karl. "Show me how it's done." He giggles again.

That fucking giggle.

I find sudden strength. I'm not going to let this man hurt me. I'm just not. As Wallace gasps and loses my left arm, I stuck it into my jacket pocket and grab the pepper spray from Owen. As Wallace tugs me harder, I raise my arm and press hard on the nozzle, right at his eyes. Pray that it works.

He screams and lets me go abruptly, falling to a hard crouch, grabbing his eyes. Rolls on the ground.

I'm screaming too, and I'm backing up. I need to run.

"Wallace, you pathetic idiot," hisses Karl. "Do I have to do everything?"

"Fuck, she got my eyes! My eyeeeees!" Wallace is sobbing and heaving. "Help me, help me, I'm dying!"

"You're right about that." With a blur of motion, Karl moves.

And now Wallace is silent, like someone turned off a switch. His body twitches, but it means little, since his head—now separated—lies three feet away in a pool of blood.

"Time to go." Karl looks at me. "Don't fight, or you'll end up like him."

I raise the bottle of spray, a feeble weapon, but all I have. Press the button.

He just laughs.

And then there's a flutter and a whir, and the area is full of energy and movement. It looks like my delay with Wallace bought me enough time because Alain is here. I've never been more grateful to see him in my entire life.

"Alain!" Even I can hear the note of desperation in my voice.

"Step back from her." Alain snarls it. Martin and Slash are with him, one on each side, and all three of them glare at Karl. "You know you can't get away from us. We will overpower you."

But Karl has me tightly in his grasp. "A fair trade. Let me go, and I let her go. If you say no, I kill her in front of you."

Everything stops.

It's like a photograph. Me with Karl's arms wrapped around me in a death embrace. The other vampires, ten feet away, staring. Frozen motion.

Alain speaks. "Let. Her. Go."

"You didn't agree to my terms, though." Karl squeezes my neck.

I cry out.

"If you hurt her…" Alain steps forward.

Karl grabs my arm. "Do you think she needs this one?" He bites down into my wrist. Hard. Tears with his teeth. Twists.

It's so painful that I swoon. "Aaaah…."

I can feel blood run out.

"Ah, I see why you like her so much. And I knew I had chosen well." Karl bends down and licks my blood, his tongue thick and sloppy on my arm. It's obscene, and yet I can't move. He stands upright once again, licking his lips. Reluctant to stop. "But look at all that pretty blood lying wasted on the ground. Like she'll be in just a few minutes, if you let her bleed out."

"Alain." My voice is a gasp. "Please."

"What a choice." Karl giggles. "You can attack me, or you can save your little human pet."

Alain stands still, staring at me. At Karl. Like he doesn't know what to do. Then he says, "Go."

Karl pushes me away hard; I stumble and fall, too close to Wallace's corpse. But I'm so weak, I can't get up.

Karl disappears. As he does, several other vampires rush up, faces I don't recognize.

"Lucius!" Slash gestures. "Tiberius. Karl just ran!"

Alain looks at me, his face tortured. "Bri." And he grabs me into his arms. He rips his shirt and binds my wrist. Touches my forehead, my arms. "You're not dying. You'll be fine. You didn't lose that much blood. It's okay."

My arm burns where Karl bit it, like it's acid. Poison. My head aches. "I…I'm sorry…."

"You're okay. Bri, you're okay." Alain looks into my eyes. "Look at me, Bri. It's going to be all right." He touches my face, feels my pulse in my neck, runs his hands over my body. "You're okay." The relief I hear in his voice slays me. The tenderness of his touch makes me feel alive again.

Slowly I regain the ability to breathe. But I still can't speak. The horror of Karl's mouth lingers in my mind, freezing my responses.

"He got away." Martin's voice is flat. "Disappeared."

Lucius steps forward. "He's faster than he used to be. And more powerful." His voice is displeased. "Alain, you said you were going to take care of him."

"I will." Alain's voice holds a note of ferocity that surprises me.

Lucius stares at Alain. "What is she doing here?" He gestures at me. "Why did you involve her in this? Humans are no match for vampires. It's folly."

"She won't interfere again; I'll see to that. I'll get him." Alain matches stares with Lucius. "You have my word."

"Stop, it's my fault," I gasp for breath and find my voice. Everyone turns to look at me. I feel like I'm on display. On trial.

"I'm sorry," I suck in air. Alain's body protects me, but

I am far from comfortable. "I got a text from my best friend. She needed me. It was a trick." I'm dizzy. "I didn't know."

"Of course, you didn't." Alain's voice is low and deceptively calm. "You don't know anything about this world." His arms are still around me, but I feel him slowly seep away. Grow distant.

"I—"

"And you shouldn't know." His shoulders are stiff. "This world isn't for you, Bri. This is all my fault. We're liabilities to each other—and that's no way to live. I've involved you in a life that's far too dangerous for a human, and for that, I'm profoundly sorry. I'm going to take you home...and then we'll have to say goodbye."

"What? But..." my voice trembles. I look up at him. "We care about each other. The things we said? Alain?" I don't even care that the other vampires are listening to everything. Right now, the only person in the world that matters is Alain. "No. We have a special bond. We have passion. You know we do."

"No, we don't." His voice is not unkind, but it's unyielding. "There's no special bond or passion. I'm sorry you felt that, and it was my fault for allowing it. I should have known you'd be incapable of resisting a vampire. But I simply can't see you again, Bri. You're going to go home and forget all about us. You'll be safe, now. No more liabilities."

Even as he speaks, I swear there's something more in his eyes, regret, maybe? Love, desperation?

But then the emotion fades, and he looks at me dispassionately, like I'm a statue.

I pull away from him, so I'm standing alone, looking at him and the rest of them.

I lash out. "Well, if I'm a liability, then you're worse. You're poison. Talk about eternal life? More like eternal hell. Trapped forever without love or kindness or friendship. I'll have more passion in my stupid, short human life than you'll have in all of your eternal one."

Alain's eyes flash, and I know I hurt him.

Good. I want to right now. I want him to remember this forever.

I continue. "I'm better alone, too. Better without people who try to run my life and make my decisions for me. Who hurt me. I should have known better. Well, live and learn. So fuck you. Enjoy the rest of your lonely life, asshole."

He opens his mouth, like he's about to say something—

Suddenly, Karl's back. "Oops," he announces. "Forgot something. I forgot to kill your little human." He giggles. "I decided promises don't mean much anymore, Alain." He's gleeful, frantic. Like a blender stuck on high. Practically vibrating with energy. So thrilled with himself, he doesn't see anything but me and Alain.

"I'm stronger than you, now. Your anger and desperation feeds me, Master." He laughs. "*Former* master. I am no longer beholden to you. I'm going to take everything you love and destroy it. And then I will have replaced you."

He grabs me and bends toward my neck. "She's just too delicious to pass up." Then, at that exact moment, he seems to see Lucius and the rest. He goes still.

His grip falters. Like he's lost confidence. Like he's surprised at this. Can't vampires sense each other? Karl must be so erratic and insane that he's not even taking basic precautions. Perhaps, in his exultation and temporary victory, he miscalculated his own future. And I sincerely hope that's so because, otherwise, he's going to kill me.

Lucius starts forward. "Attack–"

But Alain puts up a hand. "This is between me and Karl," he snaps. "We will decide it together. Right here, right now. This ends tonight." He snarls at Karl, who howls a shriek of anger and rage.

Lucius steps back. Nods to the other vampires. They form a loose circle around the three of us, but don't approach. I assume they'll step in if they need to.

Karl's fetid breath is still hot on my cheek, but his grip falters. Like he's lost focus.

I push Karl tentatively: His arms go slack, so I slither out of his grip. "Alain!"

Alain takes me and blurs me over to Martin. "Guard her with your life," he orders. He looks into my eyes. "Forgive me." He squeezes my hand softly, and then he turns away from me.

Martin grabs me and puts me between himself and Slash. I'm trembling with terror and adrenaline, barely able to stand, but I need to see. I push my head between Martin's arm, so I can peek, hanging onto him and Slash as if my life depends on it. They both support me, and not one of the other vampires suggests that I be taken away. This moment is too critical to speak or interrupt.

Alain and Karl fly at each other but stop a foot apart, as if pushed apart by opposing magnetic fields. It's not a peaceful separation--it's ugly, with power ripping and tearing and swirling around them.

They stare at each other, as if they're locked together; one being, although two parts. I can see the energy surging between their gazes. The bond between them intensifies until it's like metal bands, binding them to each other with tentacles of steel. It's mesmerizing and sick.

Then they fly at each other again, howling and slashing. It's fast and vicious and deadly. One of them is going to win, and the other will perish.

Suddenly they stop short, as Alain puts up his hand, and I swear I can almost see a burst of energy circling around, forcing Karl back.

Karl makes a little noise. Shudders once, as if cold. Then again.

Alain keeps staring, his hand up. His body trembles, as if doing this—this stare—is taking up all his energy.

And even though Alain wants nothing to do with me anymore, I'm desperate to help.

I close my eyes and try to send him every possible piece of positive energy I have to help him beat Karl. And it's not just because Karl wants to kill me. It's because I lo —it's because I care about making the world a better place, too. I want him to succeed with his medical research, even if I won't be part of his life.

You can do this. I believe in you. You're stronger than he is. You run on love, not hate. Your love for people is what drives you. He can't beat you.

Alain's eyes are glazed, his muscles so tight they might pop. I think he might have an aneurysm, if vampires can do that.

Please. You can do this. I know you can.

I'm starting to get weak from the effort to send these thoughts. With a burst of mental energy, I send all the power I have to join with him until I'm exhausted. I sink down, and Martin grabs me, props me up.

Slowly, Alain stands stronger. Taller. He makes a hissing roar, a sound of growing power, and I sense that he's beating Karl.

Alain roars. And then, with a whirl of pure energy, so bright and hot that I can see streams of red and yellow pulsing in the air like fireworks, he flies at Karl. In a move so deft it seems magic, he pulls something from his inner coat pocket. It's long, wooden stake, polished but with a wicked tip, that flashes in the light of his energy streaks. Moving like lightning, Alain jams the stake right through Karl's heart.

"I made you." Alain's voice is at once thunder and whisper. "And now I'm making up for that mistake." He twists the stake. "Requiēscās in pace."

The words I recognize from high-school Latin: "May you rest in peace." I can only assume Alain is speaking sarcastically or out of some ancient habit ingrained in his psyche because nobody here—I'm sure of it—wishes Karl peace.

The noises coming from Karl are horrific. He twists like a serpent. Writhes. His body flashes green and black, like scales. Then goes still. His eyes are blank, empty. A second later, he's dead.

I scream and scream.

"It's done." Alain's voice holds a note of finality. "I

said I would do it, and it's done. Karl is dead. I corrected my mistake."

"Good." Lucius' voice is somber but pleased. "Take her away." He gestures at me. "And clean this up." His gaze, as it flickers over me, seems dispassionate. But I sense, perhaps, a tiny bit of empathy behind his gaze.

Alain gives me a long searching look, as if he felt my help and is trying to understand. But he shakes his head.

"It will be like it never happened." Alain looks sad, and in that second, I know he's done with me forever.

The next thing I know, I'm back at my own home.

Alain stands over me, his face showing regret, but his voice full of resolve. "I won't wipe you because I know that will break your mind. But if you share details about us, other vampires will probably come for you." He hesitates. "I'll do what I can to keep you safe, but you need to keep the secret. I'll tell Dr. A. to look at your wound. Don't contact me or come to the club. We can't see each other again. It's better this way." He touches me softly with one finger, just a brush down my arm. "Your life will be better now."

He stares at me for a long second. I feel like he's about to say something else, but he just shakes his head. Gives me one soft kiss on the forehead. "Goodbye."

And he's gone.

CHAPTER 23

Bri

I'm home. And I'm alone.

My heart breaks just thinking about him cutting me out of his life.

And my angry words.

It's been two days, and it feels like it just happened.

My wrist throbs under the gauze bandage, and I swallow hard. It's getting better, but it still worries me. Dr. A. has me on a cocktail of three antibiotics and two antivirals, just in case. But she admitted she's never seen a wound like this one and doesn't know the long-term outlook.

She doesn't talk to me about Alain, and I don't ask. Knowing she still interacts with him—even though he doesn't want to see me—is excruciating. But I suppose I need to get used to it.

I had a strange dream last night. I awoke to see Alain at my window, and I let him in. He held me and bit my wound, then even let me drink his own blood, or something—I can't remember—and the pain faded. But when I tried to talk to him, he just shook his head sadly and disappeared.

I don't want to look at the wound, see that strange geode-like pattern of crystalized blood and venom, so I flip open my laptop and check the news over and over, obsessively.

There's nothing about the fight at all. Apparently, the vampires were able to wipe the minds of all potential bystanders effectively, if there were any. This is a relief, yet I can't forget that although Karl is gone, the news also tells me that the missing women are still out there somewhere.

And maybe they're going to die in captivity.

And it's all my fault. If I hadn't panicked and believed the fake phone call, if I'd just had the patience to wait like Alain asked me to—ordered me to—things could have turned out differently. Maybe they'd have been able to trick Karl, find the women's location. Instead, Karl's dead, and so are any leads he might have held.

I breathe out and stare at my blackout blinds, imagining the world going by outside. Alain, of course, will be asleep. So will Slash and Martin and their powerful ally, Lucius. Vampires I've been told never to contact again.

I miss Alain. I meant what I said, that I was better off without him. He's complicated and weird, and there's no way a human and an immortal could ever forge a life together.

But I wish it could be otherwise.

And if it can't be otherwise, I wish we could have ended things on a positive note. I'm disappointed and heartbroken that he didn't think we were worth it. Didn't want to keep me.

Even if I can't tell her the truth, I need K. She answers right away when I call. "Things suck," I say, and break down into tears.

She's immediately concerned. "Bri, what's wrong? Did the doctor call?"

For a second, I think she means Dr. A., then I remember that she knows nothing about the events that transpired or about my weird second life. She's just talking about my regular old problems. My XP.

In fact, Dr. Su did call this very morning. "Yes, and the results are good. It's clean. I don't have any markers for cancer." I take a deep breath. "They got it all...for now." I don't fool myself that this will last forever. Everyone knows that this disease gets progressively worse in 100% of the patients and that I'll be lucky if my next test comes back clean. Still, it's a reprieve.

I'm so depressed about Alain that I barely feel any relief or joy at this news. I should be exultant at this chance for a new life. Instead, I feel like I got a death sentence.

"Then what's wrong?"

"I'm...Alain broke up with me." That is but a tiny five percent of what's really hurting me, but it's the only thing I can tell her.

"Oh, I'm so sorry. What a dick. I'll come over tonight with ice-cream. Okay? I'll bring ice-cream and those pretzels you like and some wine, if you want wine, and we'll sit there, and you tell me everything, and I'll go fucking beat him up for you afterwards. Okay?"

I laugh through my tears. "Okay." I sniff. I miss her so hard it hurts. And at least I'm relieved that she and Mani are okay—there was no accident, of course. They're both fine.

"I've been worried about you," she says. "I'm really glad you reached out."

I wipe my face. "Me, too."

"Listen, you just give me his license plate number, okay? I'll bribe my brother to give him, like, a hundred parking tickets or something."

"I just want to be normal again. I just want to be normal." I'm crying.

"Bri, I'm really worried. What's been going on?"

I sniffle. I need to tell her something. But I can't tell her the truth. "It's just been—Alain meant a lot more to me than I meant to him, apparently. Now that he's gone, I don't know what to do. And I have a problem I can't solve."

"A work problem?"

"Yeah." I can't tell her the real issue. "But it's Alain that I'm sad about."

"Okay, well, I'll see you soon, and we'll talk it over. I know you'll figure it out, and everything will be okay."

K. is so sweet, so innocent, so hopeful. If she only knew the nightmare I've been living, she wouldn't be half as upbeat.

Then I realize: It's K's upbeat attitude that makes the nightmares livable. It's that emotional, quick human response that makes us effective. I can't forget that.

Maybe Alain doesn't appreciate my traits, but they're

what make me unique. And I don't want to sell myself short.

I fucked up. But I have a chance to fix things. Not with Alain; that's over. But I can help find the missing women.

I wasn't able to be a doctor. Couldn't do the right thing when it came to the fight with Karl. Messed up and believed the fake phone call. Always gave up on relationships in the past...

I'm tired of being a quitter. I'm going to be a fixer.

I can still help people in this moment.

And I'll be damned if I sit home when I could be out there trying my best to save some women in trouble.

"K?" I tell her. "Can we hang out in a few hours or maybe tomorrow? I need to go running first to clear my head and process some stuff."

"Anytime, Bri. You just call me when you're ready." her voice is so kind. "Tonight or tomorrow, whenever. You just let me know."

"Thanks." I hang up and sit looking at the phone.

I take a deep breath because I know what I have to do.

Bri

I'm back at the house where the attack happened. Where Karl died.

I thought I'd panic, but I'm strangely calm. Focused.

The street is silent, and the house quiet. The sun is warm on my arms through the UV sweatshirt as I look for the pile of mail. It's still there, uninterrupted. Seeing it sitting there almost makes me think the whole thing was a dream.

I grab the envelope that intrigued me and rip it open. It's a title to a house in Phoenix. And with every core of my being, I'm positive: This is where the women are being kept. Didn't Karl say: "Take her to the house?" It must be this one.

I immediately want to call Alain—but no. He told me never to contact him again. Anyway, he's sleeping now, until nightfall. That's just under two hours away...and the women might not have that long.

I'll go myself. I owe it to the women to do this.

It occurs to me that I should probably call my tip in to the police. But they won't do anything without probable cause; this much I know from TV shows. And what evidence do I have?

You see, officer, there was a vampire fight the other night where I was injured, and one vampire was killed. I saw this envelope and committed mail fraud to find this address. No, no proof at all. It's tied to the missing women; just a gut feeling. Oh, and you have to check it out now, during the day. Because other vampires might be involved, and they'll come kill you if you visit at night.

They'd brand me a crazy lunatic for sure. Might even put me into a seventy-two-hour psych hold at the hospital, which they have the right to do if a person seems insane and a risk to themselves or others. I shudder just thinking about it.

I don't have time to think of a legitimate story. I'll go there, and if I find them, then I can call it in anonymously...

THE ADDRESS IS on the outskirts of Phoenix, far off the I-10, and down a country road. The closer I get, the more my unease grows. This is probably not a good place to be exploring alone. Feeling the need to provide myself at least some level of safety, I pull over and grab my phone.

I bite my lip then send Alain a text. I know he can't read it until he wakes up, and he told me never to call him again, so he might delete it unread. Maybe he doesn't even have the same phone number, God knows, but I do it anyway. "I may need backup. Come here as soon as you wake up. I think the women are here." I include the address.

Then, just to be on the safe side, I send the same message to Slash and Martin. I'm pretty positive that Martin, at the very least, will have the same number. And Slash probably keeps tabs on all his old numbers because he's data-crazy...so it's a guarantee that at least one of the three will get it.

I consider sending K. a "if you don't hear from me in an hour call the police" message, but knowing her, she'd just call them immediately, and I'm not sure that's the right thing. I certainly can't wipe minds, and I don't want to have to explain what the hell I'm doing here.

After I send the messages, I continue on, and in fifteen minutes, I'm at the location.

The house is boarded up, with wooden siding that's so warped and blistered from the sun that it looks bleached. Weeds and bushes grow thick around the property, some dead and brown from the climate. There are no cars, no people, nothing. I see something rusted out next to the entry, like an old wheelbarrow, but it's overgrown with bushes.

The place is at the edge of a reservation and has no neighbors that I can see. There's some barn structure miles away, across fields, but apart from that, I'm alone.

I get out of the car and listen: Utter silence, except for a lone mockingbird in the twisted mesquite to the left.

It's eerie although the sun is bright and hot through my face mask, and there's a gentle breeze that whishes through the dried bushes. I stick my car key in my jacket pocket, my phone in the other pocket.

I walk slowly up to the boarded-up door of the house and stop, staring at it, trying to see if it looks recently used. It does not. There are spider webs, thick, extending from the door handle to the wall, with leaves caught in them, and the carcass of some dried-out insect.

I walk around the wide of the house, dead plants crunching under my boots. There's old litter here—faded pieces of plastic two-liter bottles and ripped plastic bags caught on bushes and speckled with dirt.

But then something catches my eye—something that doesn't belong. A cigarette butt—and it's plump; looks soft and recently used.

My heart starts to hammer, and I turn around fast, checking the area. I'm still as alone as ever, but suddenly I feel exposed, with my car parked jauntily right the fuck there, and me—walking around—with nobody as backup.

I keep walking, mechanically, as if by doing a full circle of the house I will instill some magical protective spell over myself. When I reach the back of the home, I see another door...but this one has been cleared of spider-webs and debris, and it has a thick silver chain on it with a padlock. No rust on this—it's new.

Instinctively I grab my phone—no texts. And zero bars. Fuck. Hopefully one of the vampires will get my text and show up. I probably should have waited for them.

The sun starts to sink towards the edge of the horizon, the sky lit up like a cinema from heaven, pink and azure and red shot through with orange and long thin clouds. It will be dark in a matter of minutes, and then Karl's vampire allies can show up at any time.

Being here alone like this may be stupid. But my life has a short expectancy anyway. And I feel a bond to these women, a need to help them. I know firsthand what it's like to be nearly killed by an evil vampire, and it's the most hellish thing, beyond all imagination. If they're here, I'm going to do whatever I can to find them and save them.

I go back to the front of the house and kick at the door with my boot. Nothing. I kick harder, and again. Again. And suddenly, like a miracle, the sideboard cracks, and the wood makes a sound like a little explosion. Dust shoots out violently, and the thing gapes open.

I scream a little, startled, my muscles locking up, my heartbeat so fast I think I'll pass out.

But I squeeze through the opening.

I don't have a flashlight, but my phone has a flashlight app. I hold it up and use it to guide my way around the dim interior.

Disappointment hits me hard. It's a one room shack, and it's empty, with just a broken chair and garbage.

There's an old tarp, the kind you might use to wrap furniture during transport, lying on the floor. Lots of dust.

I imagine thousands of black widows and scorpions—and then I hear a sound. A sort of mechanical hum coming from below my feet, like a generator.

There must be a way down to some kind of basement! I scan the area, and then kick aside the tarp with my foot. And there I see the handle to a trap door.

I stare at the outline. I should leave, drive away, call the police to come—but by then it will be nightfall. If I want to find the women before any more vampires come here, I need to do it now.

With a shaking hand, I reach out and pull the handle of the door. It opens silently, on hinges that slide smooth. There's a ladder that leads down, and the room is lit up with cool fluorescent light. The sound of the generator is louder now, and there's a rhythmic hiss and pop, too, like machinery. Medical machinery.

I stick my phone back into my pocket and wipe my sweaty hands on my jeans, and then swing down onto the ladder.

When my boots hit the ground, I whirl around and cry out. Because in front of me are three cots, the kind you'd find in a hospital. And in them, tied down with multiple restraints on arms and legs, bands across their bodies, mouths gagged, lie the three missing women, the ones I've seen on the news.

There's a fourth cot. This one is empty and has an IV pole next to it.

For a split second I feel jubilation because I was right!

I did it! They're here, and I found them, and I was right! Then the horror of the situation sinks in.

"Oh my God." My vision goes spotty, and I sway. I think my blood pressure must be spiking. "Oh, Jesus. Oh my God."

The fourth cot could have been for me. Karl said, "You will be my number four."

I lean back against the ladder for a second. The odor in the room is horrific and makes my eyes water. I gag and fight the urge to vomit. Bend down, then force myself to stand up.

The women are wearing what clothes they had when taken, I assume, although the sleeves of whatever shirts they had have been cut off, ragged. Each woman has an IV running into her arm, and plenty of bruising and marks.

A plastic bin in the corner holds stacks of gauze bandage rolls, one of them unspooled like a party streamer. A pile of wrapped needles lies haphazardly on the lid of the bin, which is on the floor too, and there are other things that I assume are equipment for blood donation bags. Glass vials catch the light like icicles in another bin, and for a horrible second, I think they look like Christmas tree ornaments.

The closest woman makes eye contact with me and lurches her body as much as she can in her restraints. "Mmmm!" "Eeeeeeelll!" she wails through her gag. Her eyes are wide and terrified, and her body looks frail. All three of them look sick, like death isn't far.

"I'm not going to hurt you," I rasp, my voice sticking in my throat. "I'll help you. We'll get out of here."

"Mmmm, mmmm!" She seems frantic. I think this

woman is Margaret Bly, the one I Googled while I sat in the blood draw office. How different she looks now from the pretty graduation picture shown in the article.

I rush over, the smell making it hard to focus. How are they alive in this foul air? I bend over her body, gasping for breath, eyes watering. My fingers are so trembly that even if I knew how to undo the ties holding her down, I doubt I'd be able to loosen them effectively.

"Are you Margaret? I'm here to help. My name is Bri. I'm going to help you, okay?"

I pull at the gag on her mouth, but it's so tight it's cutting into the sides of her mouth. I can see dried blood there and some fresh drops oozing. I reach behind her head to loosen the gag but can't figure out the knot.

"Mmmmm!" she looks to the left. "Mmmm, mmmm, mmmm."

Frantic, I follow her gaze. Oh! Scissors! Small and sharp, probably medical grade. I grab them and use my index finger to try and pull up the fabric away from her cheek, so I can insert the smooth blade and cut. She winces as the fabric pulls tighter at her bleeding mouth.

"I'm sorry, I'm sorry," I say, and cut as fast as I can. To my utter relief, I'm able to get through the material and pull it away from her skin.

She gasps, and I swear, I see new color arise in her cheeks. It's as if she was suffocating, and I helped her just in time.

But her mouth is so dry, she can't talk. "Heeeee," she wheezes. Her lips are cracked and cut. "Geeee....coooooo."

"Is there any water here?" Water?" I cry out, turning in a circle.

I cough again.

She shakes her head and tries to speak. "Heee... coooo...sooooo."

"I don't know what you're trying to say!" Desperation hits me. I take her wrist. "How do I undo these?"

There's a half-filled bottle of water on the floor, so I grab it and hold it up to her lips. It spills over her face, so I try again. Finally get her a few drops. And a few more.

She slumps back onto her filthy cot, and her eyes flutter shut. Her breathing is so rapid and shallow, I think she's about going to die. I unwind layer after layer of cloth and finally free one wrist. But she's out again, not responding to my voice.

I grab my phone, but of course it still has zero bars. "Fuck!" I scream, wanting to toss the phone at the wall.

The woman stirs, opens her eyes for a second. "eeee," she mouths, lifting her head as much as she can, then falls back like a rag doll. "He's taking the...last drops. Tonight."

"What is that?" I bend over.

"Vampire coming. Going to drain our blood...and save the last drops of it for an auction. Said it's the best."

Her body shakes with terror. "A real vampire. I'm not crazy. You have to believe me. Please get us out!" She wheezes into a cough, and her eyes sag shut once again.

"Oh, Jesus. Oh God."

I'm in over my head. Each woman is tied down with at least eight or nine bonds, all different. Some are strips of cloth, some look like BDSM cuffs. There's no more water, it's hot, and I'm going to suffocate. Even if I could untie them, how the fuck do I undo the IVs and get them to my car?

I need to get out of here, leave them, get to cell service and call 911. And I need to do it now.

"I'm going to get help," I say, bending over and touching her rank hair. It's unclear if she can hear me, but I speak anyway. "I promise I'll get help, the police and the medics, an ambulance, and we'll get you out of here. I need to go call."

But when I turn around, it's too late because someone is at the top of the ladder.

"Who the hell are you?" It's a human man.

I stare, wide-eyed.

He pulls a gun from his waistband and holds it on me while he calls on his phone, his voice oddly deferential. "I need help, Sir. Karl's not answering, so you need to tell me what to do. I've got another human trapped with the first three."

He slams the trapdoor.

I close my eyes. It's obvious to *me* why Karl isn't answering, but this man must not have heard the news. He must be talking to another vampire, Karl's ally...and as soon as night falls, we're all dead. I can try to attack him if he opens the trapdoor again, but I'm going to need help if I have any chance of real escape.

I glance around the room, desperate—and then it hits me. I can call Alain. He can get into my mind, and he seems to hear me thoughts. It's my only chance.

Alain. Help me. I focus as hard as I can. *Alain, I need you. Come to me. Help me.*

I flash images of me driving, this property, the house, the trapdoor. The women.

Please, come help me.

I don't know if it will work. But I remember how I wanted him to show up at the club, and somehow, he did; how we seem linked; and how he reads my mind during sex. Hears my thoughts. If he hasn't locked himself up from me entirely, maybe he'll still hear.

It's even harder to breathe now, and I gasp for air in this wretched place.

Alain. I found them. Come help us. Come.

I bring up the image of his face in my mind. Close my eyes again. Remember how it felt to be with him, the magic of our union.

I love you.

The thought is sent before I think twice. And then I realize it's true.

I never said it to him in person, but it's true. I mean it with every fiber of my being. Despite our differences, despite the difficulties. Even if he was cruel to me, and I to him, I love him.

And I think I always will.

lain

It's two nights after I killed Karl. We're sitting in Lucius' private office just after sundown, discussing the events, with a million-dollar bottle of McCallan 1926 whiskey and two crystal shot glasses on his wooden desk.

"So you visited Bri at night to help cure her wound?" Lucius pours the amber liquid into the glasses and passes one to me.

"How do you know that?" I stare at him. "That was a secret."

He smiles. "I don't disapprove. It's a nasty bite he gave her."

"She was injured by a vampire. She needs a vampire to heal her." I snap, then temper my voice. "She doesn't know because I come in her sleep. If she sees anything, she thinks it's a dream."

I take the glass and swallow the shot. Forty thousand dollars in one swallow, but it means nothing compared to what I've spent emotionally. "You don't need to worry about her talking."

"It's not her I'm worried about." Lucius' voice is mild. "In fact, I'm pleased...Karl's reign of terror is over." He pauses. "He will no longer rile up the vampire community. Well done." He raises his glass, and it catches the light, sending sparkles across the room.

"I thought you were displeased with me." There is no emotion in my voice.

"You took care of things, even if it got messy. It could have been worse." Lucius raises his glass. "Under the circumstances, you did a fine job. Extraordinary, even."

"Thank you." I don't touch my glass. Don't look at him.

"Are you well?" Lucius studies me.

I chuckle without humor. "No."

He nods. "It's not easy to kill one of your own, no matter how right it is."

"I'm not upset about killing Karl." I pour myself a second shot and swig the whiskey in one swallow.

"Oh?" Lucius raises a brow.

"It felt good to drive the stake through his chest, feel it go through muscle and bone and sinew. To see his eyes widen and glaze over. To watch him drain of essence until he was a hollow husk." I pour another shot and drain it, the alcohol giving me one splendid second of inebriation before it equalizes.

"That's the anger talking."

"That's the truth talking." I pour a fourth shot. "Fuck, I wish I could still get drunk."

He tilts his head. "If you're not upset about Karl, then what is it?"

"The human women are still out there, and they could be dying as we speak. And Karl's allies are probably going to hold the Last Drop auction without him. We don't know how many vampires he convinced to join his auction. Those are vampires we need to watch or eliminate."

"I agree." Lucius taps his fingers together. "Which is why I've forbidden anyone from speaking of Karl's death, yet. That way we can still rout them out if we hear chatter about the auction or anyone curious about his whereabouts."

I nod. "So far I've heard nothing, but I'm digging."

"Do you need anything from me?" His face is somber.

"Slash is on it. And a few others. We're working every possibility."

"Good." He nods. We all know Slash is the best. "When you find out, let me know. I will have my team support you in eliminating the chaff."

"I hope we can still find the three missing women."

Lucius nods. "Yes."

At least Bri is safe. Karl didn't get to take her, and for that, I will be eternally grateful.

Lucius either reads my thoughts or feels the emotion. "It's Bri. That's what's bothering you."

"What are you talking about?"

"You miss her."

"I had to protect her. I am a liability to her." I don't tell him: *Yes. I miss her so much I can't stand it. I wish we were still together. I made a huge mistake.*

"Most humans and vampires are better off without

each other in the long term. Yet there are exceptions." He tilts his head.

I examine my glass. "Not only am I a danger to her, but also—caring about her made me lose focus. I almost let Karl get away."

Suddenly something occurs to me. "But actually–" I break off, my heart pounding.

"What?" Lucius leans in.

"I need a minute." I close my eyes. Focus.

Remember exactly what happened.

Everything went down so fast that I may have suppressed some of the actions. Specifically, the part about Bri. It was too painful, so I pushed it away.

But now that I allow my memories full range, I realize something.

It was only the depth of my feelings for Bri that allowed me to overwhelm and attack Karl, ultimately. It was because of my care for her that I was able to stop him with my energy and then kill him. Instead of being a liability, she was an asset.

Lucius seems to pick up on my emotions. "Tell me."

"She helped me." The words come along with the realization. "When I was fighting Karl. I was stuck against his anger and power. Then she joined my mind. It's a thing we can do, just the two of us. I can't do it with other humans. She gave me some of her strength. And then I found mine, and I beat him."

I'm frozen. "I don't know why I didn't realize it. I think I blocked it out because I was so bent on pushing her away. But she helped me, Lucius." I shake my head. "I didn't give her enough credit. She got information all along, and then—at the most critical moment—she was there with me."

Lucius doesn't say anything for a long time. Finally, he speaks. "You underestimated the depth of your feelings for her."

"We're over."

"Alain, if you're rethinking what you said to her, you need to speak to her. And soon."

"I said things that are a one-way road, Lucius."

"Hmmm."

"I was cruel to her. You heard me. And I deliberately wasn't there for her these past few days, when she needed me more than ever. She's probably been terrified. I wanted her to hate me and prefer to be without me."

That didn't stop me from coming to her at night. Holding her for hours while she slept, whispering songs to her from centuries ago, until her body eased into dreams.

"I see."

"I'm immortal. She's not. It's impossible."

He taps his fingers together and seems to ignore all of my arguments. "Truth? Stranger pairs exist."

The truth is that I love her. Maybe she's a fragile mortal and losing her someday will devastate me. But not having the chance to spend what time we have? That's worse. I'll regret it for the rest of my existence.

This realization makes my whole body feel numb. I've fucked up the best thing that's happened to me in a hundred years.

Lucius notes my expression. "Maybe you should talk to her again. Listen to what she says, underneath the words."

I would love the chance to listen to Bri again. One last time.

Of course, it's far too late for that. She hates me now, rightfully so. As I wanted her to. I was so angry.

"I thought she was better alone, as was I. But maybe we're better together." After centuries alone, it's terrifying to think about actually committing to someone—especially a creature who isn't immortal. I love her enough to try."

"If that's how you feel, then honor it." His tone is solemn. "It's what I felt with Selene." He smiles. "And that worked out, despite the odds. Sometimes when a vampire feels this way about another creature, it means that fate plans success for you." He shrugs. "Something I've seen time and again over my many centuries."

"I don't know if she'd give me a second chance. She shouldn't." I'm disgusted with myself. "I was awful to her."

Something tugs at my mind. "Did you say something?"

He shakes his head.

I feel it again. Like I'm trying to remember something forgotten. But it's coming from outside of me—

I feel electric shock down my spine because it's her—Bri! I can hear her voice in my head. She's calling me!

Alain.

I focus hard, and her words gain strength.

Come help me.

My whole body aches with the effort.

I found them. Help me.

And

I love you. Then she goes silent.

My whole body goes numb. "It's Bri. She's in danger."

I take a breath. "She's found the missing women, Lucius. But she's in trouble."

And she loves me! She still loves me, even though I was a complete asshole—

But I can't focus on that just yet.

Suddenly my phone buzzes with a text. It's from Bri! And it's old—the satellite must be delayed. I hate when technology fails because this text is critical. And it matches what she's telling me in my mind.

"Fuck, Lucius, she's trying to find the women! She's in danger at this place." I show him the address.

I process the staticky images she sent, like flashes from an old TV. I frown, trying to make them out. My head aches. "There's a human there holding her hostage. We need to go!"

Lucius is already in action. "I can get us there faster than you can alone," he says. I know he has powers beyond mine.

I quickly call Martin and tell him to come with rein-forcements. Then I turn to Lucius. "Do it."

Lucius takes my arm and looks into my eyes. And we blur in an instant. I've never travelled like this, but it still doesn't feel like we'll get there in time.

I try to send Bri a message. *I'm coming. Hold on.*

Her messages are fading, getting dimmer. *Hard to breathe in here. The human man locked me down here and has a gun. But I have a plan.*

"She's getting weaker!" I cry out to Lucius. Cars and scenery stream by as we enter the Phoenix outskirts. "We need to go faster."

"This is as fast as I can take you," he replies.

And then we're there. The broken-down house that Bri showed me in her mind. Her car is there, along with another vehicle, an old pickup truck.

"She's in the basement," I hiss. But then I hold up a hand. "The other human is inside there." I point to the shack, a dilapidated iceberg alone in this ocean of dry grass and tumbleweed.

Lucius nods. Smells the air. "He's alone, so far." He closes his eyes. "But a vampire is coming." He goes still, then snaps into action.

"Who is it? How far away?"

"Ten miles or so. I'll slow him. You go get Bri."

But I'm already inside, even as Lucius raises his arms and closes his eyes, scanning the area with his mind.

As soon as I enter the dark house, I catch my breath. There's a human lifting the hatch. I can read from his memories that he's been told by the incoming vampire to strap Bri down like the rest of the women, so the vampire can auction off her last blood tonight, too.

I fly over to attack, and just as I do, Bri is there. She's at the top of the ladder and she has in her hand a shard of broken glass all wrapped up in gauze.

She screams and slashes at the man's arms, over and over. He shoves her, and she falls backwards to the floor of the basement room.

"Fuuuuck!" He roars, dropping his gun, stumbling. Blood runs thin and fresh from the wounds. "I'll kill you, bitch!" He scrambles around, cursing, looking for his gun.

But Bri's up already, clambering the ladder. She's fast and determined, and in a second, she's past him and to the door, limping and still running like hell. My crazy little human actually fought her way out of this! I'm as impressed as I've ever been, but I'm not going to take any chances.

Just as the human man's fingertips brush his weapon, I slam into his body, feeling pure pleasure as I drop him to the floor and hear a bone crack in three places. His shrieks are music to my eyes. I whir into action, tying him up with his own clothes.

Then I fly to the woman I love.

"Bri!" I roar. I pick her up in my arms and blur with her out to the fresh air, where she gasps. At first, she struggles, then she recognizes me and softens in my arms.

"Alain?" She's so shocked to see me, and then the most beautiful smile breaks out on her face. "You came!" The smile fades. "Is this real?" She blinks and coughs.

"Yes, it's real, baby, it's real." I kiss her cheeks, her forehead. Her lips, but briefly.

I gesture to Lucius. *Downstairs. They need help.*

He nods. *The vampire will be here in a minute. He's Karl's ally. He's alone.*

Bri looks at the things in her hands, like she's remembering what happened. She shudders and tosses the makeshift weapon into dry bushes. "The other women. They're down there, and they need help. They're dying!"

"I know, we're getting them, I promise. Lucius is down there. He'll stabilize them until the ambulance arrives." I imagine Lucius will work whatever skills he has to extend their lives and erase their most painful memories.

We hear the whoo of sirens and see lights a few miles off—the ambulances and police are near. Suddenly Slash and Martin arrive with Tiberius.

But someone else has also arrived: The new vampire. Karl's friend.

He blurs up in a burst of speed and hisses his displeasure at seeing me and Bri. The others. His eyes dart around, and he assesses the situation.

I don't recognize him. But I'm more powerful than he is, especially with my allies. This time I don't want or need to do it alone.

We work as a team, and in mere seconds, we have him pinned, all of us vampires standing over him, pressing him to the ground.

"Who are you?" I hiss, showing my fangs.

He fights our grip. "None of your business."

"Karl is dead," I tell him bluntly. "And your human friend will tell us everything we need to know.

His pupils narrow.

"Speak!" I roar.

But he won't. He closes his eyes and shutters his mind, effectively keeping us out.

"Did Karl make you?" I ask.

He doesn't respond. He goes still now, breathing slowly, almost going into a kind of torpor.

"Who else is working with you?"

But he's out.

"I've seen this before," Tiberius looks at me. "It's a way of slowing down the body, almost hibernating. He must have studied with a Zen master."

"We need the information he has." "We need to know if the operation was just him and Karl or if there are more of them. Are there more women anywhere? Who else knows about this?"

Bri calls out, "Alain, you need to waken his mind."

"I can't do that."

"You can. The way you speak with me. You can do it. Just try."

She looks at me with such confidence and pride that my heart bursts.

"All right." The sirens are getting louder as the cavalcade of police approach. We have less than a minute to finish this and get out.

I take a deep breath and push at his mind. *Wake up. Tell us what we need to know.*

It's like pushing on a wall of stone. A mountain of steel. There is no response.

Awaken.

I push with all my might, and suddenly his eyes burst open. He stares at us, dazed, with terror and a growing recognition of what is to come.

"Who else is working with you and Karl?" I demand.

"No one." He says the words slowly, as if they're pulled from him with great force, like he doesn't want to let them go. But they come anyway. "No one else. Just the human here." He twists his lip. "The other two human helpers are dead."

"Which vampires are coming for the LD auction?" I force his brain as hard as I can.

"Don't. Know." He weakens. "At least ten of them. List...is...at Karl's lair." He flashes me the image. Karl's' old lair is underneath that beat up house, where we killed him.

"Is that all?" I stare into his mind. But I know it is.

"Just do it." He closes his eyes.

I end him the way I ended Karl.

∼

I GRAB Bri in my arms, checking that she's okay. She's breathing hard, her eyes wide, but she seems uninjured. Still, I can't put her down. I keep holding her, touching her face, her arm. As if constantly reassuring her—and myself —that she's whole.

The police cars are pulling into the drive that leads to the property, so I speak to the others, even while holding Bri. "I'll leave with Bri. Martin, Slash, help clean up the body. Tiberius, get Bri's car out of here, now." I dart my gaze around. "Fast."

I look at Lucius, who's emerged from the underground basement of horror. I don't tell him what to do; he's too powerful for that. He'll tell me what he plans to do--we're lucky he's here helping us at all.

"I'll stay behind," Lucius says. "I'll tell the police what they need to know and wipe the rest of their memories of this. Make sure the women get safely to the hospital." He pauses. "I had to wipe them, too." He sounds regretful. "I only left partial images of being kidnapped and of Wallace and the dead human, but I removed everything about vampires and the blood. With luck, they'll recover without PTSD. The human here will go down for the kidnapping."

"Thank you." I send him my complete gratitude and lower my head for a second. Without him and the rest of my allies, I couldn't have done this.

And definitely, I couldn't have done it without Bri.

In seconds, we've cleared the scene—just in time for the swarm of law enforcement.

Lucius will play the innocent bystander, convince the police that he happened to come by this place and found the women. He'll convince them to believe him and wipe any evidence to the contrary from their minds, as well as wiping the necessary memories from the human helper. We may be required to help close out details later, but this is the critical moment.

It's risky and beyond complicated, but Lucius is the only one powerful enough to manage it in such a large group without loose ends. His touch, from his miraculously long life of practice, is cleaner and more effective than most other vampires.

And my only priority right now is Bri.

CHAPTER 25

Bri

"You're awake." His voice is low and calm.

I blink and look around me. I'm back at Alain's house. "What happened?" I sit up. "The women!"

"Are in the Mayo hospital in Scottsdale. They're stable. They'll recover. You will, too."

"What about the vampires who were bidding on the auction? The Last Drop auction?"

"We got the list from Karl's lair. Lucius and his team are rooting them out as we speak. I don't think they're going to be attending any more such auctions." His voice is dark. "He won't tolerate that kind of behavior in or near his area of ownership."

I shudder. But I'm relieved, too. "Good."

I move, and my wrist hurts. "Ow." I rub it where the wound is almost healed.

"Isn't it improving? I've been—I mean..." He breaks off.

I raise my eyebrows. "Yes, it's better. It was you, right? Helping it heal? I thought it was a dream. You said you never wanted to see me again."

He averts his gaze. "I, ah. Wanted to make sure you healed properly."

I don't want to hope, but this gives my heart cause to beat faster. "Why?"

He changes the subject. "You called me." He sounds confused by the whole thing. "I didn't know you could do that."

"Neither did I. But it was the only chance I had, so I'm glad it worked."

"So am I." He looks at me, and I can see the concern in his face.

He may have said ugly things the last time we spoke, but he still cares for me. I can feel it. Felt it in my mind before, and I feel it now.

I flush and look away. "You saved them." I cough, and he hands me a bottled water.

"No, you saved them first. You found them," he corrects me.

"But I couldn't do it alone. If you hadn't come, it would have ended badly."

"We made it happen together."

"So maybe we work better together than apart."

"Bri, you're right. We do work better together." His voice sounds genuine. Like he means it.

"That's not what you said last time." I'm glad he recognizes my contributions, but his past words are like rocks in my soul. If we have any chance, he needs to really mean what he's saying.

He gets down on his knees next to me and takes my hands. "Bri. I don't deserve it, but I'm asking you for a second chance." He gazes up at me earnestly. "Please."

"Why should I?" It's what I've wanted. But I need to be sure. This is so critical, so important, that I can't afford to fall for him a second time. Losing him again would kill me.

His voice is low. "Common sense says it's a mistake. Experience tells me it's bound to be a failure. Yet I…" He shakes his head. "I just don't want to be without you. It's that simple."

"You said we were over." The words still hurt.

"It wasn't because of you, Bri. It was because of me." He lets my hand go, then takes it again. "I almost got you killed, not once, but three times. If I'd just listened to you. About how much K. means to you. About your ideas. Worked with you, instead of trying to order you around. To meet my expectations." He pauses. "I thought you were better without me, so I said what I needed to say to drive you away. I just didn't know how badly it would hurt."

I remember the things I said, too. "I guess I should have listened to you, more, too. Trusted you more. It was my fault about Karl."

"No." His voice is firm, but kind. "The only one at fault there is Karl. Not you. Never you. All of us were doing our best, imperfect as it was."

I don't speak.

He squeezes my fingers. "When we first got together, at the club. I said I don't make wishes because I can make all my dreams come true. But that was a lie. Right now, you're part of my dream, Bri. And I can't get what I really want without you."

Tears come to my eyes. "Alain."

He reaches up and takes my face in his hands. "You said you loved me. Did you mean it?"

There's a note of hope in his voice.

I'm terrified, but I decide to take a chance and step off the cliff. I nod. My voice is trembly. "Yes. I do. You're part of my dreams, too."

"I love you." His voice is firm. "And I believe that if we work together, I can keep you safe. I can keep doing my work even better with you there to inspire me and greet me. And I'll do the same for you, Bri. I'll help you and inspire you—or at least I'll try. I can do better." He touches my face. "Will you let me try?"

I nod. The tear rolls down my cheek. "I will. I want to be with you. As long as we can."

He grabs me into his arms. Kisses me. Touches my hair. "Thank God you said yes." His face is full of joy, as much as I probably feel.

I put my hands onto him. "I don't care how long we have. I just want to be together. Even if it's just a few years."

A muscle clenches in his jaw. "There's a thing I can try. It's difficult and rare, and often fails but I could attempt to revert to my human form, with the right treatments."

"But it might not work?" My eyes widen.

"No, it most often does not." His voice is low. "But if you ask, I will try. You deserve to have someone by your side, who can go out during the day with you. Get old with you."

"No, I don't want you to take the chance. No!" I put a hand on my chest. "Besides, you know I'm not a day person." I smile up at him.

There's a brief silence. "Maybe I could..." I tilt my head. "Become like you?"

"Bri." His face is earnest. "I said once that I'd never want to try to turn a human into a vampire again. The truth is I would give up anything to turn you—except it fails more than half the time. Humans often die in the process. I don't want to risk losing you like that. I won't chance it. You're far too valuable."

"Oh." I look down.

"I'd do it if you were in mortal danger, and there was no other way to save your life." He takes my hands in his. "Bri, I know your disease is progressing. If it ever gets to a point where..." he shakes his head, "the doctors think..." he trails off, as if he can't even contemplate the idea. "If there's no other option, then I'll consider it."

"I want to be with you as long as I can." I squeeze his hands. "So if we get to that point, I want you to do that. To try."

"It wouldn't be easy. When a human first becomes a vampire, it takes time to learn to handle your new existence. To master the blood lust. If I made you—" he pauses, until I look directly at him. "You would really need to accept me as your Master. For at least a century. Until you equal my power and gain the ability to temper it."

That idea isn't repugnant. In fact, it's turning me on.

"I might like that." I smile.

"You wouldn't always like it." His face is somber.

"And you'd have to do it anyway. It's more than kinky sex. It's letting me guide you as a novice vampire."

"I'd like that."

"I'd be your master, Bri." His voice is stern. "In all ways."

I meet his gaze. "I'm okay with that." I smile. "Maybe that could be fun, even if I'm not immortal."

"You make a compelling argument." He raises a brow. "I like the way you think."

I touch his hand. "You know what, Alain? I have a crazy feeling that things are going to work out somehow. And I don't care what happens, anyway—I just want to be with you, no matter what."

I can't believe I'm saying this. But as the words come out, I know it's true. All of my life was preparing me for this moment. No more giving up on things I want. I'm grabbing this with both hands and never letting the fuck go.

"Okay." His voice is hoarse. "We'll make it happen. Say yes, Bri. Say you'll be mine, and we'll figure it out."

Alain

We haven't yet made a decision on what to do. And I know I have to make a lot of changes to my attitude and behaviors to really deserve this gift I've been given. Luckily, I have lots of time to make it right.

But knowing we've chosen each other gives me incredible strength and joy. I can see it in her face, too.

Tonight, we're celebrating at my house, with champagne…and a little BDSM. She's wearing jeans and a T-shirt, and she's never looked hotter.

Of course, soon she'll be naked. And I plan to push her submission tonight, the first start of having her accept me as her master. Good thing she likes it that way.

"One of the best parts about choosing to be together," I tell her, running my hand over her thigh, "is that we can do this. Any time we want." I brush my fingers over the crotch of her jeans.

She sighs and spreads her legs a little. "That is a really good point. Tell me more about it." She leans into my body.

"I could do that. But first you'd need to get naked." I bite her ear. "And get down on your knees in front of me. Now that you've agreed to fully submit to me."

"All that for just a little conversation?" She reaches down and cups my cock through my pants. I'm already rock hard, straining against the fabric. Dying for her body.

"You know you have to earn your pleasure," I whisper. I wind my hand up under her shirt and squeeze her nipple through her lacy bra.

"Ow." She sucks in a breath. "Alain." Her voice is lower, already tinged with desire.

"I think you mean, Yes, Master," I correct her, squeezing harder. Pinch a bit longer before I let go.

She wiggles on my lap and moans.

"Because how can I properly punish your nipples if they're not bare?" I squeeze the other one for good measure.

"Why am I being punished?" She makes a face.

"Simply to remind you who's in charge." I slap her

inner thigh lightly. "Since you're going to accept me as your true master."

"Then is it truly a punishment?" She pushes her body closer.

"Perhaps it's more of a training session, then," I say. "Teach you discipline. But there will be punishments, too, when you disobey."

"Mmm…" she moans.

I can smell her arousal through her jeans and panties. She's wet for me. Her temperature rises, and her heart rate increases. I can hear her blood rush through the veins, her heart pump with desire.

"Don't try to hide it," I chide her, slapping her thigh again. "You know I can read you. You want this. Say it."

She moans a little bit and closes her eyes.

"Bri." I make my voice stern. Partly because it's fun but also because I'm going to need to train her to listen to me, obey me. Part of me says it's just to be on the safe side: If I ever have to try to turn her into a vampire, and it works, I can help her stay in control of her new existence if she's used to being submissive.

The other part of me just fucking likes being a dom.

"Remember the cane?" I put my hand to her crotch and hold, letting the warmth of her body mingle with the heat from my hand. "You struggled with one. If you don't start obeying, I'll strip you down and give you five to start."

She can hear the note in my voice.

She sits up straight, and her eyes fly open. "Alain–"

I shake my head.

She swallows. "Yes. I want this." Her voice is small

but irritable. She does want it, and she doesn't like to have to say it.

I chuckle. Fuck, it's fun to train a submissive.

"Clothes off, then." I slide her from my lap. Lean back and cross my arms. "Give me a good show."

She narrows her eyes, then the heat takes over. She wants to play as badly as I do. Of course, now it's more than a game. Finally. She's mine to master.

"You like?" She smiles at me as she removes her garments, one by one.

When she's only left in her silky panties, she turns around and looks at me over her shoulder. "Should I leave these on? It is a bit cold in here." She giggles. Pats her own ass with one hand.

"Worried your ass will freeze? I'll warm it up for you." I growl and grab her. "After your spanking, I promise your ass will be red hot." My cock throbs with need.

"Alain!" She squeals and grabs at my body, but she's no match for my strength. I bring her into the bedroom and deposit her on top of the comforter.

"Part of being my submissive," I tell her, watching her nipples pebble up at my words, "is being nice and obedient. Let's see how well you do."

Her chest heaves. "Yes, Master," she murmurs.

"Slide those panties down to mid-thigh and roll onto your stomach," I tell her.

She blinks at me. "Why?"

I move fast. Flip her over. Smack her ass once, twice, three times. Hard spanks. "And you don't ask why. You just do it."

"Ow!" She reaches back to rub her ass, and I grab her hand.

"No, now you get three more for trying to interfere."

I take both of her wrists into my hand. "Lift your ass up a little bit. Yeah, like that." I wait until she gets into the pose I want. "Like you can't wait for the spanking. Keep it high."

I bring my hand down hard with a crack.

She flinches. "Oooh."

"Ass back up. In position."

She quickly tilts her hips up. The thin cloth of her panties is barely any protection at all, and as I spank her again, even harder, she whimpers. But I smell her arousal grow. It hurts, but she likes it.

"One more. As high as you can get that ass now."

She pushes her body up, and I whack her across both cheeks.

She sucks in her breath. Just from those few spanks, pink blooms on her skin below the panty line.

"Now do what I asked you before," I order her.

She reaches back and tugs the panties down. "Like this?" She twists her head to look at me. "Master?"

"Perfect. Now stay there and keep your hands above your head."

I go to fetch a few things. She wiggles a little bit, probably feeling the sting on her ass, wanting to rub it. I chuckle. She's going to feel a stronger burn before we're done…and not just on her ass.

When I return, I've got a medium sized butt plug and some lube. I crouch down to show it to her. "See this? It's going into your pretty little ass, and you're going to keep it there for a while. Part of that time, I'll be spanking you, and part of the time you'll be waiting. Just enjoying the sensations."

She makes a little oooh.

"And this lube is a ginger based warming solution." I lean in closer and speak into her ear. "It's going to sting and tingle a bit."

"Alain, I've never…" She bites her lip.

"There are many things we're going to do," I tell her, "that you've never tried before." I flip the bottle open, and she flinches a little at the sound the cap makes. A little pop.

"Spread your legs as far as you can in the panties." I smack her ass once again.

"Yes, Master." She's a little breathless. The panties go taut on her thighs as she moves her legs apart. Moisture glistens on her pussy, and I can't wait.

I discard the plug and bottle, flip her over, and grab her hips in both hands, so I can plunge my tongue into her cleft.

She cries out and stiffens, then relaxes into my touch. I flick her clit with my tongue, over and over, using techniques I've perfected over decades of play. First, I ramp up her desire with soft touches. Then I flick harder, almost too hard, teasing her where she's most sensitive.

She wiggles, but I hold her firm, forcing her to take exactly what I want to give her.

"Alain, it's too much, oh, God," she murmurs.

"Relax into it," I order. "Soften your body because I'm not stopping yet."

I use my tongue to slap at her clit, push it back and forth. Draw circles around it.

She moans and struggles against me, but I don't stop until I've had a good taste, and she's frantic with need. Playing with her like this has me so hard that I want to fuck her right now. But it's even more fun to draw it out... so I do it some more.

Then I flip her back over. "Now let's get to that plug. Legs wide again."

She does it, and I immediately drizzle a generous amount of the lube on her asshole. Use the plug to start massaging it around, pushing into her anus just lightly with the tip of the plug. Showing her what's to come.

"Keep your ass relaxed," I instruct her. "Don't clench up." I tap her cheek. "I brought the cane over, in case you need a reminder." I reach over and grab it, toss it onto the pillow above her head. "Let's just keep it here, shall we? Look at it every now and then if you feel like disobeying me."

She whimpers, possibly at my words but maybe because I've pushed the plug in deeper for the first time. She clenches up, then relaxes her ass.

"Good girl," I praise her. I insert the plug further. I let the widest part of the plug stay right at her anal ring, stretching her out.

"It burns," she mutters, shifting her hips. Moving her hands.

I pull the plug back out and reinsert it, again leaving the widest part at her anal entrance.

"Get used to it," I whisper, kissing her neck. Biting softly. "My cock is much bigger."

She immediately clenches up, squeezing her ass cheeks around the plug. "What?"

"Relax your ass," I remind her. "You're getting my cock eventually, you know. Maybe not tonight. After all, we have forever to do this."

I play with her, pulling the plug out, pushing it in, all the while adding lube as necessary. But now the lube is starting to heat up, the ginger essences coming out with the warmth of her body.

"Ooooh," she moans. Her body shudders. "Alain, it's burning my ass." But the way she's moving her hips tells me she likes it as much as she hates it.

"Good." I smile and push the plug all the way in, going slowly, so I don't overwhelm her. It's long and thick; I chose a solid sized plug, so she could really feel it in there while she waits for her spanking.

"Now I want you to lie still for the next five minutes while I prepare. No moving those hips. I'll know if you do."

She moans, and I swear her pussy gets wetter than I've ever seen it. I can also tell how much control it's taking for her to keep her body still. Her ass looks so fucking delicious with my plug in there, still pink from the spanking I gave her earlier. I can't wait to give her a harder spanking, put down marks I can still see tomorrow.

I strip my clothes, keeping any eye on her. She's winding her fingers together, squeezing her toes into the sheet—but so far, she hasn't moved her hips.

I smile. Time to amp up the challenge.

lain

Now naked, I take a few more items from my dresser and approach her bed. "You're doing well so far. Let's see how you handle these."

Moving like lightning, I reach under her body and attach a small silver clamp to each nipple.

She cries out as they bite into her soft skin and twitches. "Alain!"

"Don't move, remember?"

I run a hand down her ass, stopping to push on the plug a bit. Twist it. "Keep those pretty breasts pushed into the bed, Bri."

"It hurts," she whines. With an undertone of desire to her words.

"I know," I agree. "It's supposed to. Over time we'll train you to wear them for longer periods of time. Sometimes I may put them on under your bra while we go out for a drink at the bar. How would you like that?"

I can practically hear how hard her nipples get, and

how this makes the clamps sting even more. She's so turned on right now she could practically come with just my voice.

"We can't have that." I lay a hand on her ass. "If you come before I give permission, I won't let you come again for three days. Do you want that?"

"No, no, I promise I won't come," she begs. I tap the plug again. She shifts a little bit and stiffens. I love how the nipple clamps will make stay still for her ass play.

I push the plug again and twist, and she moves more. Twitches her hips.

"Oh, Bri." I make a tsking sound. "You moved. Were you supposed to do that?"

"No, but you tricked me!" She turns to look at me. "That wasn't fair."

"Well, get used to it." I chuckle. "And now you're going to suffer the consequences of disobedience."

"Are you going to use the cane?" She sounds apprehensive. Hopeful, too. My little human likes to play hard.

"I have something else in mind." I bring out my crop. "A few of these on your thighs and ass, I think, will remind you who's your master."

I flick the crop at the back of her legs. It doesn't take much to leave a bright red mark.

"Oh!" She flinches, then stops sharp as the clamps pull at her nipples. "Alain, please."

"Twenty." I flick her again, right where the curve of her ass starts to swell. And again in the same spot. "On each side, for each count. If you move, I start over."

She groans, but it's a sound glazed over with desire. My sweet Bri likes her pleasure mixed with pain. And she loves obeying me. I can read it in her body; how her submission is making her sensations heightened, forcing the impending orgasm to gain in strength.

"Count." I flick her again, a few sharp slaps with the crop on each cheek. "Start with one."

"But–" She thinks better of arguing.

I bring the crop down harder than before on her left cheek, then once on her right.

"One." She forces it out.

"Good. Keep your hips steady."

I whip her with the crop again, just next to the first marks on each side. Nice and hard. Making it burn.

"Two." She gasps and her arm twitches, like she wants to reach back.

"No, "I caution her. "Don't touch your ass, or I'll add the cane at the end."

"Nooo," she whispers.

"In fact, grab the cane with both hands," I tell her. "Maybe that will help you stay in position. Think about how you want it to stay right there in your hands. Not in mine."

She does what I say, pulling the cane closer and latching onto it. "Alain…" she trails off.

"I know, this stings." I whip her with the crop in the middle of her left cheek. The middle of her right.

"Three," she whispers. The crop marks are gorgeous red blotches.

"Now the rules have changed," I say. "You're getting two on each side for each count. Don't argue."

She opens her mouth, bites her lip. "Yes, Master." But her voice is irritated. Pissy.

I chuckle. Give her two hard crops on her left cheek, nice and high. Two on her right cheek, low. "What's the count?"

"Four…" she gasps. I can tell she's dying to move her hips. It's hard for her to stay still. I know I'm putting her through a difficult situation with the plug, the clamps and the crop. But it's good training for her. She needs to learn discipline.

Plus, she's going to have a hell of an orgasm pretty soon.

I can read her feelings. Her pain threshold is high with her excitement and endorphins. I'm pushing her, but she's into it.

By the time we get to twenty, her ass and thighs are a gorgeous mix of red and pink, and she's panting with the exertion of staying still. When I finish, I toss the crop aside. Pick her up. Kiss her.

Our lips lock, and I thrust my tongue into her mouth, and grapple with hers. She kisses me back wildly, eager for me. Crazy for me. My cock pushes into her soft belly, and it's all I can do to hold back. But I still want her to wait a little more.

"Some masters make their submissive stand in the corner for a while as part of their training. I think I'll try that with you."

"But I don't want…"

I look at the cane. Her eyes follow and get wide. "Yes, Master," she says.

"Not for long." I look into her eyes. "Just a few minutes. It's about the experience of doing what I say."

She blinks. I know she's at war with herself. It's not easy to submit like this.

Finally, she says, "Yes, Master."

"Good." I'm beyond pleased. I point. "Go to that corner, please. Hands behind your head, tits nice and high. Back straight. Don't let the plug come out and don't fidget. I'll tell you when you're done.

And keep the panties around your thighs."

"But I…" She bites her lip.

"Figure it out." I cross my arms.

"Yes, Master."

She manages to get it done; she squeezes her ass cheeks together, hard, while walking with her legs slightly spread to keep the panties in place. When she makes it to the corner, she turns once to look at me.

I nod at her.

She turns back to the corner and puts her hands behind her head.

Fuck, this is phenomenal. Having this woman at my beck and call, at my command, doing it willingly, is so intoxicating. The fact that she's accepting me voluntarily as her master is euphoric, better than any drug I've had.

I don't make her stay there long; just a few minutes. It's not about the time. It's about the mindset.

"Bri, come on back to the bed," I order. "Drop the panties and keep the plug in. I'm going to fuck you with it still in your ass."

"Yes, Master." She allows the panties to slide down her legs and manages to get into the bed, somewhat awkwardly, without losing the plug. It's fun to watch her contort and figure out how to move to keep it in. I'm definitely going to make sure we do lots of anal play during her training.

And now I can't wait a moment longer.

I blur over to her and make sure she's on her back, legs nice and wide for me.

I straddle her body and lean down, carefully lifting each arm above her head. "Keep them here," I say. "While I fuck you."

She tosses her head back and forth. "Alain, I can't wait any longer." She's desperate. "Please. I need to come."

Waiting in the corner ramped up her desire to a level she nearly can't handle. I can see how hard she's struggling to hold back her pleasure. Her body quivers with need.

I adjust her hips, spread her thighs a little, and pull up on the back of them. Ease my cock to her entrance. "It will be tighter with the plug." I push the tip into her warmth. "See?"

As I push in, she cried out. "Oooh." Closes her eyes, makes fists. "Fuck." Her thighs tremble. "Alain."

I can feel the pressure of the plug squeezing against my cock, making her pussy impossibly tight. It's fucking incredible to push my way in, inch by inch, until I'm seated. "Fuck, Bri, you're so tight."

She makes a strangled sound. A whimper. "Please," she whispers.

I adjust my body and pull out. Thrust back in.

She catches her breath. Her pussy clenches.

"Not yet," I warn her. I pump again, faster. Again.

She starts making little sounds, little cries and calls.

I fuck her harder, faster, until we're going at a frantic

rhythm. My cock is ready to explode, and I can tell that she's not going to last much longer, no matter how hard she tries.

Another day, it would be fun to make her come without permission. But today I just want to make her come.

I adjust my movements, so I'm rubbing her clit too, and soon her whole body starts to vibrate. Just as she's about to come, I reach down and pull off the clamps.

She screams and bucks around me, her pussy so tight it's like a fist, shuddering with pleasure.

Oh, God, oh, God," she cries, and continues thrashing as her orgasm goes on and on.

As she's about to climax, I allow myself to come, and push into her mind, making her orgasm even wilder. Then I bite into her neck, taking her blood, and letting my essence permeate her body to enhance all of her sensations.

She cried out again and again, and so do I, as we both share a moment of phenomenal bliss.

Bri

I'm sweaty and exhausted and my pussy is still sparking with pleasure. That was literally the best orgasm of my entire life, hands down.

My nipples and neck throb with a combination of plea-sure and pain, and I don't know where one ends and the other begins. It all feels so good. Even the plug feels full and sexy in my ass. And I'm not even sore from his spanking.

I think it's his bite. It does something to me—takes away the pain, adds pleasure.

I shift, and he puts his arms around me. "Sweet Bri. You were quite obedient, for your first time as my submissive."

I pretend-bite his shoulder. "Maybe I need another lesson, Master. Just to be sure I get it."

He growls. "With pleasure."

And he's right. The pleasure is out of this world.

*B*ri
 The day is hot, the sun bright. I'm sweating, and the cap is poorly balanced as it has to fit over my protective headgear and face shield. But I don't care. This is the best day of my life.

It's crowded but everyone is quiet, focused on the speaker at the podium, who is leading us in the final pledge as we graduate.

I repeat the words of the oath with my classmates, all of us in unison: *"I solemnly pledge to dedicate my life to the service of humanity."*

My gown is heavy and feels royal. Standing with my graduating class, I'm amazed at far I've come; what I've accomplished.

"…I will maintain the utmost respect for human life…"

The audience is full—hundreds of family and friends have come to the graduation. I know K. and her wife Mani are out there somewhere cheering for me. I can't spot them in the vast crowd of excited onlookers, but I feel the energy of everyone together. It's uplifting.

"I will prevent disease whenever I can, for prevention is preferable to cure."

Having suffered with my disease for so long, I'm ready to commit to a life of preventing disease in others. Like Alain, I will also dedicate myself to pursuing cures to help humanity.

"May I always act so as to preserve the finest traditions of my calling, and may I long experience the joy of healing those who seek my help."

We finish the pledge and look around at each other with joy, a new class of physicians ready to go out into the world and help humanity.

Alain isn't here, but we will celebrate tonight. He's almost as proud of me as I am of myself. It turns out it wasn't too late for any of it: Applying to med school, getting in, and graduating *summa cum laude*, even with my disability. All it took—well, *all* is a simplification, but all it took was determination and resolve not to give up. I don't give up anymore on things that matter.

Alain was incredibly worried about my health and safety. He's fussed over me the past years, often using his saliva and his blood to keep my advancing disease at bay while I attended medical school. He assigned me bodyguards, ones I could see, and ones I could not. Helped protect me the entire time.

And I did it. With Alain's love and protection, with the help of Dr. A. as my mentor, with Slash and Martin as my friends, and with K. and Mani as my never-flagging besties, I did it.

K. and Mani find me.

"Congratulations!" K throws her arms around me, and I hug her small, strong body.

Mani joins in. "We're so proud of you."

I wipe a tear from my eye. "I couldn't have done it without you two supporting me."

My disease, despite the help from Alain, has started to worsen, and the two of them have been my daytime rocks, always being there for me no matter what. It's scary, but I'm focused on living my best life. I want to make every moment count.

"We'll be right back!" K. and Mani are pulled away by the undulating crowd, and I bump into a woman.

"Excuse me, I'm so sorry." I smile up at her, squeezing my diploma. "Oh! Amber. *Amber*? Oh my God, thank you so much for coming!"

Amber is besties with my web design buddy, Foxfire. We've been to more than a few group happy hours together, and although we're definitely friendly, I didn't expect her to come to my graduation although she RSVP'd for the party. Yet here she is.

"Congratulations!" She gives me a huge hug. "So excited for you, and I can't wait for the big bash."

Amber is a human like me...sort of. As I became integrated into Tucsons's super-human crowd through my bond with Alain, I learned that Amber is mated to one of the most powerful alpha wolf shifters in Tucson, Garrett, and has some intense powers of her own—psychic visions. This is obviously something I can't share with Mani or K... but I've gotten quite good at managing my double life.

I've never asked Amber to *see* anything for me, even

though she helps others when she can. If Alain and I have six days left or six years, I just don't want to know ahead of time. Maybe that's why I've avoided forming a stronger bond with her, even though she seems like she'd make a great friend.

"I have a graduation present for you." Amber smiles at me, warm and excited. "Right now. I think you're really going to like it."

"Amber, you didn't have to do that." But I notice that her hands are empty.

She leans up and whispers into my ear. "I see the worry in your face sometimes. I know you never want to know, and I won't do it again, but just this once, okay? I recently got a vision of you and Alain. You're standing outside at night, talking to someone, looking just like you do today. Young, I mean. Then you get into your car together and fly off."

"Fly? Like, we go really fast? Speed?" I frown.

"No." She winks. "You heard me."

"I'm sorry, I don't understand." But I think I maybe do. My heart starts to beat faster.

She touches my arm. "It's a pretty sophisticated machine, Bri. My best guess? It won't be common usage for oh, say, over a hundred years from now."

My heart pounds. "Are you saying…" I put a hand to my mouth.

"Just from one woman to another. Things may be rough in the short term, but eventually they are going to be okay."

My eyes fill with tears. "I think this may be the best present anyone's ever given me."

"This isn't an easy life." I know she means life as or with a creature with extra-human powers. Her expression is sympathetic. "Sometimes a piece of good news can really help. Anyway, I think you have two things to celebrate tonight."

She squeezes my hand and disappears into the throng. Then Mani and K. are back with balloons and smiles and more hugs.

As we make our way to their house for my graduation party, I send out my thanks to whatever Gods and fates and karmic forces rule the universe and promise to give back as much as I've received.

THAT EVENING, as I approach our home, holding my diploma, I'm charged with a new electricity. I've already been working with Dr. A. as an assistant. Now that I have my full degree, I can take on expanded responsibilities and help create even more exciting research. Plus, there's the tantalizing story that Amber told me—and what it means. The one person I want to share it all with tonight is my love, Alain.

When I come in and see Alain, the love and relief in his face fills me with extra joy.

"You did it." He reaches out a hand. "You still want this?" He raises a brow. Gestures at himself and me. "Doctor Briana Shaughnessy, M. D. You still want to spend your life with a vampire?"

"Of course, I do." I take his hand. "Because I love you. Always."

He smiles. "I love you, too." He nods. "Then come."

I close my eyes for one second and let my life thus far flash before me. Then I open my eyes. Smile.

And walk into my future.

WANT MORE?

Read all the books in the Midnight Doms Series

Alpha's Blood by Renee Rose and Lee Savino
  Her Vampire Master by Maren Smith
  Her Vampire Prince by Ines Johnson
  Her Vampire Hero by Nicolina Martin
  Her Vampire Bad Boy by Brenda Trim
  Her Vampire Rebel by Zara Zenia
  Her Vampire Obsession by Lesli Richardson
  Her Vampire Temptation by Alexis Alvarez

-Join the Midnight Dome Facebook party room: https://www.facebook.com/groups/701925946969115/

—Sign up to get news of the Midnight Doms releases: https://www.subscribepage.com/midnightdoms

ABOUT THE AUTHOR

Alexis Alvarez writes hot kink with doms so sexy you'll swoon! She's into photography and travel, and when she's not figuring out ways to get her main characters together, she's out with her camera looking for inspiration. Find her under her other pen name, Rebel West, where she writes kinky alien romances and the Zandian Bride Series with her writing partner Renee Rose.

Find Alexis Alvarez (aka Rebel West) on Social Media

Alexis Alvarez Amazon Author Page: https://www.amazon.com/Alexis-Alvarez/e/B0107LJQEM

Rebel West Author Page: https://www.amazon.com/Rebel-West/e/B07B866MY9

Newsletter: https://goo.gl/forms/iVRhZbk2s0mz8v6h2

ALSO BY ALEXIS ALVAREZ

Read More by Rebel West / Alexis Alvarez

Zandian Brides Series (with co-writer Renee Rose)

Night of the Zandians

Bought by the Zandians

Mastered by the Zandians

Zandian Lights

Kept by the Zandian

Claimed by the Zandian

Sci-Fi Romance

Conquered by the Alien Prince: Luminar Masters, Book 1

Steamy, Contemporary Romance

Perfect Match

A Handful of Fire

Boston

Dream Girl

Kinky/BDSM Romance

His Firm Direction

Casey's Choice

Capturing Kate

Myka and the Millionaire

Return

READ THE BAD BOY ALPHA SERIES
THAT LAUNCHED MIDNIGHT DOMS

Bad Boy Alphas Series

Alpha's Temptation

Alpha's Danger

Alpha's Prize

Alpha's Challenge

Alpha's Obsession

Alpha's War

Alpha's Mission

Alpha's Sun

Shifter Fight Club

Alpha's Desire

Alpha's Bane

Alpha's Secret

Alpha's Prey